Feisty, erotic and metaphysical . . .

"In *Yoga of the Impossible*, a series of journeys of the mind, the heart, and the whole spirit dance, punctuated by the most amazing imagery. At some place in this picaresque work, the reader will stand up and cheer. I guarantee it."

—Mary Norbert Korte, Author of *The Persephone Poems*

"Diane Frank has that amalgam of poetry and prose just right. She has perfect pitch. It's a knockout."

—Robert Scotellero, Author of *Measuring the Distance*

"One of life's greatest teaching tools is paradox, as people have to deal with paradoxes every day in order to grow. Diane Frank's *Yoga of the Impossible* weaves the paradoxical teachings of union to show how to find the gold buried within. Diane is a master tantric weaver in the way she slips a man into a woman's mind to feel the power of relationships from a woman's experience. Her rich, sensuous imagery enlivens me to my core."

—George James, Author of *Copperhead: Tantric Lessons on Love*

"Diane Frank has written a novel that is wise and exquisitely lyrical! Both love story and spiritual odyssey, *Yoga of the Impossible* is addictive, leading to hours on a cushy sofa, feeling delighted and enthralled."

—Anya Luz Lobos, author of *Wild Knowing*

"I am once again swept into poetic prose and metaphors that make objects and the yearning for love come alive within me and I am transported ... recalling especially Stokes State Forest as well as loving the journey to Montreal and the Jazz Festival. I am truly loving *Yoga of the Impossible* and Diane Frank's literary prowess! It's a sacred gem."

—Alyssa Miller, President, *AM Mediaworks*

"*Yoga of the Impossible* is clearly written by a poet. The language is spare, allowing the images and story to come alive. Like *Blackberries in the Dream House*, the novel is infused with a sense of magic as it reveals the life of a sculptor who loves to create art as much as she lets her experiences mold and transform her."

—Stewart Florsheim, author of *The Short Fall from Grace*

Yoga of the Impossible

Diane Frank

1st WORLD
PUBLISHING

Yoga of the Impossible

Diane Frank

Published by 1st World Publishing
P.O. Box 2211, Fairfield, Iowa 52556
tel: 641-209-5000 • fax: 866-440-5234
web: www.1stworldpublishing.com

First Edition

LCCN: 2014902257
Softcover ISBN: 978-1-4218-8682-4
Hardcover ISBN: 978-1-4218-8683-1
eBook ISBN: 978-1-4218-8684-8

Rainer Maria Rilke's third "Sonnet to Orpheus" is reprinted from *Selected Poems of Rainer Maria Rilke*, translated by Robert Bly (HarperCollins, New York, 1981). By permission of Robert Bly.

Quotes from Caroline Casey reprinted from *Making the Gods Work for You* by Caroline Casey (Harmony Books, New York, 1998); the Visionary Activist Show on KPFA; and her talk at the Phoenix Theatre in 2004, Petaluma, California. By permission of Caroline Casey.

Quotes from Rob Brezsny's *Free Will Astrology* reprinted from the *San Francisco Weekly*. By permission of Rob Brezsny.

Special thanks for sharing ideas about contra dancing to Kirston Koths, Charlie Fenton, and Stephen Bennett.

Special thanks to Erik Ievins, Julie Thomas, Diane Porter , Anya Luz Lobos, Susie Niedermeyer, Stew Florsheim, Jeanne Glennon, Lynne Rappaport, and my Tuesday Night Workshop for great suggestions and careful proofreading.

I want to express my deep appreciation to
Grandma Helen,
Robin Lim, Melanie Gendron,
Christopher Seid, Larry Kassin,
John Gregorin, Jo Mortland,
Erik Ievins and the
Dance Gypsy Community of the Midwest.
You have all inspired me.

This book is my prayer for
the polar bear, the honeybee,
and our lovely green and blue planet
flying like a jewel through the universe.

Many of the birds, flowers, plants and trees
celebrated in this book are endangered species.

Contents

Part II – My Year as a Dance Gypsy

Part III – The Yoga of the Impossible

About the Author

Books by Diane Frank

Music and Recipes

Between my love and my heart
things were happening which
slowly, slowly
made me recall everything.

You arouse me with your touch
although I can't see your hands.
You have kissed me with tenderness
although I haven't seen your lips.

You are hidden from me.

—*Rumi*

Part I

Swimming Back from the Light

Chapter 1:

His Emotions Were Slippery like an Avocado

It rained between conversations. We were in a café on Judah close to the beach where sand dollars pile up after the low tide. We sat by the window waiting for breakfast – avocados and eggs before a journey into the underworld.

When the rain stopped, the light turned green at the corner, reflecting on the puddled streetcar tracks. "I'll be keeping the light on inside for you," he said.

I told him, "I'll remember that," whispering to myself, "table crumbs," wanting to slide my hands inside his shirt.

He paid for my omelette, which is a signal in this part of the country. He said he'd been painting all morning and ranted about what the fumes do to your nose. I could see it – green paint on the hairs inside his nostrils.

On Friday night he kissed me on the street, gave the half-Japanese man two dollars to buy himself a beer and go away. We talked about how strippers in West Palm Beach are like the geishas in Kyoto. He told me men like to give their power to these women and let the woman be in charge. I told him about the Noh actor in Kyoto who thought I was a geisha. He took me out for tea late at night, which is expensive, because he needed to tell his secrets to a stranger. Someone he'd never see again.

American men don't tell you what they mean. They give signals. They think about seducing you in airplanes but pretend they don't care. They don't tell you the truth until you are gone.

Later that night, we walked on the beach. I found a slice of a nautilus shell, the fractal spiraling to the edge of my emotions. We stepped over a pile of sand dollar fossils – etched orbits of the pentagram pressed to stone between sand. I wanted to put my nose against his skin. Then my lips.

I remember the night in San Francisco when we went to Ebisu for sushi and got a little drunk on sake. That was my first signal. The wind was blowing fog from the Pacific Ocean, swirling around a telephone booth in the Inner Sunset. We tangled around each other on the streetcar and loved each other for hours that night.

His plane leaves at six o'clock in the morning. I let the hug he gives me imprint like oak leaves. Bamboo over a koi pond, his eyes eggshell blue full of messages. My emotions – spider webs on leaves tearing apart. And what does it mean to have a man inside you? I act like Scheherazade. I tell him stories.

Chapter 2:

The Snake Charmer

Life begins with the stories your mother tells you. My mother played oboe in the Cleveland Orchestra before I was born. She was a snake charmer of a musician, and her party act was singing like Billie Holiday. Sometimes at symphony celebrations, some of the brass and woodwind players improvised jazz and swing tunes. When they needed a vocalist, she would stand by the piano and do her diva act. The story my mother tells is that I ruined her career. You didn't get up on stage with a pregnant belly in the fifties.

My parents were high school sweethearts. To make sure he noticed her, my mother joined the hall patrol to station herself by the door of his sixth period physics class. She was smiling every afternoon when he walked out of the door. On weekends, they'd escape to the West Village in his red convertible, to the apartment he shared with his half brother in a loft filled with etchings. They went to night clubs where she pretended to be eighteen years old to hear Billie Holiday, Ella Fitzgerald, Count Basie, Tommy Dorsey and the musical mahatmas of their time. Years later, I loved wearing her vintage evening gowns.

After my father graduated from high school, he shipped out with the Merchant Marines as a radio operator on a Liberty Ship. This was during the Second World War and added the spice of long distance intrigue to their relationship. While he was gone, my mother studied oboe at Juilliard and sang with a swing band in Manhattan. When my father came into port, she'd sing to him directly with bedroom eyes, *How High the Moon* wailing out of Tommy's trombone and then cascading from her mouth. Who could resist such a song? She kept a scrapbook of those times – concerts in Harlem, photographs from nightclubs, and gardenias my father had pinned in her hair.

When she was twenty years old, Mama auditioned for the Cleveland Orchestra and made second chair. She played with them for three seasons. On her twenty-first birthday, my father proposed with his grandmother's diamond ring. They married in June with a string quartet playing Pachelbel's Canon as they walked down the aisle. By then, my father had a job in Manhattan and spent his evenings in pubs and cafes with left-wing political beatniks in the West Village. My parents couldn't agree where to live, so they lived like gypsies for a while. It was unusual in those times, but it was exciting. Even though they were married, they still felt like they were dating. It was always a celebration when they got together, and in between, they had their own lives.

When Mama became pregnant with me, my father moved her to New York. He opened a bookstore where the politicos gathered and rented a small apartment in the West Village. Women followed men in those days, but she took a suitcase of resentment with her. Before I was born, my father put two photographs over my crib – one of Karl Marx and the other of Albert Einstein. Of course, my mother added her touch with a mobile of floating boats and origami cranes hanging from the ceiling. Sometimes, I still see them floating in my dreams.

My story is that I was a firefly flickering over the door to a forgotten alcove in her soul. They conceived me in a cabin by Caroga Lake in upstate New York. The night I came into being, they shared a bottle of wine, threw the glasses into the fire, and made passionate love with moonlight streaming through the window. Nine months later, she named me Katarina in honor of her gypsy grandmother and hoped my name would invoke the blessing of her gypsy spirit.

My birth was her initiation into fully being a woman. In the photograph on my birth announcement, she is wearing a Japanese kimono. My father smiles at the camera as he wraps his arms around her. My mother has a transparent face. As her arms cradle my tiny body, I see her completely happy.

When I was two years old, Mama auditioned for the New York Philharmonic but didn't make the cut. Soon after that, she was pregnant with my brother Seth. Two years later, Jessica was born. While Jessica was still in diapers, Mama started performing with a chamber group and a local symphony. I was always happy to see her on stage, playing the solos in Beethoven's Fifth and the New World Symphony. My father graduated from night school with a degree in physics and worked for a Nobel laureate. By then we had moved out of the city.

When I was six years old, Mama gave me a silver flute and sent me to one of her symphony friends for lessons. I loved the flute, and music filled me with joy. Mama found a ballet studio near our home and walked with me to lessons twice a week. When I danced in the Nutcracker, she played in the orchestra. For months after that, I danced around the house in my mouse costume. When I danced in Swan Lake, my mother's music swirled like incense around me.

In many ways, Mama was like a fairy godmother. She took us to see the dinosaurs and the whale at the Museum of Natural History, to special exhibits at the Museum of Modern Art, to children's concerts at the New York Philharmonic, and of course, to the ballet. She took us to parks and taught us the names of flowers, birds and trees. Seth played piano and tablas, and Jessica played violin. On Sunday afternoons, we had a family chamber group, led by my mother, the music goddess. She chose the music and always played with us.

But sometimes my mother had a sadness in her face, born of an abandoned dream. There were periods when she would yell at her children every day – it was astounding to me that she was able to sing after straining her voice that way. When I had my own way or sassed her, as every pre-teenage girl does, her story was, "I wish you were never born." But that was a lie, a momentary lapse of matriarchal integrity.

My mother has the soul of an artist and the delicacy of an oak leaf in October tearing apart. I am my mother's daughter.

Chapter 3:

Swimming Back from the Light

Christopher lived down the street from me. A few days after we moved from Manhattan to our new home in Saddle River, I adopted him as my older brother. Our families went on vacations together every summer. Christopher was really good at math and an amazing artist. He could draw anything, and it looked like the person, the cat, or the tree. From the time I was eight years old, he gave me drawing lessons. After school, he walked me home and helped me with my math homework. As the youngest of six boys, Christopher enjoyed having a little sister, even if she lived in another house.

When I was twelve years old and Christopher was fourteen, our families went on vacation to Lake Hopatcong. Two summers ago, we went out on the lake in a rowboat, but this year his brothers brought a beautiful red canoe. From the dock, Christopher showed me how to use the paddle with different strokes to make the canoe go forward, backward and turn. Then my mother let him take me out on the lake.

It started out as a perfect day. Sky blue as a robin's shell, with puffs of clouds like mashed potatoes or floating boats. The canoe so red and beautiful. I loved paddling with Christopher over the water, rippled with the reflection of the trees and the sky.

A group of bigger boys in a silver canoe paddled up to us and started teasing Christopher. He was a little bit smaller than some of the other boys from his school, and these boys weren't in his group of friends. He tried to ignore them at first, but they wouldn't go away. They teased him about having a girlfriend, which was ridiculous. I wasn't old enough for that yet, and he was like a brother. Then they called out, "It's war!" and started heading for our canoe to ram it.

Christopher did his best to defend the boat. He yelled out, "Hey, she's younger than you! Leave her alone!" We paddled as fast as we could toward the shore, but the boys were older and stronger. They came close to us and started ramming the canoe.

Christopher took his paddle to try and push them away, but he leaned over too far and the canoe turned over. What happened after that is confusing to me. I knew how to swim, but one of the paddles hit me on the head. I must have blacked out and started going down. Later, Christopher told me he went down after me but couldn't find me in the water. It was too green and muddy.

I saw a tunnel inside the water. I left my body and started walking through. Or maybe floating. In the distance beyond the tunnel, I saw a light. Almost like a skylight inside a geodesic dome filled with music. There was a radiance inside the light. I felt this as a steady stream of love. I flew into the light and was gently embraced.

I heard music that felt like memory and saw my future inside a field of calla lilies. The calla lilies were lit up from inside, as if by sunlight. I felt God as a steady flow of love and light. Then I felt gentle hands pulling me back to a world I knew.

Inside the tunnel Christopher took my hand, and we started swimming back from the light. Swimming underwater, swimming through light, swimming through green waves toward the world. There's an animal part of us that needs to breathe, and the air came rushing. I floated through my skin and found myself back inside my body. Somehow we were on the earth again.

When I opened my eyes, we were both on the shore of Lake Hopatcong, surrounded by our families and a crowd of strangers. My mother was crying. She was holding me, stroking my face. I returned to a world where everything was sparkling, but I felt different in a way I couldn't explain. Christopher was on the ground next to me. Our eyes met inside the silence.

Chapter 4:

In the Language of the Birds

Christopher and I spent a lot of time together that summer. We had shared an experience that other people couldn't understand. At least not the people we knew. We walked in the woods, hiked in the mountains, and rode bicycles to deserted places.

Christopher told me when he was in the light, he saw his life like a movie. "There was a being of light who looked like a bird or an angel, and she watched the movie with me. We could communicate by telepathy. What surprised me most was so many things that felt wrong to me – with my brothers, my friends, and at school – were actually right. I could see that everything was really the way it was supposed to be, even if it didn't feel that way at the time."

These were words that would never leave me. He let me know, "I tried to rescue you, but I couldn't find you. It was too dark and muddy at the bottom of the lake."

The story my mother told me was the lifeguards pulled us out. When we went under, we were close enough to the shore. That summer, I often dreamed about Christopher – the same dream, over and over. *We are in a water tunnel, swimming towards the light. Christopher takes my hand and we both swim free.*

That summer my mother looked at me in a different way. I could see it in her eyes and hear it in her snake charmer music. One night, she cooked a special meal for the lifeguards and invited

Christopher. As a gift, she gave them tickets to the New York Philharmonic. Christopher and I were quiet. We didn't know what to say. After dinner, we played music for them, selections my mother chose by Vivaldi, Telemann and Bach. I think my mother wanted to show them something about the lives they had saved. I played flute and put my feelings into the music. But what Christopher and I liked best that summer was walking in the woods and listening to the voices of the birds. The birds reminded me of angels, and we could communicate with them by telepathy. We spoke the language of the birds – a private symphony of wood trails, silence and bird sounds.

Christopher and I lived close to nature, in the woods of Stokes State Forest, High Point, and the Delaware Water Gap. We camped on Long Beach Island, walking early in the morning on the isolated seacoast. Christopher was my friend, my teacher, my guide. He felt that in solitude, one absorbs the personality of nature. We both chose to live, inspired by Thoreau and the ideal of the *sanyasi* from India, deliberately, alone, in the classroom of nature. Being with Christopher did not diminish the feeling of being alone. It felt like hiking with a soul companion, inside the music of my own soul.

At times, Christopher would disappear for days. His grandmother sensed his need for solitude and asked him to be caretaker of the family's summer house on an Appalachian mountain slope in eastern Pennsylvania. While the rest of his family sailed her boat to Key West, he stayed alone in a cabin over a hundred years old, close to a small lake. It was very isolated. Christopher cooked on an old wood stove, cut the lawn with a scythe, walked in the woods for hours, and watched the sun set over the mountains. Then he'd write in his journal or watch foxes and deer lurking around the edges of the woods.

The shelves of the cabin were full of books – literary classics, *The Bhagavad Gita*, Whitman, Thoreau, Emerson, Annie Dillard, Mary Oliver and a whole shelf of nature guides with illustrations of wildflowers, trees, stones, shells and birds. Christopher discovered three illustrated albums of bird songs and played them over and over on the old phonograph until he had each call memorized. One afternoon, he watched a falcon fall out of the sky like an arrow, diving on some poor unsuspecting chipmunk. Later that day he read in *The Bhagavad Gita* about the cycle of life, death and rebirth. Everything in the world was mysterious and filled with light.

In her quiet way, his grandmother was an inspiring mentor to both of us. She was a real life Demeter who loved birds, animals, growing things and getting her hands dirty. After she returned from Key West, she came by my house in her old Pontiac station wagon, and after a chatty tea with my parents, drove me to her cabin. The next morning, she taught us how to attract chickadees with a dry whistling. She showed me how to weave on the handloom in her cabin's loft. On the side of the mountain, we sat in silence listening to the birds. She'd identify every one of them by their songs, which is how I learned their language. What I most remember about that summer is encrypted in the language of the birds.

It was pure joy to see Christopher again. Both of us felt a distance from other people we didn't feel with each other. In the forest we were in touch with the larger rhythms of life, death and rebirth. One event I will never forget. We were standing by an upstairs window, and there, no more than fifteen feet in front of us, was a tiny squirrel crawling out to the edge of a branch of an old apple tree. We were amused by his clumsiness, entertained by it, when all of a sudden, out of nowhere, a hawk flew by, snatched the rodent and flew off, like he was picking an apple. Who could not be forever shocked and amazed by birds after seeing that? It was a beautiful thing, a horrible thing, and a gift from the gods to witness.

We continued hiking in the woods close to where our families lived – our private weave of nature, innocent love and pure solitude. I grew profoundly close to the rhythms of the big chaos. When you're alone like that, nature becomes your companion. The nuthatches, waxwings and redpolls who fly in the forest and visit the feeder in your yard become your friends. The skunks who snorfle around under the feeder, the blacksnake we caught snagging eggs from the catbirds' nest, the raccoons weaving down the street under the moonlight – all of these became my friends. Their personalities are subtle, beautifully in tune with the rhythms of the earth. It was pure luxury to live like that. At the same time, I realized I needed to return to civilization and learn about people or be forever branded as peculiar.

Chapter 5:

Life Continues without a Filter

The start of the new school year came too early that September. In my seventh grade classroom, I discovered I didn't have a filter. Most people are very careful about what they say and never say what they really feel, especially at school. For me, that was impossible. Christopher and I were out of phase with the other students. Neither of us saw a reason to speak unless it was the absolute truth, or at least the truth as we saw it. This got me in trouble constantly with my teachers. My mother, trying to give some gentle guidance, told me to think before I speak. Her advice seemed stupid and annoying. Why should I think before I speak, when I know that what I say is true? I heard her tell one of her friends that I had become a teenager, and like most teenagers, was starting to sass her. I didn't see it that way.

I think the light in the tunnel did something to my eyes, and now the light of the world filtered in differently. Bright lights and loud music were close to unbearable. One tiny consolation was that Christopher felt the same way, and we could talk about it. I started having dreams that would later come true. Birds flew into my dreams and spoke to me – sometimes a cardinal, sometimes an owl, sometimes a wood thrush. Their colors were important, part of the message.

Christopher and I knew things we didn't know how we knew. We had an inner knowing, a subtle, visceral feeling when something was true. If people were talking to hide what they truly felt,

I'd respond to the hidden message. This scared people, but when I listened deeper, I didn't hear their words.

I filled a sketchbook with pencil and charcoal drawings of what I saw in the forest. I had a powerful urge to create things, and my art teacher, Miss Vardi, was very taken with me. She looked like an Italian goddess, with beautiful green eyes and flowing black hair. Miss Vardi encouraged me to use color, first with pastel crayons and then with paint. I made a mural of the birds I loved – cardinal, bluejay, wood thrush, veery, and owl – in the branches of a towering maple tree. The wood thrush and veery are absolutely stunning singers – I had already learned to play their songs on the flute. A few weeks later, I did a painting of swallowtail butterflies in a garden of irises. My third painting was a tunnel of light with dolphins swimming in and out of turquoise currents of water. Miss Vardi looked at that one for a long time, and for some reason I could not completely explain, I felt she understood.

The real explosion in my hands came when Miss Vardi let our class work with clay. The other students made twelve-year-old versions of dogs, cats and horses. I sculpted a horse leaping in front of a huge rising moon. I glazed the horse blue and found the perfect shade of yellow for the moon. I mounted them on a star covered in midnight blue silk and called it, "Night Horse Leaping to the Moon." The other students thought I was a little bit strange, but Miss Vardi loved it. After that, I sculpted an owl in a tulip tree with large, embellished flowers blooming.

My third sculpture portrayed my mother playing oboe. I took the clay home and asked my mother to pose in her black chiffon dress with rhinestone straps, the one she used to wear when she played in the Cleveland Orchestra. For three nights, I studied my mother and found her shape in clay while we listened to Bach's *Goldberg Variations*. My hands knew what to do. They could find the shape I saw.

In middle school I loved my science classes, especially biology. I was fascinated with every detail of every leaf and insect, and in some way I couldn't explain, this was helping me find my way back to the world. I drew illustrations for all my science projects, even when it wasn't required. I loved astronomy because I loved the night sky. My art projects were filled with insects, leaves and planets. When my science teacher let me, I stayed after school and put murals on the board for the next day's lessons.

My body started changing, and I found myself in that in-between place where I was no longer a girl but not yet a woman. I saw my body as sculpture, changing shape in the clay that is skin, muscles, and bones. My blood came every twenty-eight days, just before the full moon.

Christopher was learning karate and continued until he became a black belt. But there was another side of him few people knew. On weekends he'd hike out to Bear Mountain, Stokes State Forest, Pinchot Falls, or the Appalachian Trail. He'd fill his backpack with trail mix, granola, a few apples, binoculars, a sketchbook, lemonade, and two bird books. He could communicate with the birds by whistling and telepathy. Sometimes he took day hikes, and sometimes he'd sleep in the forest. Sometimes he needed to be alone. Other times he'd take me with him.

Some of my happiest times were hiking in the forest with Christopher. He was getting taller now, stretching to the trees we saw. He was handsome, and I wanted to paint him – cornsilk blonde hair, blue overalls, no shirt, surrounded by the birds he loved. His karate practice was making lovely sculpture of his muscles. Sometimes we'd walk in silence; other times we'd sing in harmony. Music in nature waves out, is magical, has elves.

One night we were out in the woods with our sleeping bags, camping under the stars. Christopher put his arm around me, and we fell asleep that way. It felt like we melted into each other all night, and music came from the trees. In the morning at dawn, the birds in the forest joined the song. First the phoebe, then a robin, then a vireo, and after that a whole weaving symphony of bird songs. Each time a new bird joined in, Christopher told me who was singing. What I most remember about Christopher is the way he knew the names of all the birds by their songs.

Chapter 6:

Music from the Other World

In my dreams, I kept swimming through the tunnel, talking by telepathy with angels. My nights were filled with music from the other world, a steady stream of love and guidance. Every morning, I'd wake up filled with light. I wanted to express my visions in my art in a female form because I was becoming a woman. For one of my world culture projects, I read early Greek mythology and was inspired by the stories of ancient, powerful women. With Miss Vardi's encouragement, I starting painting goddesses – goddesses emerging from trees, goddesses in wildflowers, goddesses with brightly colored birds flying through their arms.

There are certain things you need to forget to continue living in the world. Toward the end of middle school, the river of love and guidance began to fade. My inner light wasn't a constant companion, but I could feel it in quiet moments. This has continued through my life, although I forget to listen sometimes. Like most teenagers, I wanted to be normal, even though the summer at Lake Hopatcong had set me up for being out of phase.

In the spring Miss Vardi gave me a book of photographs of Italian sculptures, and I started sculpting nudes. She would let me paint or sculpt anything I dreamed about, and she always gave me praise. If she was sculpting me, I didn't know. Her suggestions were always gentle. In the fall I was assigned to a different art teacher, and from the first day of class, I had the impression she didn't like me. She was quite a bit older than Miss Vardi and had a formal way of teaching. The projects she assigned had strict rules which didn't fit my style. On my own I studied anatomy and continued painting nudes, but my teacher told me, "This is not what a young girl should be painting!" I responded with a flood of tears.

After school, I brought my painting to Miss Vardi. She praised my use of color and offered suggestions about painting hands and feet. When I told her what my new teacher said, she gave me some private space in her storage room, next to the window, and told me, "You can paint anything you want, including nudes."

I sat on a table in the closet and looked up at Miss Vardi's green eyes. The warmth I saw there comforted me and I felt permission to pour out my pain. "When someone doesn't believe in me, something inside freezes. I start doubting myself and wonder if they're right."

She looked me in the eye and said, "Katarina, you're going to be a great artist. Keep trusting yourself."

With her gentle guidance, the world started speaking to me again. Back in my high school classroom, I painted birds, sketched charcoal portraits of students playing music in the orchestra, and sculpted what I saw in the forest. This gained my teacher's praise, but there was a deeper part of me she never saw. After school, I went to Miss Vardi's classroom several times a week and painted what I dreamed in the style that felt right to me. Miss Vardi offered suggestions to help refine my style, but always from a level of love and appreciation. Her belief in me made me feel hopeful and inspired. Her classroom was a place of permission, and what I created there filled me with joy.

During the summer I twisted copper wire into horses. Nobody taught me how to do it, but my fingers knew.

Chapter 7:

Blue Overalls, No Shirt

t's amazing to watch a boy swim into a man. As the months passed, Christopher grew taller. His muscles widened, his shoulders became broad, and something deepened in his eyes. He was sculpture unlike anything I had seen in this world. On paths in the back woods, I liked to walk behind him so I could watch him. His muscles were like roots and branches in an old growth forest. In his presence, the world was illuminated. Everything spoke to me. My eyes were still sensitive to bright light, but I loved the filtered light of the forest.

When we went back to school in the fall, Christopher started having girlfriends. First Elena, then Robin, then Joella. At seventeen, he had become a black belt in karate. He was president of the Karate Club and generous with his knowledge, but the special things I knew about him were always hidden. Christopher assured me that he still thought of me as his sister, but every time I saw him with his new friends, I felt invisible. I felt an ache I didn't understand. My small consolation was that I was the only one who knew about the tunnel and how he could speak the language of the birds.

Birds flew to my hands, but I was alone now. On the way to school, I walked past his house every morning. Sometimes his mother would call me in and give me a blueberry muffin, but Christopher was never there. What really bothered me was that Christopher wasn't available anymore for our walks in the forest. I tried hiking in the forest alone, but the simple pleasure I felt there was gone.

In June I went with my family to his graduation party, and I helped him load his VW Microbus the morning he went off to art school at the University of Kentucky. Just before he left, Christopher put his arms around me and said, "Take good care of yourself, Katarina." He massaged my shoulders and held me for a long time. Then he drove away.

My dream was like an echo that night – the flapping wings of an egret flying to the ocean. Something inside me felt like the hollow of a tree where a downy woodpecker nests. For the next week, I consoled myself by sculpting Christopher, then painting him inside a profusion of birds. I heard bird songs all around me, and the music came out through my fingers. I didn't need him to pose for me because I knew him.

Chapter 8:

The Cloisters and the Unicorn

I had no idea how often Christopher thought about me after he left for Kentucky, but a note was missing from the chord of my soul. Christopher's life had followed another river, and I wondered where he was hiking and where his art was leading him. Sometimes his mother invited me to visit on my way to school. She always gave me a blueberry muffin and asked to see my sketchbook. I always hoped to hear a few words about Christopher. Sometimes his Grandma drove me to her cabin so we could weave together, and for my birthday, she gave me a long purple scarf with knotted tassels.

Painting and sculpture continued to lead me into an expanding universe of joy. In my junior year, our new art teacher took our class to the Metropolitan Museum of Art. He told us stories about the painters and encouraged us to incorporate some of their techniques in our own expression. He asked us to experiment, which sometimes fell on its face and sometimes was amazing. Life became an experiment in new forms.

My other passion was playing flute, and our school had a strong music program. The orchestra rehearsed before school three times a week and each day during the third period. The choral classes performed a Broadway musical every spring, and for six weeks before each performance, the orchestra was excused from gym to rehearse with them. I was very relieved to miss rope climbing, since I felt more comfortable on the ground than close to the ceiling, but I enjoyed volleyball, soccer and gymnastics. At the urging of my music teacher, I tried out for the All State Orchestra. So many students from our school were accepted that we had a school bus taking us to rehearsals. Before the concert, one of the boys who played clarinet asked me out on a date. Since we lived in different towns and neither of us were old enough to drive, I wasn't sure if it was a good idea.

David starting calling me a few times a week, and he kept asking me to meet him in Manhattan. He said, "We can take the train into the city and meet at the station. Or we can meet at the Museum of Modern Art."

I thought about it, then told him, "Actually, I've already been there several times this year with my art teacher."

"How about The Cloisters? We can see the Unicorn Tapestries! Last time I went to The Cloisters, my friends and I discovered an amazing bead with more than a hundred carved figures inside. Have you ever been there? You take the A Train to Washington Heights and we can walk from there."

I told him, "I'll have to ask my parents." I loved unicorns but I felt that David was being too pushy.

He was encouraged and said, "Okay then. I'll call you back tomorrow."

David was a year older than me and lived closer to the city. He and his friends took the Path Trains to Manhattan almost every weekend, but I had never gone there by myself. I enjoyed talking with David, especially about music, but when it came to planning a date, something inside me hesitated. For some reason I didn't understand, I had quiet misgivings. I decided to ask my father what to do.

His first question to me was, "What do you want to do?"

I thought about it, then said, "Actually, I don't want to go. I just don't know why."

He gently replied, "You don't have to go out on a date just because someone asks you."

"That makes me feel better. I like having a friend at the All State Orchestra rehearsals, but going on a date is different."

My father smiled. "It's okay, Katarina. You don't have to go. It's important to listen to your feelings about this boy and to trust yourself. If something doesn't feel right, don't do it. You don't need to know why."

"But what should I tell him?"

"Tell him your father will not give you permission to go on a date in Manhattan, but you'll see him again next year in the All State Orchestra."

I felt relieved. Then I asked him, "Do you think anyone else will ask me out?

"Of course, Katarina. Even if it doesn't happen in high school, you'll have plenty of time to meet someone special when you are in college. When the right guy comes along, you'll know."

"It's nice to be noticed, but something about David makes me feel uncomfortable."

"Whenever you feel that way about anyone, listen to that quiet voice inside you. You'll stay out of trouble that way."

After school the next day, I went to visit Miss Vardi. When I told her about David, she agreed with my father; however, she thought I should visit The Cloisters before I went to college. She walked to her bookshelves and pulled out two books about the Unicorn Tapestries, *The Unicorn in Captivity* and *The Virgin and the Unicorn*. She said I could take the books home for a few days.

At home that evening, I was fascinated as I read: "Unicorns are glorious creatures, gentle and good, at least toward those who are innocent, and filled with grace and splendor. They are magical in their appearance and character, also in their abilities. The tale of the virgin's ability to tame the unicorn seems to have arisen in Medieval times. As the legend goes, if a virgin is led to a place where the unicorn has been seen, upon seeing her, the unicorn will rest his head in her lap and fall asleep. The unicorn was the symbol of chastity and was sought after by kings who wanted to display it as a symbol of power."

The photographs of the Unicorn Tapestries were enchanting, with symbolic birds and flowers, and I wondered about the artists who created them. Since unicorns had not been seen on the earth in recent times, I wondered what it was like to be the last unicorn. During the summer vacation, I'd ask my mother to take us to The Cloisters, since Jessica wanted to see the unicorns too.

David's parents took him to see our high school's performance of *West Side Story*. We talked for a while at the party after the show, but he stopped calling me after that night. He was getting ready to go to a summer music program in another state. I had no interest in the boys at my school. They couldn't shine in the light of Christopher's star. If anyone from my school was drawn to me, I didn't notice. My strength and my refuge were in my art. Following Christopher's lead, I knew I would go to art school after graduation.

Chapter 9:

Night Stars and the Aurora

After visitors' weekends at four universities, I decided to major in art at Cornell. My requirements for choosing a university were an outstanding art department, a music program with an orchestra, and a location where I could feel connected with nature. Hiking was my meditation, my way of finding peace. The gorge next to the campus was exquisite, and the surrounding countryside was abundant with lakes and waterfalls. After the tour of the campus and a hike into the gorge, I knew this was where I wanted to live for the next four years.

Early in September my parents and I loaded the station wagon for the drive to Ithaca. We left a day early to visit one of my father's high school friends in Gloversville, a small town west of Albany on the slopes of the Mohawk River Valley. I looked forward to seeing his daughter, Celeste, whom I had known since I was eight years old. Although she was two years younger, Celeste was precocious in a way that I was not. She had, in her own words, "gotten into trouble" with an athlete from her school. Her father grounded her for three months after a late night joy ride when she and her boyfriend drove on the curb and knocked over several rows of garbage cans. This seemed so funny and strange to me.

I asked Celeste to tell me about her boyfriend.

"Johnny's a year older than me, captain of the soccer team. We met at the Valentine's dance last winter – it was love at first sight.

He's tall, handsome, and my father never liked him. Said he didn't want me marrying someone who works in a gas station."

"But he's not going to do that all his life. . ."

"Well, who knows? He doesn't have a plan yet. But when I told him what my dad said, he drove down our street and knocked over the garbage cans. Dad was so angry when he found out, he hit me with a hairbrush."

"Your father hit you? With a brush?"

Celeste nodded, like it wasn't anything unusual in her house.

"My father would never hit me. Just thinking about it makes me feel sad."

We had a long silence after that. I remembered my father's stories about skiing to high school after winter storms. One February the snow was so high, he had to climb out of his second-floor window. Celeste's father and my father were best friends back then, before my dad shipped out with the Merchant Marines. Celeste's father never left Gloversville, and clearly, he and my father had different values now.

While our parents played bridge downstairs, Celeste and I traded fantasies about our future. Now that I was going to college, I was hoping to have a real boyfriend.

Celeste didn't have the doubts that troubled me. She told me, "I'm sure it's going to happen. Tomorrow, you're going to college and you're so beautiful!"

"Beautiful? I've never thought of myself that way."

"Go look in the mirror."

Celeste was still grounded, but since I was visiting, her dad let the two of us go for a walk in the early evening. She was wearing torn jeans, and her blonde hair fell to her waist. She pulled on black leather boots, and as soon as we were out of sight, she kicked over a garbage can. We turned left on a small street lined with elm trees, then went straight to her boyfriend's house. His parents weren't home, so he lifted her into a bear hug. After Celeste introduced me, they disappeared for twenty minutes while I sat on the sofa in the living room. I turned on the radio, looked around the kitchen, ate an apple.

After they reappeared, we took a walk in the woods, which made me think about Christopher. Celeste and her boyfriend walked arm in arm, and I walked with my memories. After about a mile, the trail ended in a park in his neighborhood. We sat on the swingset, the two of them cuddled on one swing, with me pushing off on the other. They shared a hand-rolled cigarette with an unusual aroma and started giggling. Then Celeste got chatty.

"Katarina, you're almost eighteen years old, and you've never had a boyfriend?"

"Well, he wasn't exactly a boyfriend . . ."

"Ah-ha! I knew there was something you weren't telling me! And his name was . . .?"

"Christopher, but . . ."

"And you've known him how long?"

"Oh, I was maybe eight when I met him. . . Fifteen when he went to art school at the University of Kentucky."

"An older man! How cool!"

"We were neighbors; he was like part of my family. The two of us almost drowned together when I was twelve . . ."

"You almost what?"

"Oh, let's not talk about it. Christopher and I spent a lot of time together that summer. We had a secret language that nobody else could understand. We liked to get away from other people and walk in the forest. We hiked together in Stokes State Forest, Pinchot Falls, the Delaware Water Gap, and the Appalachian Trail. His grandmother taught us how to understand the language of the birds, and she showed me how to weave on her handloom. We hiked in the woods with sketchbooks and our eyes so wide open. It was like everything in the forest was speaking to me."

"That sounds like a boyfriend to me."

The air was crisp and cold with the sky splashed with the aurora borealis. Above us the stars were huge, and I was hypnotized by the curtains of light that flowed and changed color – sometimes white, sometimes green or pink. They would intensify, fade and change shape. It felt like an omen, mysterious and beautiful.

"Well, thinking about it now feels different. I never looked at him that way, but I loved watching Christopher walk in the forest with sunlight in his hair. His hair was like a halo lit up with a gold fire. I loved the shape of his muscles, and I even knew what he was thinking most of the time."

Celeste and her boyfriend shared a private glance. Then she said, "It sounds like love to me. And he was an artist, like you!"

"If you're meant to be an artist, it's that way from the time you open your eyes to this world. Christopher was the one who taught me how to draw, and I have his sketches all over my room. Animals, trees, birds, a self-portrait, my hands, a waterfall.

"You know, I've never talked about this before, but one weekend we went hiking on the Appalachian Trail with sleeping bags. When it got dark, we watched the stars for a long time. Then, we rolled out our sleeping bags in a grove of pine trees, and he fell asleep with his arm around me. It was such an amazing feeling. All night, our dreams wove into each other, and in the morning, it felt like the trees were singing."

Celeste and her boyfriend stared at me with the widest eyes. "You mean you slept together?"

"I never thought about it that way."

"That's amazing!" Celeste and her boyfriend shared that knowing look again. "And don't go telling me you've never had a boyfriend."

Celeste looked at her watch. "Uh-oh. Getting close to curfew. We'd better go back now."

She kissed her boyfriend goodbye, then took my arm and we started walking home. Above us, the aurora was spraying a sky show between the stars. A waterfall of light around the constellations. I thought about Christopher in Kentucky. Perhaps right now, he was staring at the same stars, his eyes filled with the same light. Millions of light years away, every star was speaking his name.

When we got to her house, we walked through the back door and straight up to her room. Celeste had bunk beds for sleepovers, and she gave me the top bunk. That was really nice of her. In the bathroom, we played with our reflections in the mirror, made faces at each other, laughed until we ached. On the left side of her mirror, Celeste's blue eyes. On the right side, my brown eyes. On her side of the mirror, blonde hair falling straight along her back. On my side, dark hair wavy and wild. I thought about her dad hitting her, and it didn't feel right. I hoped that in two more years, she would leave home and go to college.

Before we went to sleep, we made a pact. First of all, we would keep in touch – one postcard a month, but I'd put mine in an envelope so her father couldn't read it. I promised my cards would be hand painted. Second, we would keep this evening secret. And since we were sleeping on the same bunk bed, she would dream about Johnny, and I would dream about Christopher. Before I fell asleep, I thought about Christopher, remembered our night in the forest. Something we had begun felt unfinished. Somehow, I wanted to find him again, but he was hidden from me. When I woke up in the morning, I couldn't remember my dreams.

After breakfast, my family loaded the station wagon and headed toward Ithaca. We drove by dappled fields of cows, silver lakes and hills reflecting sunlight. Memories of Christopher were tugging at me – an arc of a planet's orbit, a bird's song in the forest, a question that lingered so long I wondered if it had ever been heard.

Chapter 10:

The Greenhouse and Other Hidden Places

My total immersion in art at Cornell was an elixir to my soul, and I woke up each morning in a wave of happiness. Since the summer at Lake Hopatcong, the deepest part of me had always been alone, except when I was with Christopher. Now I had the opportunity to create a new life for myself in a world that was art-centered. This was a world I loved and, perhaps for the first time, felt I belonged.

Cornell had a special dorm for first year art students, and I was surrounded by kindred spirits. My friends and I confided in one another and stayed up late painting, drawing, and reading art history books. I loved my sculpture workshop and found important mentors for painting, graphic design, and art history. When I wasn't up to my elbows in clay, I enjoyed art films and lectures by visiting artists. We went to concerts to hear Joni Mitchell, James Taylor, Simon and Garfunkel, Jefferson Airplane, and folk musicians from upstate New York. Graduate students introduced my circle of friends to the women's movement. On weekends, I carved out time to go hiking in the gorge. My friends and I went to the Goodwill store and dressed ourselves in velvet, lace, and antique dresses. We were the flower generation.

My art was unusual and attracted attention. I already had a distinctive style and delighted in finding new ways to express myself. At an opening for a group show, one of my professors introduced me to a gallery owner from Manhattan. She asked if she could show some of my sculptures at her gallery in Soho, and I was thrilled. This gave me a source of income and a certain level of freedom.

I expected to meet my boyfriend in one of my art classes, but I met Jonathan in the honors biology lab. Jonathan had a strong interest in ecology, which I shared, but I didn't want to take calculus, a prerequisite to understanding the curves of succession of species. Jonathan was able to help me there, translating complex mathematical formulas into human, even artistic, language that I could understand. In the lab we sat next to each other and became study partners, with a lot of kissing in hidden places we found around the campus. The greenhouse was one of our favorite winter cocoons. During snowstorms, I loved to lie on my back, looking up at the sky through a lacework of tropical leaves.

Jonathan was a year ahead of me, with a major in film and broadcast journalism. He hosted a program on the campus radio station and spoke in a deep, resonant voice I enjoyed while working on art projects late at night. My girlfriends teased me about this and insisted that Jonathan wasn't a real person. They said I was dating a radio, a disembodied voice, which sent me into waves of laughter. His dorm room was filled with totems, masks, found art, old coins, Inuit sculptures, and thrift store treasures that were usually old, slightly flawed, and carried intricate histories.

For his birthday I gave Jonathan one of my sculptures – a bronze woman becoming a mermaid, along with a handmade book of quotes about mermaid life and language. I wrote the quotes on rice paper with a dancing script. In the sculpture studio, I made her hair long and modeled the mermaid's eyes after my own. I gave particular attention to the scales where the transformation to mermaid was taking place, made them large and full of waves. Jonathan put my sculpture in the center of his room, which was already like a museum. He put the book on a pedestal by her feet.

My favorite quote was by H. Bowen: "Some Mermaids possess powers of prophecy, and all have the ability to protect their loved ones from harm. They can also bring bad luck, and even great catastrophe, to any who betray them."

Chapter 11:

Grandma Helen's Summer Porch

During our summer vacation, I went to New Jersey to live with my family and hike in the Appalachian Mountains. Jonathan went home to Montreal. At the bus station, Jonathan hugged me, then whispered something sweet in French. I knew he was tired of speaking English. His French Canadian accent had been erased in broadcast journalism seminars, but as summer approached each year, he longed for the part of himself that English cannot describe. "Every language has nuances that are lost in the gaps of translation. One day," he said, "you will visit my family in Montreal and see what I have not been able to share completely."

Our agreement that summer was to call every two weeks and share our best stories for fifteen minutes, to stay connected but avoid a huge international phone bill. As we spoke, I sat with a sketchbook on my knees and let his voice create his image. In charcoal I drew the fine bones of his French Canadian lineage, added a white shirt with a few buttons undone, sleeves rolled up just past the wrist. Dark blonde hair, gold wire-rim glasses, large brown eyes. Something about his eyes was innocent and knowing at the same time. His skin, light with a darker tone underneath. I could paint it more easily than find language to describe it. His body, thin and muscular, made for dancing. His hands, sensitive and artistic. Time condensed and expanded during these conversations. Late at night I would fall asleep with the image of his arms around me.

Finally, after my junior year, we decided to spend the summer together and travel across the United States and Canada. We would start at my grandma's house, drive west to the Mississippi River, follow the river north to Minneapolis, cross the Canadian border, and then head east toward Montreal. Jonathan was eager to show me the city where he grew up and introduce me to his family. He had just graduated but would be returning to Cornell in the fall for his Master's degree. Except for his thesis, he planned to finish the program in one year, and I knew he was enough of a genius to do it.

We started the trip by driving from Ithaca to Pennsylvania to see my grandma, who had moved back to the farm where she grew up. Grandma Helen treated Jonathan like family from the moment we walked through the door. He delighted her by taking her in his arms and waltzing her around the kitchen of her farm house. He praised her paintings of the barn, the pond, a wooded path by a bridge, and he had intelligent comments about all of them. By the end of the afternoon, I found myself looking at her paintings in a different way. Jonathan encouraged her to start painting again and promised to buy her an easel, brushes and new tubes of paint.

Grandma Helen laughed and told him, in that straightforward way she had, "I can't see well enough to paint again that way."

Jonathan would not accept her excuse. "You can be an impressionist now, like Monet or Van Gogh. My art history professors believe a significant change in eyesight was the catalyst for all impressionist art, so this is a perfect time for you to paint again."

"Only if you promise to waltz with me after my first new painting!"

For the next few hours, the three of us had a long conversation about ways of seeing the world and how that translates into art. We agreed that art always involves a transformation. This was something I knew intuitively, even in high school, when I began to ripple the legs of the women I sculpted. The ripple of the legs had become an important element of my style.

In the early evening we picked mint leaves from the garden, made tea and drank it on the porch. As the sky grew dark, Jonathan and I enjoyed the cascade of stars, intensely visible away from city lights. We found the summer constellations around a long splash of Milky Way. We pointed to Orion, the Pleiades and Cassiopeia, but Grandma Helen told us she couldn't see the stars anymore. They were too small and too far away. This made me sad.

Later that night, Grandma put us in separate bedrooms in the back of her house and slept on a cot in the sun porch – far away from us. Usually when I came to the farm, she slept in the room with me, but on the porch, she could watch the moon between her dreams and listen to the crickets by the pond. I started giving Jonathan a back massage, which I felt he deserved for driving me from Ithaca to Pennsylvania. The massage progressed into an intricate verbal and non-verbal discussion of boundaries and edges.

That night, Jonathan and I were faced with a decision. We had already slept together in his dorm room many times when his late night radio show or one of my art projects didn't interfere. We were both very affectionate, but there hadn't been a penetration. Even with the sexual revolution blooming all around us, I hadn't initially felt ready. Then it became a habit to be affectionate but not all the way. Now, with the Milky Way above us, and a symphony of crickets and frogs in the late night summer mist, I wondered if this was our night.

As I massaged him, we talked about encoded messages in the body. Jonathan said something about my feet and my hands that I didn't understand. He said they gave him a message he couldn't explain to me. He also mentioned a promise he made to his French Canadian grandmother. In the end, after talking and touching for hours, we decided to wait for consummation until our wedding night. Jonathan said that since we had already waited this long, we may as well keep things simple and wait a while longer. I felt pulled in both directions. Our decision felt simultaneously right and not right, but at three o'clock in the morning, any intuition I had drifted into an uneasy sleep.

In the morning, over a tall glass of Coca-Cola, Grandma Helen studied me. She asked, "Did anything happened last night?"

I said, "No, Grandma."

She took a sip of her coke, scratched her shepherd behind the ears, and looked at me again. "Maybe there's something you want to tell me?" But when I told her we decided to wait until we were married, she smiled and said, "Okay then."

"Grandma, he said something about my feet and my hands. He said they don't give him the right signal." She had no idea what he meant by that, and I didn't either. To me bodies were sculpture, and every one in its own way was beautiful.

Grandma Helen took out her waffle iron, and I went out to pick strawberries from the garden. Later, when Jonathan joined us for breakfast, she entertained both of us with stories about the Great Depression. I especially liked the story of how her father put rabbit fur on the seat of the outhouse to keep their little bottoms warm during the winter. She and her mother canned apples and cherries from trees by the stone well, stored corn for the animals in the shed, and canned vegetables for the winter. With hens and their small herd of cows, her family always had enough to eat. When there was extra, my grandfather brought food to the hobos in York.

Jonathan coveted my grandma's antiques, the tin wash board, the slag glass, the treadle Singer sewing machine. He promised to come back and dance with her next summer if she would share her secret recipe for beets and pickled eggs. She said, "I might consider that."

Grandma Helen found Jonathan totally charming. He made her want to get on her feet again. He made her want to put up an easel. He made her want to dance.

Chapter 12:

We Navigate by the Flowers

ater that morning, Grandma Helen packed us a basket lunch and we continued west. I was so thrilled to have time alone with Jonathan that I let my misgivings from the previous evening float away. We passed through the mountains of western Pennsylvania singing in harmony to Jonathan's collection of madrigals and shape note music, which he had recorded especially for our vacation. Then, as we descended to the open skies of the Great Plains, he was full of information about cloud formations, weather patterns and the edge that creates thunderstorms.

After a picnic by the Mississippi River, we followed the river north. Jonathan had filled the back of his car with yard sale treasures and antiques to present to dealers in Minneapolis, Toronto and Montreal – his contribution to the finances of our travels. We navigated by the flowers – tiger lilies by the side of the road, foxglove in the meadows, and Queen Anne's lace at the edges of the ponds. Each night we read out loud from *The Egyptian Book of the Dead*. Isis, Osiris, Horus, and giant ibises floated through our dreams. We camped below the Big Dipper and the Pole Star, with fireflies blinking possibilities.

Each night we lit a kerosene lantern for our readings from *The Egyptian Book of the Dead*. Our evening ritual was putting up the tent, preparing a modest dinner, and then reading this ancient script. Jonathan's voice was deep and musical. As he read to me, the night shadows of branches etched his shoulders. I sketched him naked in charcoal with leaves and branches climbing his arms and legs. As we fell asleep together, I tumbled into a larger place, where I waited for messages in hieroglyphs from Egyptian dreams.

Jonathan was full of information about everything, and I found his intelligence deeply attractive. Actually, he was modest about his knowledge, said it was what he needed to develop his radio career. We took small country roads instead of large highways, and each day found hidden treasures – a tea shop with home-baked scones in a small midwestern town, a used book store with an amazing collection of art books, and eighteenth century china in the attic of an antique shop. The next day, a vision of swans floating under an early evening moon, a box of chocolates, and a boating dock to a lake when we needed to cool our feet from the late July heat and humidity.

Jonathan narrated our journey with his FM radio voice, and as we discovered the landscape day by day, I shared with him the things that artists see. Shoulder high in prairie grass and midwestern wild-flowers, I played my flute. We traded backrubs, shoulder massages, and a secret foot washing ritual. Jonathan massaged my feet with almond, jasmine, and lavender-scented oils. Which oil we chose depended on what kind of dream we wanted to create.

After a few days of exploration and savvy deals in antique shops and used book stores in Minneapolis and St. Paul, we crossed the Canadian border. We camped for a week in the Canadian Rockies, then continued traveling east below the Great Bear's left shoulder. I drew black-eyed Susans and white pines at the edges of the horizon, evergreen forests rippling the mountains, and aspen leaves shimmering silver.

We ate Indian food in Toronto, explored the art museums, and stayed a few days with Jonathan's friend in a neighborhood called "The Beaches." Richard was a few years older, a radio talk show host with a popular program on relationships. As he explained it to Jonathan, "Depending on the caller, I alternately play a sensitive male, an intuitive genius, or an exasperating jerk. It depends on my mood and the theme of the program. The juxtaposition of the caring, intuitive male with my impossible side makes me extremely attractive to women."

Jonathan's eyes lit up in a way that made me viscerally uncomfortable. Richard continued. "Through the radio station's voice mail, three or four women come on to me every week. Perhaps I'll choose a partner one day, but right now I like seeing two or three women at the same time. Since my ex-wife has dark hair, I prefer blondes." As I listened, I felt invisible, even though Jonathan held tightly to my hand.

On Tuesday night Richard took us to the radio station. With headphones we listened to a radio sex therapist who took calls on the airwaves. She was bold, funny, and full of information. Ten minutes before his program, Richard took us through a narrow passageway, up a small flight of stairs, through a red door, and out onto the roof. He asked Jonathan to look around at all the buildings in the city center and beyond and to feel the energy of the people in these buildings. "In ten minutes, I'll be sharing my voice with over ten thousand people out there. After you graduate, I hope you will return to Canada. This is your future."

Jonathan walked to the edge of the roof to admire the urban landscape. He imagined his voice reaching into the secret lives of people who lived there. With Jonathan turned away from him, Richard used the opportunity to take my hand in elegant ballroom style, lead me into a spin and dip me. On the way back up, he pulled me into a rough embrace and tried to kiss me. I turned my head and used the momentum to maneuver myself away. On the other side of the roof, Jonathan watched the sun falling over the edge of the city.

In my twenty-one years, I had no idea that a man would choose to treat his closest friend that way. I didn't know that Richard was incapable of seeing the disgust in my eyes. I moved to the far side of the roof with the instinct of an animal in the forest but didn't have the earth wisdom to know whether I should tell Jonathan what had happened. In that moment, I was too shocked to speak. If I had found a voice for my feelings, perhaps it would have changed the future.

It was now three minutes before broadcast time. Jonathan and Richard walked arm in arm through the red door, down the stairs, through a maze of corridors and back into the broadcast studio. I followed behind in silence. On the other side of a large glass window, Jonathan and I put on headphones and listened.

Chapter 13:

The Tunnels in Jonathan's Attic

As we drove into Montreal in the late afternoon, a flock of cedar waxwings flew into an arc of overhanging branches. Cedar waxwings are magical, treasured birds, with bright yellow feather tips on the tail and red feather tips on the wings. As they fluttered around the branches of a cherry tree, their feathers were illuminated in sunlight. I pulled the bird guide out of my backpack and read to Jonathan: "The cedar waxwing has a striking black mask and an elegant crest. They're affectionate birds that sometimes pass berries back and forth among themselves as love offerings, at times getting intoxicated on fermented berries, then flying wobbly and acting silly."

Jonathan started laughing. "Sounds like two people I know! We'll have to find some raspberries after dinner." As we continued toward his neighborhood, I was intensely curious about everything we saw.

Jonathan's home was in a neighborhood with outdoor cafes, narrow cobbled streets, and nineteenth century houses. Since everyone spoke French, I was hoping to learn some new words and fine tune my accent. Jonathan spoke English when he introduced me to his family but a few minutes later switched to French. I couldn't understand much of what they said, but it felt exotic. After an early evening meal of soup, double cream brie and bread, Jonathan pulled me into the night – an odyssey we would continue for several days.

He showed me a tiny jazz café, his uncle's antique shop, his school, three cathedrals, his favorite used book stores, a flower shop with the largest sunflowers I had ever seen, and the bakery with the best French pastries. On long walks through mazes of narrow streets, we developed a litany of secret places.

Each morning, we drank tea in his mother's kitchen. Her kitchen was a cocoon woven with beeswax candles, copper pots, flea market treasures and hand-painted China. The window ledges were lined with Inuit sculptures of bears, whales and arctic birds carved from stones you could hold in your hand. She let me know the rosebud plates I admired were a gift from her great-grandmother and would one day be Jonathan's.

Around his mother, Jonathan sometimes revealed a melancholy I hadn't seen before. It felt like a secret language between them. Their conversations were always in French, and I could feel the emotions. His moods would come and go like nimbus clouds. One afternoon, the three of us drove to a lake north of the city. We hiked down a long slope to the water, then rowed across the lake in a green wooden boat built by a local fisherman. Later, I walked with his mother, carrying a basket of ripe pears, with wild vetch and sorrel blooming at our ankles. We built a fire near a shoulder of rocks studded with garnets. Later we climbed over boulders below a tangle of heirloom roses.

Each night we read out loud from *The Egyptian Book of the Dead*. The shining ones from the Egyptian myths appeared in moonlit waves, then swam through unfinished dreams to the back rooms of his mother's home. We walked to a concert of early music in a stone cathedral, followed by a solo performance of Bloch's *Schelomo* on the cello. I was smitten with the cello and the music put me in a rapture. Over a charcoal outline of the cello, I drew a cascade of cedar waxwing feathers spiraling between light and shadow. Music from the cathedral lit up my dreams.

Jonathan's mother, a French Canadian Catholic, put us in separate rooms on the third floor of her house. This arrangement had implicit rules, but the rooms were connected by a tunnel that led from the closets through the attic. Jonathan crawled through the tunnel to my room every night, and at some point during the week of the Montreal Jazz Festival, we passed through the gateway to another world. We were lit up with each other, under slatted stripes of moonlight, playing with the edge for hours, and finally we went over. It was mysterious and magical. I was flooded with a tide of light, something I had only seen on my brief journey away from this world. Memories were revealed inside the petals of calla lilies, the scent of pink roses, the light of wild orchids.

The Montreal summer was a sauna of relentless heat, an origami enigma unfolding inside a cryptex of tunnels. In the dark, I couldn't see Jonathan's face but we were always touching. We met in corridors that revealed themselves in dreams, secret attic passageways, a game of hide and seek. And I, the woman in his fantasies, was in that in-between place. Not a girl anymore, but not yet fully a woman. Jonathan floated through the melody of a mountain violin as I climbed the pyramid tunnels of an Egyptian dream. I was the beating of a heron's wing, the footprints of a cormorant dissolving in his hand.

Chapter 14:

The Yoga of the Impossible

I entered my senior year of college with a new knowledge. I felt quietly confident but intensely vulnerable. From the center of this mystery, I saw everything in a deeper way. In the mirrors of the ballet studio where I danced, I saw my body transforming into a woman, filled with secrets I hadn't known before. When I worked in clay, I found a powerful new expression in my hands. I sculpted women with their heads thrown back in ecstasy, lovers in passionate embrace, goddesses with orchids in the center of the holy place. My hands were in an altered state of consciousness.

One night, at a dorm room gathering with a friend who had painted her walls like a Tibetan temple, I heard about an honors seminar called "Selected Topics in Contemporary Mysticism." That was where, my friend informed me, she got the idea for the temple of sacred art we were sitting in. During her summer vacation, she had studied Tibetan tanka painting with exiled Tibetan monks in Nepal, and sacred art was now the center of her spiritual practice. In a prayer circle around her walls, she had painted more than one hundred Buddhas. To add a contemporary touch, she accented their auras with flourescent brush strokes, so that under a black light, they glowed in the dark. I had been searching for something new and obscure to study during my final semester. Clearly, this was it.

The professor was a Tibetan monk and a practicing shaman, having recently returned to New York after a sabbatical in Nepal.

His course was so popular that every seat was taken, and the aisles were filled with people sitting on the stairs. First we read selections from the *Zohar* to explore the cosmological structure of the Kabbalah. After that, we read *The Tibetan Book of the Dead*, watching for parallels between Tibetan Buddhism and Kabbalah. Toward the end of the semester, he introduced us to an obscure spiritual discipline from India called the *Yoga of the Impossible*. It was a way of getting enlightened by exploring paradoxes and contradictions.

"Every contradiction," our shaman professor explained, "has an underlying unity that pervades it, and every paradox is contained by a consciousness large enough to solve the riddle. If you follow a contradiction to its edges without resisting the mystery, you will break through to something larger. If you follow every contradiction until it reveals its mystery, you will become enlightened."

This was a larger idea than I could sculpt. Even Jonathan, who was usually the one to share radical ideas with me, was fascinated. We talked for hours about the *Yoga of the Impossible*, walked with it, breathed it, ate it, drank it, lit candles over it, made love to the paradox. I woke up dreaming about contradictions and filled a sketchbook with paradoxes circling yin yang signs.

I knew I couldn't solve the paradox which was obsessing me, but I explored it. I shaped a wild dancing goddess and glazed her sunshine yellow on one side and late night blue on the other. Over her heart, I painted a red and blue yin yang sign, surrounded by a thousand-petaled lotus. Her legs rippled into a river, and around her well shaped arms, I carved circlets of mysteries. For the installation, I hung two rows of Tibetan prayer flags over her head. On the sand by the river, I wrote an eight line poem:

Goddess of Night and Morning

She is a Flowing River.
She takes us beyond the dolphins
to the Fire
where we are burned but not consumed.
She leads us into the secrets
of ecstatic Love
where fingers of clay open to reveal
the Great Mystery.

My body was in a constant state of longing and embrace. Another paradox. I felt connected to Jonathan with every cell in my body, but when I was away from him, another part of my soul started singing. Sometimes, in those meditative moments, I felt a quiet whisper, but I couldn't translate the message. Maybe it would be revealed later. During late night marathons to complete our graduation projects, we shared the fabric of our visions and naked moonlit hours of making love. I loved Jonathan with every shade of my emotions, my art and my dreams. At the same time, there was a part of me he didn't touch, and that was a mystery.

Chapter 15:

After the Montreal Jazz Festival

When I graduated without plans for a summer wedding, my mother was disappointed. We hadn't talked about it before, and I didn't understand her expectation. When my mother pressed me for more information, I told her, "Jonathan feels that we need more time to make such an important decision."

My mother looked at me. "This worries me. When I was twenty-two years old, your father and I already knew."

Trying not to worry myself, I told her, "Times are different now."

I tried to put her worries out of my mind, but all young women are shadowed by their mother's stories. Well Mama, maybe you taught me that getting married too early ruins your career. My art is important to me. I am willing to make that sacrifice.

Even though I graduated Magna Cum Laude from Cornell University, my mother didn't comment on my Dean's List honors, which included academic subjects as well as art, and my 3.8 GPA. If she had noticed, she neglected to tell me. She seemed more focused on my younger brother and sister, who in her words, still needed her guidance.

I expected my mother to play oboe at my senior exhibit, to do her musical snake charmer act from a pillow nest inside my sculptures. She had prepared excerpts from *Scheherazade* and *Swan Lake*, but my sister, Jessica, had the flu that weekend and my mother stayed home with her. My friends from the Cornell University Orchestra filled in with a string quartet, but my mother's absence tugged at me. The pillow nest was for her alone – my tribute to the nine months she carried me. My mother never saw my goddess sculptures rippling out of wood, rock and ocean.

My mother was convinced that I was not a virgin, but I refused to talk about it. If Jonathan needed more time, I would wait for him. The catbirds in the oak tree in our yard were feeding three tiny chicks. They had mated, nested, and in the coming weeks, their babies would learn to fly. Maybe I would have to wait another season, but Jonathan and I would find our time for nesting. At the same time, I kept hearing the echo of our heart-to-heart talk on graduation night when Jonathan told me, "We are too young to be engaged. I still don't know myself well enough to make such an important decision."

I hadn't made a decision about graduate school yet, but about Jonathan, my heart was not confused. My reply was, "When the right time comes, I know it will be you."

Early in July we spent a week at the Montreal Jazz Festival, this time traveling up through New England and Maine before crossing the border. We shared an intense week of heat and music. Since we weren't married, Jonathan's mother put us in separate rooms again, but every night, he climbed through the attic tunnel to fall asleep in my arms. When the dawn light hit our faces, he crawled back through the tunnel to finish his sleep.

A few weeks later Jonathan came to see me in New York. After three days of stifling August heat, we packed his car and headed up to Maine, where we camped outside Kennebunkport and Bar Harbor. Just before the full moon, the sky was flooded with the aurora, which we took as an omen to follow the constellations north to Canada. Across the border, we looped back to Toronto to visit Richard, spent a day at Niagara Falls, then headed to Montreal. Every moment was full, but it worried me that we didn't have plans for the future. In a café in Toronto, I tried to talk about it. Jonathan immediately took my face in his hands and kissed me. Then, looking deeply into my eyes, he told me, "Enlightenment takes place in the present. We shouldn't ruin this moment by taking ourselves somewhere else."

In September I rented a studio in a Manhattan loft with a group of sculptors. Autumn descended early with a chilling wind, and even in the city, I felt the earth move into the quiet time of the year. Jonathan and I had weekly phone calls, every Sunday in the early evening, but no plans to visit on my calendar. Jonathan was unemployed, which made him feel uneasy, and he wanted to move out of his mother's home before inviting me across the border. He was thinking of moving to Toronto, where Richard could help him find an apartment in The Beaches, his favorite neighborhood.

On an impulse, Jonathan signed up for Sufi camp, an October retreat by a lake north of Montreal. By intuition, he felt he might meet someone important there, and perhaps after that, make the move to Toronto. I had reached the point where I couldn't stand being away from him, so I bought a plane ticket to fly to Montreal a few weeks after his return. If he moved into Richard's guest room, I could take the train to Toronto.

Two weeks after his retreat, I called Jonathan to tell him about my plans. I was so excited to tell him about the ticket and to hear the surprise in his voice.

There was a long hesitation across the border. Then slowly, "I'm not sure that's such a good idea right now."

"Why not? I can hardly wait to see you again!"

I felt his silence, with rivers freezing to the north for an early winter.

"Jonathan, what's wrong?"

"Well actually, nothing's wrong. I have some amazing news. On Monday, Richard offered me a position on his radio show. I'll start as his assistant for a few months, and in the spring I'll have my own show. I'll be moving to Toronto in a few days."

"Wow! Just what you wanted. We should celebrate. I'll take the train to Toronto after my plane lands." In the long silence that followed, I could almost hear his heart beating. "Jonathan?"

"My situation has changed in the past few weeks."

"What do you mean?" I was holding the phone, but my hands were shaking.

"Something unexpected, but then again, not."

"You're speaking in riddles . . ."

"I'll be clear. I met a woman who intrigues me at my Sufi retreat, and I'm getting to know her."

"Is this something serious?"

"Katarina, I'm not sure how to tell you. . ."

"Tell me the truth."

"I haven't known her for a long time, but the connection is deep. She's a Sufi dancer with long blonde hair and stunning blue eyes, which is really what I had envisioned all along."

I was so shaken that I could hardly speak, but I had to know. "Have you become lovers?"

"Katarina, don't ask me these questions."

"I need to know."

"Yes, we have."

Jonathan and I had taken such a long time before crossing that border. It was a gift I had given after more than two years of consideration, and my intentions were not casual. I pulled my grandmother's quilt around my shoulders. I remembered her blessing. Now, my life was shattering, rose petals in supernova explosion, angels scattering into the unseen. But it was my promise, and possibly nothing Jonathan ever intended or shared. Had Jonathan, in two months become someone I didn't know anymore? Even though it felt like thorns ripping my skin, I needed the truth.

"And you did this at Sufi camp?"

"No, not at the retreat. After the Sufi camp, on Richard's couch in Toronto. Every night, we've been reading Rumi and Hafiz, and the whole world is speaking to me. I should mail you a few books by Rumi and Hafiz. You would love their poetry."

Now it was my turn to be silent. Long blonde hair, blue eyes, and yes, of course, Richard's sofa in Toronto. With Richard cheering them on, his ear pressed to the wall.

"Katarina? . . . Katarina, I'm sorry about the ticket. Let me know how much it cost and I'll send you the money."

"Don't bother."

"I'll be making a good salary at the radio station. In a few weeks, I can easily afford it."

"It was my decision to buy the ticket. I don't want your money."

Jonathan was not quick to speak but continued in a tone I did not recognize. "Katarina, you are my closest friend. I hope you can wish me well. I want your blessing."

I put down the phone and looked in the mirror. Rainbow skirt, embroidered peasant blouse, gypsy earrings, earth colored eyes, dancer's body, and wavy raven hair down to my waist. What was wrong with me?

Chapter 16:

Let the Bird Fly Free

That week my family and everyone I knew tried to comfort me. Even my little sister baked cookies and left them on my bed. My first love had flown away, and I was covered by huge waves of dark water. In the room of my childhood, I rediscovered old friends – my childhood art and Christopher's sketches, charcoal renderings of birds, trees, a waterfall and my hands. What was wrong with my hands? Why did Jonathan say something was wrong with my hands? And what kind of vision was underneath it? Christopher felt a reverence for everything he drew. I remembered walking in the forest with our sketchbooks, late in the morning, when Christopher gently positioned my hands over a pattern of leaves so he could sketch them. Miss Vardi had been sharing techniques to draw feet and hands with both of us, as it takes a level of mastery to render them well. A few days later, Christopher framed his drawing as a gift to me. I had to trust his vision.

This was the first time I'd thought about Christopher in quite a while. I wondered where his life had taken him and how he was expressing himself. It would have helped so much to be able to speak with him now. When I was twelve years old, I had fallen in love with Christopher, but it was a different kind of love – the love a girl has. Jonathan was the only man I loved, and with the heart of a woman, I thought we would share our lives until my final breath. It shattered my world to find out I was wrong. I was a luna moth with my wing in a web of night weaving. I was caught in a visceral rending that put my whole body out of balance.

I bathed myself in the events of the past two summers. I was flooded with images of our odysseys across the United States and Canada. In my mind, I relived the details, over and over again. The part of my mind that holds logic kept trying to figure out what had happened as I cried myself to sleep every night. My soul felt hollow and empty. I kept searching for a flicker of a candle, but the light was gone.

Even my grandmother had fallen in love with Jonathan. I knew when she let us sleep so close together in her farm house, she was making it easy for us to open doors and change rooms at two o'clock in the morning. I remembered the afternoon she played her favorite swing tunes on her antique Victrola and asked Jonathan to dance with her. I saw them waltzing over her Amish braided rug. I threw a handful of clay against that image. I threw a clay image of Jonathan against the Canadian Rockies and watched the pieces shatter.

I thought about Grandma Helen and the way she had loved one man all her life. Jonathan had been enchanted with my grandmother's farm house, the sunflowers by the barn, the fuchsias and four o'clocks in the garden, and the sweet taste of the white corn she grew. He loved her slag crystal collection, the Amish hex circles on the sheds, and her two shepherds. He coveted her collection of Depression glass and the Andrew Wyeth painting on her wall. We spent hours talking about her teenage rebellion years, her flapper crowd in the early twenties, and her feisty behavior when my grandfather was courting her. These images would not leave me.

Last summer, as she was stitching a Pennsylvania Dutch Star Amish quilt, Grandma Helen told me, "I know that Jonathan is the right one for you. I'm saving this quilt for your wedding." Grandma Helen was the matriarch of our family, and she gave me her blessing. This was the first time in my life she had been wrong.

Late at night I questioned everything. What does it mean to be a woman? And what does it mean to have a man inside you? There was an aching in my body. An emptiness. A wound. Life wasn't supposed to be like this. Everything felt wrong.

Chapter 17:

The Altar over my Red Pashmina Shawl

or several months I had no interest in sculpture. I avoided my loft in Manhattan. There was no art in me, but I took a yoga class twice a week and kept a journal. I read poetry – W.S. Merwin, Pablo Neruda, Mary Oliver, Jane Hirschfield, Stephen Dunn, Denise Levertov, Robert Bly, Rumi, Kabir and Mirabai. I kept a dream journal, which I sometimes used to write poems, as I wasn't ready to express my emotions with my hands. I saw friends in Manhattan and played flute with my mother, but nothing made me happy.

It was becoming clear to me that something had to change, and the change had to be inside me. Jonathan was happy with his new life and he wasn't coming back. He'd send letters from time to time – multi-paged descriptions of his new life that I'd take to a quiet place in the woods behind my parents' house and burn. He said I still felt like family but more like a sister now, which was certainly not the way I felt about him. He still wanted to share his stories with me. I was struggling to find my way, but I couldn't see a path. In an act of desperation, I drove out to my grandmother's farm. She was the one with common sense in our family tribe of musicians and artists. Maybe she could help me.

This was the first time in three years I had been to her farm without Jonathan, and every night I dreamed about him. We'd make love in the garden, behind a silo, or next to the pond. Then

I'd wake up empty. In the garden I shared my dream journal with my grandma, but I hardly knew what to say anymore. Three days of silent breakfast was as much as she could stand. The fourth morning, she took authority in a stern but loving voice and declared, "Go back to your room and write about what you are feeling. Don't come out until something changes!"

For twenty minutes I sat in silence. I did a set of yoga *asanas* – the tree, the fish, the peacock, the plow. I prepared an altar over my red pashmina shawl, lit candles. Then I took out my journal – batik cover, handmade paper, ribbon of red silk – and wrote in calligraphy: "The Yoga of the Impossible." The poem did not provide any answers but the language revealed itself in a flood – a river of image and emotion. I had to tell the truth. Three hours later I read this to my grandmother:

The Yoga of the Impossible

We might be traveling cross country,
but that's possible.
We fill the back seat of the car
with antiques to be traded
in Toronto and Montreal.

We navigate from the midwest
by the flowers – foxglove and chicory
on the banks of the highway,
tiger lilies and Queen Anne's lace
at the edges of the ponds,
at night *The Egyptian Book of the Dead*
floating through our dreams.

In the kitchen of my grandmother's farm house,
I massage the asphalt and fatigue
out of your legs and your shoulders.
Below the Big Dipper and the Pole Star,
fireflies are blinking possibilities.

Swans float under the full moon
in the pond on the far side
of the sloping cornfield –
the pond with the belly of mud
and the heat of the inner tubes
I used to swim in as a child.

Night shadows of branches etch your shoulders
in a pattern you long to discover,
perhaps in the attic of an antique shop,
or a message in hieroglyphs
from an Egyptian dream.

Silently, we shift positions –
gestures of the *Yoga of the Impossible*.

I wonder if you will touch me
in a way I haven't known before
but you say it's impossible.
Something about a promise to your mother
and something about my hands,
an encoded message,
edges charred around the scar of a cave.

We continue traveling northeast
below the Bear's left shoulder –
black-eyed Susans and white pines
at the edges of the horizon,
larch pine forests rippling the mountains,
aspen leaves shimmering silver.

In Montreal we drink tea in your mother's kitchen –
her cocoon, woven with gifts
from flea markets,
beeswax candles, rosebud china,
and Inuit sculptures of bears,
arctic birds
and shamans in flight –
sculptures carved from stones
you can hold in your hand.

She asks you about your life
as you tell her,
"What I had in mind isn't quite possible."

In the late afternoon,
we hike down the long slope to the cove,
launch a boat your father built
in the estuary water.
I walk with your mother,
carrying a basket of ripe pears,
wild vetch and sorrel blooming at our ankles.
We build a fire of beach wood
near a shoulder of garnet rocks
and mussel shells.

Later we climb over boulders
below hedges of wild roses.
I watch waves swell and break for hours
before I close my eyes.
I am the wild goose shadow
etched into glaciers,
wide Atlantic waves crashing into a high tide.

The shining ones
from *The Egyptian Book of the Dead*
curl through unfinished dreams
from moonlit waves
to the back tunnels of your mother's home.

I melt into a transformation
from fractals
into extended textured plains –
rock heather,
mother of pearl,
sea lavender.

You float through the ivy melody
of a mountain violin
as I climb the pyramid tunnels
of an Egyptian dream.
I am the beating of a heron's wing,
the footprints of a cormorant
dissolving in your hand.

You are looking for a hand
as familiar as the antique cups
in your mother's kitchen,
as we dream of shark fins,
shoulder blades,
two feathers spiraling between
light and shadow
only fingertips away,
but that would be possible.

Chapter 18:

Coda in Soho – The Elusive Bird

On the drive back to Saddle River, I talked to myself in the car. The kaleidoscope of the past few weeks was swirling. I had the imprint of my grandma's hug to comfort me, along with a basket of blueberry muffins. My ears were annoyed by words which kept echoing. I was thinking out loud, remembering:

Is there a cliché that bugs the hell out of you? Something too many of your friends say at exactly the wrong moment? Something your mother told you? Try this . . . You've just split up with the man you thought you would marry. It felt like an ambush. It caught you by surprise. You need simple acts of kindness – a walk in the forest, a shoulder massage, a cup of sassafras tea. You're in a café in Soho with your sketchbook, trying to make sense of your life with charcoal between your fingers. One of your girlfriends comes to your table, and you tell her what's on your mind. She says, "You have to let the bird fly free," and goes on and on about how he'll come back if he's supposed to. Obviously, she's not paying attention.

Two hours later, a stranger sees the sadness in your eyes. He listens to your story, then offers his vision about the elusive bird. Strike Two. When you've had enough of Soho, you take the train home to the hugs of your father, who says, "Let the bird fly free." I'm sure it's true, but right now, it's totally useless.

My father was sitting on the porch when I returned from Pennsylvania. He was working on a crossword puzzle as evening settled into the sky. I interrupted and asked him, "How do you know when someone is really right for you?"

His answer, like so many of my father's answers, was a bit of a riddle. "When all the ducks are pointing in the right direction."

I wanted to ask him if all the ducks were pointing in the right direction when he met my mother, but in that moment I didn't want to know. My sister had just baked a dozen chocolate chip cookies, but my appetite was gone.

I climbed the stairs to the second floor to watch the sunset through the branches of my favorite tree. As I sat in the room of my childhood, my attention was drawn to Christopher's charcoal drawings. They pulled me to the Appalachian Mountains, to the voices of the birds, a language I could still understand. I watched a cardinal fly to a branch on the oak tree by my window and asked for a message. Maybe the cardinal would speak to me in a dream before the sun rose in the morning. I thought about Jonathan and the nuances of our riddle conversations. A hint dropped here and there with omens I didn't want to hear – the many ways he told me we didn't have a future. But he was never direct. His words were full of art, philosophy, and images of enlightenment – words that would shake me to the bone. Every time we reached his threshold of intimacy, Jonathan would find a way to deliver one of his cryptic messages – words that would sting and pierce but not release me.

I had my way of navigating the paradoxes he'd present. In the echo of the enigma, I'd let myself feel his words completely. They'd scrape my skin and settle in my bones. The undertow would pull me below a thick green wave, and I'd tumble for a few hours. But wishing to find my happiness again, I'd put the paradox on a raft and release it to the ocean. Hours would pass and Jonathan would knock on my door before midnight. He'd offer a massage, which would lead to a deeper way of touching. The happiness in my body would make me forget what I had been thinking.

Time would pass and then we'd have another riddle conversation – words that would sting like bees, words with long shadows. Late at night, I'd have riddle conversations with myself, asking the words to leave or change their meaning. Someone with a more sophisticated shit detector would have picked up the subtext right away. Especially when he was with Richard, whom I detested from the moment I met him. Richard was now Jonathan's mentor and best friend. Jonathan's life was working on his terms, and my life had become a riddle.

It was getting more and more clear that I had to find my way out of the labyrinth or succumb to the Minotaur. I walked out to the porch, where my father was sitting on his favorite chair, and asked him if he knew how to make the pain stop. He said, "The only way is to let go."

I thought about this for a while. My mind, a whirlwind of oak leaves in a distant wind, as I told him, "I don't know how to let go."

He said, "I know it isn't easy, but try to find a way to open your hands."

This was something I could do physically, but emotionally, something was holding tight. Life was a cryptex, a maze without an echo. Letting go was something I had not prepared to do, something I didn't want to learn.

Chapter 19:

My Japanese Plates Enter Other People's Lives

The next morning, I returned to my loft in Manhattan, but everything was painful there – the bed where Jonathan and I had dreamed together, the shower where we had massaged each other with almond-scented soap, the Japanese plates with memories of special meals we had shared. Everything was speaking to me in a visual language of unbearable messages.

I walked around Soho and the West Village. I carried my sketchbook on the subway, into museums, and into my loft with a candle late at night, but my confusion kept getting deeper. I walked the galleries of the Metropolitan Museum of Art to see if the sculptures would inspire me, but the stones from ancient civilizations were silent. Sometimes I got lost in Italy, Japan or Greece in those halls, but then I had to go home again. What became clear over time was that I needed to start over somewhere else. A location where places and objects did not have associations. Somewhere unhaunted by memories.

Since I didn't know where I wanted to live, I decided to travel cross-country. I gave notice at the loft, then started unloading things. A week before I left, I sold my tea set, my Japanese plates, seven large clay pots, my hand weights, some clothes, and most of the gifts Jonathan gave me at a sidewalk sale in the West Village. I liked the idea of having these things leave me and enter other people's lives. Lives I would not see. I sold several sculptures with complete faith in my ability to create new art.

Two days before my trip, my brother drove into Manhattan in his old pickup truck. Seth was disturbed about how I had been treated. During a long walk in Central Park, he offered to let me use his truck for my vision quest to discover my next stop on the map and find my happiness again. While a friend kept guard, we loaded my clothes, my favorite sculptures, a futon, a pillow, my flute, two boxes of books, a wooden crate with my sculpture tools, some candles, and a cedar chest with photographs, gifts, and a few family heirlooms into the shell over the truck bed. My brother had devised an elaborate series of locks so these things would not be stolen, but as a precaution, I spent the night with my family in New Jersey before I headed west.

My books were mainly art books, bird books, poetry, a few novels in the genre of magical realism, and five or six spiritual books from India. As my brother and I drove across the George Washington Bridge, I thought about the *Yoga of the Impossible*. My life was about contradictions, and I had not yet discovered something larger to unite the gap between my visions and my life. I did not have the kind of peace that can only come from inside.

My grandmother came for breakfast the next morning, and two hours later, I headed west. As I pulled away from the life I knew, my parents, Seth and Jessica waved goodbye. In the map pocket of the truck, I had a collection of postcards from friends and artists I met at Cornell. For almost two months, I visited everyone I knew as I traveled west, hoping that one of these places would feel like home. None of them did, and I kept feeling more and more lost. In the midwest, the sunsets were astounding, but the flat terrain did not inspire me. The Rocky Mountains had a dramatic beauty, but I didn't know anyone in Colorado, New Mexico or Arizona. I kept going farther west until I landed mid-September in San Francisco.

Something felt different here. As I walked around the city, I was delighted by the profusion of flowers on the streets and the elegant beauty of Victorian houses painted in three-tone color schemes. On the paths in Golden Gate Park, people smiled at me, and I spent an afternoon sketching the herd of bison with a charcoal pencil.

On Haight Street, a woman who lived in a commune invited me to a macrobiotic dinner. All of her friends had long hair and wore colorful clothes made of batik fabric from Bali. One of the men in their group had recently flown back from Bali with a suitcase of sarongs. Most of the people I met that night had traveled to San Francisco from other parts of the country. Meadow, who had moved here from Mississippi, shared that living in San Francisco gave her the freedom to create a life in tune with her soul. When she found out I was searching for a place to live, she invited me to sleep on her sofa for a few days. In an intuitive way, I felt comfortable and decided to stay. To thank them, I baked a few loaves of cinnamon raisin bread in the morning.

In less than a week, I found a house share in Noe Valley and set up a sculpture studio in a loft in the warehouse district south of Market Street. It was before this section of town became popular, and the streets were gritty. Inside the loft, I created my personal heaven. For companionship, I bought myself a betta fish with a beautiful fantail. I named him Fishface and gave him a home inside a delicate glass globe in the cupped hands of a mermaid. To surround him with beauty, I put two dozen blue glass stones on the bottom of the bowl and a stem of orchids in close viewing distance.

During this period, Fishface became my closest friend. Every morning when I came to the loft, Fishface swam to the top of the bowl to greet me. Then he'd swim in circles to create a bubble nest. I think he mistook me for a larger fish. Judging from the size of the bubble nest, his instincts were probably telling him I was female. He just had the species wrong. At the feet of the mermaid who held his globe, I planted tiny redwood seedlings in terra cotta pots. I knew I would plant them outside one day, somewhere.

After I settled in, my brother flew out for a San Francisco vacation before reclaiming his truck and driving east again. Perhaps the love I felt for my brother kept me from falling into anger towards men as a whole. For the next two weeks, we walked through all of my favorite neighborhoods in San Francisco, then crossed the Golden Gate Bridge to hike in Muir Woods and Point Reyes. We watched improv in a comedy club, visited galleries, and the night before he left, we treated ourselves to a concert of the San Francisco Symphony playing Shostakovich's Fifth Symphony, which we both had played as university students. When I was nineteen years old, this symphony had revealed an emotional intensity beyond anything I had previously known. Hearing the symphony from the audience was a new experience, as an orchestra sounds different from inside. Later that night, the symphony cascaded through my dreams, especially the flute.

The next morning, my brother and I had breakfast at the Acme Café on 24th Street. Then he headed east. After that I moved at the mercy of public transportation.

Chapter 20:

Fog on the North Side of Golden Gate Park

aomi Wolf describes San Francisco as a city of sensual mysticism – a place of intense permission. I found myself in a culture so openly spiritual that you could go to a temp job and hear talk of deja vu, astrology and reincarnation in the lunch room. This was clearly a place where you could be completely who you are and still fit in. I fell in love with San Francisco the night I was invited to play chamber music with a group of new friends who shared a house on the north side of Golden Gate Park. We played Handel's Water Music in the early evening. During a break we looked out the bay window to Fulton Street, where fog was filling the street and weaving through the trees. It was so mysterious.

All of the people in the house played in the Berkeley Chamber Orchestra, were vegetarian and practiced meditation. One of the men especially intrigued me. Playing flute with Jeffrey was like walking down a mountain barefoot, with moss and lichens revealing themselves on the bark of tall trees. We continued with a piece by Telemann. As the flute, oboe and violin braided themselves together, a forest of emotions revealed itself. The colors of early music flowed through rivers, moved from underneath the moist earth, dismantling my shield. My emotions were a wild improvisation, almost on the ground but lifted.

A few hours later, Jeffrey and I were sharing kisses on a foggy balcony. What astounded me about this man was the way he gave himself completely to the music. He got lost in the music, went into a trance, and it made the hairs on my arm stand on end. I felt him giving himself to me that way. His hands revealed the same musical passion I knew from his virtuoso violin, and in his presence, I found myself deeply happy. With his arms and legs around me, I dreamed of light flowing through windows, holograms of planets, and doors mysteriously opening and closing.

At six o'clock in the morning, a woman opened his door and became hysterical. Jeffrey hadn't told me about Mary, a willowy blonde who played the English horn and had been somewhere else last night. As he held her hands and attempted to calm her, speaking in a whisper, I fell back into my inner world and resurrected the shield around my heart. Under the sheets, I pulled on my jeans and sweater. As quietly as possible, I put my flute inside my backpack, walked out to Fulton Street, and waited for the #5 bus in the early morning fog. I took the bus to Divisadero, then hiked up the Castro Street hill and back down to 24th Street. When I got home, I took a shower and finished my dreams in Noe Valley.

How could I trust my heart again after such a disappointment? And what was love, really? It took all the courage I had to try another time, and I had failed. The other musicians in that house must have known that Jeffrey had a girlfriend. I wished that someone, anyone, had been honest with me. Something between the visible world and my heart was hidden from me, or perhaps my inner world held a deeper truth. In my art, I had easy access to a universe which constantly amazed me. Prisms of color revealed themselves, and my hands understood the sinews of everything I touched. I was the goddess of a universe I created, and I knew how it worked. With men, it was different. I had offered a gift that was stolen from me. As an act of self-preservation, I abandoned my plans to audition for the Berkeley Chamber Orchestra.

In January I started graduate studies in art at San Francisco State University, not because I needed a mentor, but it was an easy way to have access to studio space and a foundry. At first I worked alone, but much to my surprise, I found myself surrounded by a community of artists. We sat on rooftops together, planned group shows, and shared blueberry cheese pastries at Tassajara Bakery on Cole Street. If I wanted to hear jazz, see a foreign film or go to the Symphony, I didn't have to go alone.

I'm not sure exactly how and when it happened, but I got into the habit of seeing my life as an art form. It didn't matter whether I was using my hands to shape sculpture or if life was using me for a larger work of art. On Tuesday I might be casting bronze, but by Thursday, life was casting me into a sculpture too immense for my daylight comprehension. These two worlds breathed together, embraced like the branches of trees, spawned rivers that rippled into other dimensions. My dreams gave me messages, visions, and images that informed my life and released my hands to find their form in clay.

On weekends, I hiked in redwood forests and returned to a pleasure I had embraced earlier in my life – dancing. I started with ballet, branched out into swing dance clubs, then discovered folk dancing at Ashkenaz in Berkeley. I dressed in bright colors and met a parade of men, but they didn't make me happy. No one could make me happy because my heart was somewhere else.

From time to time, I had boyfriends – a muscular auto mechanic who worked in the Mission District, a sculptor from one of the galleries in North Beach, a paratrooper from the Israeli army, a dancer from the San Francisco Ballet, and an acrobat from the Pickle Family Circus. We might see each other for a few weeks or a few months, and then they would disappear, the way a dream does in the morning. I didn't open up the way I did before. Even the thought of that was far too painful. My real romance was with my art.

Chapter 21:

The Mating Behavior of Betta Fish

ome artists have to pound on the door to have their work accepted, but I was lucky that way. My first wave of West Coast art, a series of sculptures and paintings based on Fishface, was well received in galleries and a few shops on 24th Street, Union Street, and North Beach. I modeled betta fish in various sizes, exaggerated the fantail and the fins, and painted them in both realistic and exaggerated colors. After a few months, I crafted a series of tropical snakes and dream snakes, mainly poisonous.

I brought Fishface to gallery openings in a chalice held by a goddess. This led to my second wave of creative expression, inspired by requests for goddess sculptures surrounded by snakes and leopards for pagan priestesses in San Francisco and Berkeley. Working the clay kept me in a rapture, along with dancing and mysterious dreams that gave me messages and visions for my art. Fishface amused me by swimming in flamboyant mating circles whenever I put a mirror near his bowl.

After a few weeks of watching his mating dance, I became worried that Fishface might be lonely. So I found him a consort at the California Academy of Sciences in Golden Gate Park – a spectacular blue and red female with long flowing fins and tail. She swam in visual contrast to his tropical orange and silver, and I hoped they would like each other. I brought Cleopatra home in a goblet, which I placed close to Fishface, and discovered a new dimension to my friend. In her presence, Fishface loved to strut his stuff.

One evening I came home from Ashkenaz to discover the spectacular mating dance of the betta fish. I had purchased a special tank with a plastic divider in the center. Fishface and Cleopatra were separated by a thin plastic sheet, so they could see each other but not touch. Fishface built a huge bubble nest about an inch above the water line and probably three inches in diameter. On the other side of the divide, his consort was swelling with eggs. When I looked carefully at her belly, I could see pink eggs through her skin. I left the divider in place for several days until the night of the full moon. Finally, I took out the divider and let them come together.

Fishface continued his posturing, with flared gill covers and a dramatic showing of his beautiful tail and fins. Cleopatra seemed hypnotized by this display. He circled her briefly, and then wrapped his body around her, enfolding her with his fins. Their bodies vibrated and undulated together for maybe five seconds. He then released her, dazed in a belly up position. Below her, I could see tiny pink eggs falling through the water. Fishface caught the eggs in his mouth and took them to his nest. He made several trips to catch and transport the eggs, and then blow them into the nest. I'm not sure if they embraced again, but I was careful to separate them when their mating dance was complete – for her protection.

For the next several days, Fishface protected his progeny by staying near the nest, catching any eggs that came out and carefully blowing them back into the nest. After a week or so, I could see the undulation of tiny tails hanging down from the nest, and later, when the baby bettas were swimming on their own, I removed Fishface and placed him in a hand-blown goblet.

Inspired by the miracle of birth and the new little beings swimming in my loft, I sculpted fish globes in the upturned hands of mermaids. Inspired by the mating behavior of Fishface and Cleopatra, I began to think about having a consort too. Occasionally, I would meet a man who inspired me at a gallery or a dance – especially the dancer who impressed me by lifting me over his head and turning me upside down. I'd fantasize about being alone with him in a forest or a field of sunflowers, but then I'd worry about the three month breaking point, which had plagued me since my move to San Francisco. No matter how promising anyone seemed, he was gone by the time the season turned, and my heart was not wired for casual encounters. Love was a foreign country, mysterious and terrifying. Nothing made me feel more vulnerable.

What was most important to me at that time was my friendship with Fishface. I never felt lonely in his flamboyant presence.

Chapter 22:

What My Betta Fish is Dreaming

ishface was lonely when I went to work today. He was thinking about the orange flamboyance of his fins and whether that really makes him the center of attention. Orange and silver fanfare, circling and circling. And can a betta fish be the eye of a spherical galaxy in a bowl with no one looking, dancing for his pleasure alone?

Fishface contemplates issues of audience. Is the stage a platform for connection with an audience or a bowl to swim in circles of the self? And does music come from colored stones, glassy and transparent? Fishface dreams he is a rainbow trout, cascading down a waterfall. He dreams he is an echo in an abandoned redwood forest.

Fishface is dreaming about his consort in a mountain pool. A light rain is falling, or maybe it's snow. He dreams he is in Nepal, sixteen seconds before an avalanche. The world is getting colder, and the branches of rhododendron trees are sheathed in ice. The sun fills the icefall with light until the edges fall from their own weight. Fishface has past life memories of being a trilobite. The Kali Gandaki River Gorge is an ice-littered war zone.

Fishface thinks I am a flying fish in a larger tank. He watches me eat breakfast. He'd like to swim to me if he could float through glass. He reads *The New Yorker* and admires a poem by Rustin Larson. He flashes my reflection on his silver fin. He dreams of swimming in Alaska with the northern lights spilling across the sky.

Fishface doesn't take personal growth seminars. He doesn't get blamed for the things that go wrong in his life. In his singular bowl lined with blue glass stones, he is unaware that betta fish in pairs fight each other to the death. His fins are beautiful.

Fishface isn't a part of anyone's late night mythology. He doesn't send holiday gifts, and he won't surprise you with a phone call after too many years have obscured the memory of his face. He doesn't ride the Tilt-A-Whirl or distort himself in fun house mirrors.

Fishface will dream of eels tonight taking shapes he hasn't seen. A thousand bettas, newly born, swim out of a coral cave, unaware of snow, branch or stone. In the morning, he will wait patiently for tiny globes of fish food that fall like stars from my fingers. In my quiet joy, I will listen to the tiny crunch of his teeth.

Chapter 23:

Crossing the Appalachian Mountains

espite my success as an artist, this was a time of loss in my life. Every night I went to sleep alone, except for the company of two hand-sewn bears I had taken cross country – Thelonius and Honeysuckle Rosie. I was missing my Grandma and longing to see her. Grandma Helen was losing her sight, and her doctor suggested a move to a nursing home. It wasn't a place where she could bring her shepherd puppy, and she didn't want to go. That was late November.

On the night of the winter solstice, I fell asleep in my loft and woke up on a mountain. I built a fire in a snowy field surrounded by white pines and blue spruce trees. Above me, there was a clearing where I could look up to a river of stars in the silent cathedral of the sky. I saw my grandmother flying with huge white birds. In a silent field of snow, I watched as they crossed the Appalachian Mountains and ascended through the northern lights.

In the morning I knew she was gone.

The week that followed was a collage of intense emotions, vivid memories and dreams. Grandma Helen had given strict instructions to my father – she didn't want a funeral but wanted us to gather in her memory. The next morning I flew east and could not hold back my tears for most of the flight. The flight attendant from time to time stopped by my seat and asked if I needed anything. It was sweet of her.

Grandma Helen's wish was for her family to toast her memory with a bottle of good champagne. She wanted us to celebrate her life and the many years we enjoyed together. December was cold in Pennsylvania, even colder without the comfort of her wise woman words when we gathered in the snow. I knew she didn't want us to be sad, but I couldn't help myself. I was devastated and unprepared to return to California, so I stayed with my family for ten days after the memorial.

During those ten days Grandma Helen was the major character in my dreams. When I fell asleep each night, she was always with me. Each night I climbed a mountain to a snowy field where huge white birds were waiting for me. I flew with the birds to leave this world in a spiral of light. We flew above the clouds where the stars were singing.

I walked with my Grandma through rows of blossoming white corn, cucumbers and tomatoes on the vine. I saw her standing in grey suede pumps and a tailored suit, the way she looked when I was a girl, holding my grandfather's hand. By her heels, her two dogs, Gretchen and Freda, followed our footsteps. We watched a lazy group of dappled cows grazing in the green and shimmering distance.

I watched my Grandma weaving a linen of sky and clouds, the blue thread like a jet stream expanding into the shimmering dawn. She had the innocence of a small child gazing up at a dragonfly, with an arc of dew beaded on a morning glory leaf in the early morning sunlight. By the edge of the pond, her two shepherd puppies chased each other. I held her hand and watched two meadowlarks. For a moment, we forgot everything except how to sing.

Where I met my Grandma, it was always summer. By the stove inside the screened porch of her farmhouse, she was canning green tomatoes with the recipe she learned from Great-Grandma Lena. She sliced onions, stirred a marinade of dill seeds, brown sugar, and sweet cider vinegar. We sunned ourselves on the dock of the pond that seemed so big when I was a child. We swam in black inner tubes to cool ourselves from the summer sun, dragonflies skimming the water inside a cacophony of bullfrogs.

My days became lighter, infused with light from the other world. Especially in the shower, I felt my Grandma's presence. During the day I couldn't see her, but she was so close I could speak to her. I asked her questions, and in my mind, I heard answers. When I asked her about Jonathan, she said, "Enough of this now. You gave him your best, and it's time to move on."

Part of me knew she was right and part of me was still deeply confused. I sat down in the tub and let the water spray over my head for a long time. Maybe the steam would dissolve his tenuous presence.

Grandma Helen interrupted me. "You were in college and you gave it the old college try. Let go now."

In the shower I begged her to tell me if I had done anything wrong.

She replied, "Don't blame yourself."

"But... But..."

She interrupted. "Trina, honey, child, you have my blessing. There is someone for you. I just can't tell you who or when."

That night, after I fell asleep, I saw my Grandma walking through a field of sweet Williams, four o'clocks, and tiger lilies. She turned and waved to me, then kept walking.

Chapter 24:

Tunnel Hum at Taraval Beach

On the plane flying back to San Francisco, I decided to plant a garden. In a few months, it would be April. I didn't have a yard where I lived, but my fire escape had an extended landing with huge possibilities. In my sketchbook I started designing an urban garden in terra cotta pots. Next to each pot I penciled names of plants and flowers – redwood tree seedlings, succulents, cacti, fuchsias, columbines, two or three pots of the requisite nightshades, and my grandmother's favorite flowers – pink dianthus, sweet Williams, four o'clocks, and tiger lilies. At the feet of a sculpted goddess, I drew an herb garden – sweet basil, parsley, oregano, dill weed and mint. Three more months of winter storms, but then I would bless my grandmother with a garden.

With my grandmother's encouragement, I started meeting men again. Her presence was around me and I kept hearing her say, "There's a surprise for you out there." I longed to find him. At the Avenue Ballroom, I met a Yemenite man with warm blue eyes and dark skin. Even on the dance floor, I knew his muscles were worthy of sculpture, and later with a jasmine candle glowing, I was eager to uncover them. But in my dreams, the branches were heavy with blackberries. I'd travel east to a place where wild orchids were dying.

Every Wednesday night, I'd go to Ashkenaz in Berkeley. I'd dress in colorful clothes, daub patchouli on my wrist, and invoke an aura of bohemian bravado. This was to cover the truth that I was still shaking in my boots. On Thursdays, I'd go to Mandala for international folk dance with exotic men from other countries. For some reason that was hidden from me, it wasn't the right time in my life to meet a soulmate, but something about dancing put me back in touch with my soul. As I walked through the urban landscape, I began to notice a quiet joy. In the morning, I'd wake up in a wave of energy, often with an image I would pull into a painting or sculpture. Life was full of music, but this time from inside.

On the streetcar I'd sit by the window to observe the kaleidoscope city morning collage as the "J" snaked down the Church Street hill. The sun slid in from the east through the Mission District. I'd think about the way my Yemenite dance partner grabbed my hip, how it was more seductive than an American man. When his visa ran out, I was sad but didn't take it as a rejection. I welcomed the new season and found a new dance partner from another country. On the streetcar, I'd think about sex. I'd think about how we are all animals, and how sex brings the animal into the angel. With men from other countries, I could feel the animal more.

The wheel of the year kept turning. Winter rains cleared into an early spring bloom, with calla lilies and birds of paradise. At that time, there were still pedestrian tunnels under the Great Highway at Judah and Taraval. On the afternoon of the summer solstice, a huge crowd of artists and musicians gathered in the Taraval Tunnel for the Tunnel Hum. They clustered in swarms of friends and strangers. A choral conductor began the chant, and the swarm hummed intervals resonant with the amazing chords at the end of Beethoven's Ninth Symphony – the ones he wrote after his hearing was gone and the music totally went interior. We chanted chords Tibetan monks sing along a tunnel of two hundred voices. Every few minutes, the chord would change and pulse.

That night in my dreams, I revisited the tunnels at Jonathan's house in Montreal and charted different exits and entries. Maybe another maze, but a different journey, where I would make it through to the end without being devoured by the Minotaur or by Jonathan's wife, whom I heard was pregnant now. I woke up shivering, with the moonlight streaming through the slats of my windows.

After drinking a cup of hot peppermint tea, I returned to another dream. This time I was in the desert. I didn't know when or where, but it felt like a long time ago. Or maybe the future. The sand was warm to my feet but not burning, and the place where I stood was infused with light. A procession moved towards me, and I felt the presence of a soulmate. I watched the caravan, camels with cobalt and ruby blankets, bedouins dressed in white with gold bands woven into the cloth. The procession was long and I felt his presence, felt him longing for me, but the dream dissolved before I saw his face.

I could almost touch his collarbone. In the soft light of a seashell lamp, I took out my sketchbook to see if my hands could continue the dream, but my hands were blind. Even when the dream faded, I knew someone was looking for me. I tried to discover him and filled a whole sketchbook. I could feel his soft embrace, but his face remained hidden.

Chapter 25:

The Dreaming Room

*Y*ou can only discover the Dreaming Room by accident. It is *open only at night, and only on nights when the Icon Keeper decides to open the gate.* Twice before, I had noticed Tibetan Buddhist icons in the window when I was walking down Columbus Avenue. This particular night I was walking in North Beach with two friends from the dance community and, for the first time, discovered the door was open.

You enter the Dreaming Room through a long corridor filled with icons and tribal art. The air is filled with incense and music by Taipei Lounge, highly seductive. As I walked through narrow rows of Buddhas and sacred art, my attention was pulled to a huge bronze mermaid. I felt her speaking to me through my intuition. A flock of green hummingbirds from Bali shivered on strings and hovered over my shoulder. As I continued through the labyrinth of Malaysian batik and Tibetan prayer wheels, I discovered an antelope carved in white stone and etched with sacred symbols. Inside the labyrinth, rows of Buddhas from Nepal, Tibetan bells, sacred animals from Africa, saris from India, flying puppets from Thailand, and batik orchids from Bali hid and revealed their secrets.

I felt a tropical wind, perhaps from Hawaii. This was a signal from Demian, curator of the gallery, a mysterious man who kept himself in the background. This was a thin disguise, as he was highly aware of everything and everyone in the room. Demian moved around the Dreaming Room with light and shadows on his face, illumined by rows of beeswax candles. He walked silently, like a Shoshone warrior in the forest. Something about him was highly seductive, sensual in a guarded way. I saw a sensitivity in his eyes. You could get lost there – a river, a sky, a forest. I knew that Demian was in touch with an intense artistic and spiritual power. This was something he concealed and revealed, but you could pick it up from a look in the eye.

The Dreaming Room is a sacred temple of sensuality, a time warp full of art and little altars, each of them piled with coins. When I asked Demian about the coins, he told me, "People make wishes here." He did not explain but handed me a card. On one side of the card, I saw an image of Manjusri, the Tibetan God of Wisdom, illuminated with red light. Above the icon, the words: THE DREAMING ROOM, A Gallery of Tribal and Exotic Art. On the other side of the card, I found these words:

In the legends of the Mwokipai people of the Mpo Islands, there was a place where their ancestors could go to dream magical dreams. For when dreaming in this place, they had the ability to move both forward and backward in time, and to go to any place in the world whenever they wished to do so. And once each year, when the stars were lined up just right, they had a special power. They could reach in through their dreams and extract just one thing from the place and time of their voyage. The rules were few. The items must possess great spiritual power, or they must display a magical level of craftsmanship. And one more thing. The items could never leave the stone walled place where these dreams were made possible, unless taken by another dreamer. One thousand years later, we welcome you to enter... The Dreaming Room.

A huge candle with three flames was burning as I wandered through corridors of mysterious totems – carved African gazelles, Tibetan lovers embracing, Balinese jewels and silver. The Dreaming Room was hypnotic and full of a beauty that opened the viewer's awareness to hidden corridors in their own soul. Everyone who walked there entered an altered state of consciousness. Every moment was a mystery and a gift.

Suddenly, the air was vibrating with the toning of Tibetan bowls and silver bells, a memory of rain. At the end of a row of candles, I gazed into a beveled mirror, where I saw my grandmother. Her image dissolved into a vision of my future, the outline of a shoulder, the echo of a collarbone. My memories were deconstructing, blindfolded with a green silk scarf. Or maybe it was purple. Dragonflies pushed my body into distortions. I was wild inside gauze, crawling in the dark towards a flicker of light. A mystery covered by a cocoon while meteor showers exploded over my shoulders.

I was free falling from the air with prayer flags drifting around my ankles, floating in the dark. Yellow and black stripes of light and shadow drifted across my feet. Banded bees were trying to tell me stories, but all I heard was a buzzing in my ears. My lover and I were dancing barefoot after midnight. Someone whose collarbone I saw in my dreams. We were both covered with oil inside a steam of jasmine flowers. My heart was shaking, or maybe it was the walls.

A tunnel was streaming with gauze as I crawled in the semi-dark. The bees were humming softly on the other side of a parachute. The tone was silk or translucent, and floating – a new kind of music that I refused to listen to before. *The bees say the erotic is in the shadows, and nobody can love without the wound. They tell me we all need to be pierced to know the mystery.*

Bees flew in and out of the shadows, then bells and a light rain. On a Persian rug in the Dreaming Room, I reached into my backpack and took out a bronze goddess with six arms, thighs that rippled, hair like snakes, and a tiny ruby in the sacred place on her forehead. I kissed the ruby, then placed her in Demian's hands. He gazed at me with loving eyes, then placed the goddess on an altar of red silk. He disappeared, then returned and surrounded her with gardenias. He gazed at me and I fell into the shimmering lake of his eyes. As his face emerged from the water, he said, "You will have a dream worthy of your goddess tonight. And in this dream, you will be given a gift of great spiritual power."

A few moments later, he pressed a small velvet bag into my hand. Inside it, a delicately crafted amethyst ring. Something about the ring made me feel that my life was changing.

Chapter 26:

Nautilus

Back in my loft after midnight, I felt deeply at peace. Months ago, I had given up on men, but I questioned it now. From a nearby loft, I heard the wide vibrato of a cello – a musical prayer in a minor key, played close to the heart, held between the legs with the passion of an embrace. I rolled out my futon, lit a triple candle. The amethyst ring, on my left hand now, sparkled in the light. Something deep inside was telling me my soul had a path and a purpose. I knew this in the core of my atoms. I knew the love inside me would find expression in the world. I just didn't know how or when. With the candle burning, I slipped onto my futon and put the ring under my pillow. Through the open window, I felt the cello embrace me with its ethereal music – a promise and a vision as I fell asleep.

When I began to dream, a series of images were revealed to me. First, a dream about Noah's ark and a flood of water. Then a tropical island with mangos, hibiscus and silver water – a peaceful place for art-centered souls. After that, a long mysterious dream about a nautilus. It started out as an exercise gym, then became a seashell. My dream swirled through me like a whirring from a hummingbird. The dream was larger than life, ethereal as a rainbow gently shining its colors into the world. This is how I was given a mysterious gift.

I walked into the Nautilus in a lavender leotard and turquoise shadow pants from Bali. I had never been to an exercise gym before, and I was curious how it would feel to work out on those big machines. Like the Dreaming Room, the entrance wasn't obvious. The number 18 was clear enough, but there was no sign on the door. I stood in the street searching for entrance to a world that had not been open to me before.

A man with green eyes, curly black hair, and well-defined muscles walked out from Building 18. Something about him reminded me of Demian, but he was one or two years younger, slightly taller and darker. His eyes were warm and electric. Something about him felt familiar, so I asked, "Are you Demian's brother?"

"We get asked that a lot. We're kindred spirits, and we work together at the Nautilus. I'm Noah."

"Hi, I'm Katarina."

Silently, Noah led me through the door. Something about him made me feel like I knew him. I entered a circle of exercise machines, where a cluster of urban athletes were pumping iron below waves of music. Inside the circle of metal, Demian was dancing with an invisible partner as "Higher Love" spiraled out of elevated speakers. As soon as he saw me, he danced over and hugged me as though we shared a secret. I wondered if he hugged everyone that way. In the periphery of my vision, Noah went back to helping a woman with red lipstick and short red hair.

The phone rang before Demian had time to work with me. While he was talking, I looked around. The Nautilus came from a different part of the universe than the Dreaming Room. The machines were not arranged artistically and the floor was dirty. Two changing rooms had sarongs tacked to unfinished boards. Noah gave shiatsu massages in a loft, which was embedded in white sheets like a sailboat. Still, the warehouse had the charm of the older architecture in San Francisco, and the bricks on the wall curved into a spiral pattern. After a song by Jai Uttal, Demian got off the phone and gave me a few instructions. Then it was tiny body to big metal. Exercising this way felt awkward, and I couldn't imagine wanting the kind of muscles these machines were sure to build.

A woman rowing across the room had legs as thick as my waist. Noah ignored her; he was assisting the red-haired woman. I imagined Noah with a series of beautiful women, each one positioned on a large machine. Noah let Demian take care of the men. Almost against my will, I found myself watching Noah whenever his attention seemed to be absorbed somewhere else. He was a peacock, a slinky song, and I was drawn to him.

Demian was surprised at the strength in my dancer's body, especially in my hands. Most of my body did what he asked me to, but my eyes kept staring at Noah – his green eyes, his hands, his shoulders. Noah magnetized me into an altered state of consciousness, a green tide pulling me into a current I didn't understand. I liked the cut of his pants and the way he walked in his brown, wooden clogs. I liked his energy, intensely sensual like Demian's, but younger, more green, more pure. Something inside me felt confused in his presence. At the same time, I felt him calling my attention in a silent, powerful way.

I moved from machine to machine, unsure about whether I liked working out this way. I didn't think my body was suited to these large pieces of metal, and the exercise I liked best reminded me of swimming. I liked the way it made my muscles feel and decided to find a lake or a river. Moving my body this way would be more enjoyable in the water.

After working out on four machines, Demian said, "This is enough for the first time."

I heard the snake charmer chant of an oboe fluttering down from the ceiling. Following the music, I looked up into a sculpture of steel girders and silver light. The longer I stared, the more it deconstructed. The light became diffuse and then changed color, the way it does inside the aurora borealis.

Everything dissolved, the way dreams do, then reappeared differently somewhere else. The snake charmer, Demian, Noah and I were sitting in full lotus around a fire inside a vortex in Sedona. We filled ourselves with starlight from the four directions. The fire became a glowing nautilus shell, and Demian became a Mayan bird.

He flew around us, then flew out of his feathers into the form of a man again. We walked through a door in the desert, which led back to the Nautilus gym, with a café and a shiatsu room in the loft.

As an art-centered soul, I visioned the Nautilus differently. I saw walls draped with sarongs from Bali and a café full of shaman art from the Dreaming Room. I wanted to paint Italian frescos on the doors and texture the light in the loft with stained glass and huge sculptures. I knew it would be amazing to get a shiatsu massage from Noah. Sometimes my back hurt, especially when I felt lonely. Every time I looked up, I was dazzled by silver light from the lace-work of steel beams. I wondered if Demian wanted to take the oboe player to the Dreaming Room. At the same time, I knew he enjoyed his freedom. As she played her snake charmer music, she worried about the next pretty woman who would walk into the gym. She had her genders confused.

Demian offered me a cup of pomegranate juice. I sat on the balance beam and drank it slowly. Noah stared at me a little too long, and I spilled what was left in my cup into a dripping red moon. My emotions poured onto the floor, then swirled and became the sky. My secrets became the constellations. The season changed as flocks of pelicans migrated south. It rained and California had its flood of winter storms. Later, a clear blue sky with the Marin Head-lands in the shimmering distance. The pelicans flew back and it was spring.

A river of light poured out of an early morning sky. I was dancing inside a dream within a dream. In the distance, I heard the toning of Tibetan bowls and silver bells, a memory of rain. At the end of a row of candles, I gazed into a beveled mirror. I was in the Dreaming Room. On the other side of the mirror, the door to the Nautilus was open.

I walked through the open door into one of the changing rooms, which became a circle, then a pentagram. I put on an emerald leotard and wrapped myself in batik silk from Bali. I liked wearing fabric that swayed the way my long hair did when I turned sud-denly. From the beams of the café, I knotted rope to hang ferns, orchids and hibiscus. I framed posters by SoMa artists, and on a series of wooden stools, arranged a group of nautilus shells with a blue glass dolphin. This was political, for Green Peace. I became the apprentice of a French pastry chef, and when the Paradise Lounge poets stopped in to cool out, I flirted shamelessly with my dark Mediterranean eyes.

The café was popular with the South of Market crowd, even with people who didn't use the gym. I served them salads, chai, macrobiotic soups, fruit smoothies and French pastries. In the loft I forgot about sculpture and men for a while, but sometimes visions would surprise me. A surprise embrace in the tunnel, swimming back through the light. I was breathing again.

Noah and I rarely talked, but we were always aware of each other. Something inside me shivered whenever he walked up the stairs. At night I went folk dancing at Ashkenaz or the Avenue Ballroom. I never knew what Noah did in his free time, but I heard rumors that he was studying theatre and playing fiddle with a Cajun band. Why not live life to its extreme edges?

My grandmother whispered to me inside a swirl of sandalwood incense. We walked on the silver light of cumulus clouds. Visions appeared and disappeared inside a curtain of light, a river of butterflies, a sea of dreams. The wheel of the year turned.

On the night of the summer solstice, I crossed the Bay Bridge to hear Robert Bly read poetry in Berkeley. In a small theatre on the U.C. Berkeley campus, I found an aisle seat and sat by myself. Bly read for hours, wore masks, and chanted Rumi to chords on a mountain dulcimer. After the reading, I asked him to sign my copy of his translation of Rilke's *Sonnets to Orpheus*. He wrote his name and drew a picture around the third sonnet, my favorite one. I sat on the floor and read the sonnet to myself:

A god can do it. But tell me, how can a man
follow his narrow road through the strings?
A man is split. And where two roads intersect
inside us, no one has built the Singer's Temple.

Writing poetry, as we learn from you, is not desiring,
not wanting something that can ever be achieved.
To write poetry is to be alive. For a god that's easy.
When, however, are we really alive? And when does he

turn the earth and the stars so they face us?
Yes, you are young, and you love, and the voice
forces your mouth open – that is lovely, but learn

to forget that breaking into song. It doesn't last.
Real singing is a different movement of air.
Air moving around nothing. A breathing in a god. A wind.

As I turned around to walk to the door, Noah reached out and gave me a long, sensual hug. Then he disappeared into the silk sheet of a dream, which became the aurora borealis.

Noah and I started having little encounters, but only in secret places revealed in dreams. We shared a private night language that didn't translate into images of the morning. At the Nautilus we were silent, but his eyes revealed a universe of intuition. Every night as I fell sleep, I felt someone kissing me in the dark.

The Icon Keeper opened the gate of visions, then bells and a light rain. I was dancing at the Gaskills Ball with a partner from the San Francisco Ballet. The ballroom was transformed into an Alpine palace, with beeswax candles in silver candelabras. Our costumes created a magic spell that took us back in time. Everyone was dancing. My partner's style was technically perfect, but his heart wasn't open. Our midnight waltz was amazing, with dips and lifts embellishing the music, but something inside me was not satisfied. I longed to return to my loft, to take a bath and be alone. I fell asleep feeling agitated and empty.

At four o'clock in the morning, I danced in a dream as the door to my loft cracked open. Normally, I would have been frightened, but it didn't feel that way, even before I saw Noah standing in the door with a yellow rose. He was taking his boots off when I opened my eyes.

Noah was a tiny bit drunk on sake. Quietly, he told me, "I was planning to leave the rose outside your door and go away, but I had to touch you." He said this as he stepped toward my bed. "I was on my way back from a cast party in a warehouse south of Market, playing Cajun fiddle for some experimental theatre, a re-enactment of the Persephone myth with dancers, poets and musicians. It opened tonight at that new theatre on Mariposa Street." I felt his hand curving gently around my shoulder.

We held each other in silent embrace as a hummingbird fluttered in the window. Noah's touch was strong but very tender, full of feeling, as he moved his hands slowly along my back and my arms. His green eyes spoke silently to my hesitation before he kissed my neck, then my face.

"I've been watching you for months," he said. "I know you have strong emotions, a fiery passion, and a heart full of love you keep hidden. You're at the gateway. It's time to step through the door."

I was still too amazed to speak, but my hands knew who they were touching. I felt his muscles like roots and branches. Yes, this was the place where the animal meets the angel, an angel I heard whispering, "Yes, this is the one your soul has chosen." In the tenderness of his embrace, his spirit came so far inside me that my heart opened to him completely. My heart opened like a lotus and I remembered how to love again.

Sometime before morning, I dreamed I was at the ocean. I was walking on a beach in Baja and the waves were huge. The beach was narrow, almost jammed into the high cliffs that ran along the coast north of Ensenada and covered with rocks washed smooth by water and sand. The stones felt deliciously warm, as I curled my arches and toes around a litter of agates and stone eggs, jade and jasper. My feet had an extraordinary sense of touch, as though they were making love to the stones.

I wandered onto a beach with a fine, white sand. A cadence of amethyst waves rippled from the horizon. I knew that one of these waves might crash over my head, but I wasn't afraid. In fact, I had never felt so peaceful. A giant wave washed an enormous nautilus shell onto the sand. Hummingbirds fluttered to the fractal, which was so immense and inviting, it felt like a gateway to an invisible world.

Without hesitating, I walked inside the shell. Each chamber contained a different dream, luminous as a watercolor painting, and I swam through each one. Sometimes Noah embraced me in mountain pools of steaming water. Later, I couldn't find him as I swam with dolphins and rode on the backs of painted sea turtles. Angels were whispering to me, asking me to remember – a yellow rose, an ancient promise. It was comforting, like water, as though I were being held and would continue to be held forever. I was wrapped in a profound and inexplicable sense of peace.

Part II

My Year as a Dance Gypsy

Chapter 27:

Escape from San Francisco

I first began to notice it in my hands. One morning I stared at them and saw the hands of an older woman. Hands that had planted tomatoes and arugula in the garden. Hands that had shaped sculpture and played Vivaldi on the flute. Hands that know things. No yellow roses on my table; no photograph by my bed. Twenty years had passed without a whisper of my Grandma's promise.

In San Francisco I enjoyed success as a sculptor, with gallery exhibits, commissions, and a few of my sculptures in museums. In quiet moments, however, a restlessness pulled at me. I thought of the gifts I had been given by my teachers and wanted to give them to the next generation of artists. Perhaps it was the edge of a change choreographed by snow angels, but when I accepted a tenure track position at a small university in Mt. Pleasant, Iowa, I had no idea of the consequences this would have in my life.

My voyage to the midwest was an astounding rite of passage. When I fully realized what I was doing, I cried for twenty-four hours behind the steering wheel. This started on the San Francisco Bay Bridge and continued as I ascended the Sierras. Something inside me knew I was surrounded by an astounding level of beauty, but I saw it through a veil of tears. I noticed the elevation as I approached Donner Pass – my grandmother's station wagon didn't have the power I was used to at sea level. I attributed this to the rack on top of the wagon, loaded with sculptures.

Driving was easier after the summit. As I sped through a forest of ponderosa pines, I felt the pull of my friends in San Francisco. Nobody wanted me to leave, and one of my favorite dance partners showed up in tears at my front door while I was packing. All of this burdened me now. At the same time, something deep in my soul had been asking for a new direction, which I felt in quiet moments and a flood of dreams. My life was an unfinished sculpture, a jigsaw puzzle of an enigma with a piece missing. I wanted to create something more in tune with my soul, and I wondered if I would find the missing piece in the Great Plains. This is what kept me from turning my wagon around and driving back, along with classes I had committed to teach in two weeks.

My decision was easier to live with after I crossed the state line into Nevada. I drove as far as Winnemucca the first night and just after ten p.m. pulled into the Budget Inn, where I was welcomed by a family of East Indian motel entrepreneurs. They assured me they would keep watch over my station wagon during the night. As the high desert moonlight poured through the window, my dreams were edgy collages, like a Max Beckmann triptych, crowded with images of the life I had lived in San Francisco – galleries, sculpture, dance partners, lovers, and friends. I walked through museums, sat in the first tier at the San Francisco Symphony, watched the constellations shift over a hot spring on a mountain.

The rooms of my dreams dissolved into images of my exit from San Francisco – crossing the San Francisco Bay Bridge, the Carquinas Erector Set steel cantilever bridge near Crockett, the cascade of trees in Auburn and the Sierra foothills, the ascent to Donner Pass, and the "No Hitchhiking" signs by prisons in Nevada. I had a few moments of raw anxiety, then sunlight through the rust-orange curtain of the motel window. Time to eat oatmeal and start again. After I loaded the car, I put a Grateful Dead cassette into the tape player. My plan for today was to wash my soul in music, surround myself with beauty, and stop thinking.

Memory is idiosyncratic, but there are things I remember clearly. On the way to Elko, I was stunned by a low hanging cloud the shape of a flying saucer. It looked like a transport from a far place in the universe. Every time I crossed a state border, I observed an immediate change in the landscape. The salt flats in Utah looked like a portal to the moon – one of the strangest places I've seen on this planet. On top of the salt, graffiti artists had embedded a code in stones – a giraffe, a spaceship, letters inside a stone heart.

Past the Great Salt Lake, I wove through the maze of Salt Lake City, then was astounded by the beauty of mesas and red rock mountains. In the late afternoon, I crossed into the high desert of Wyoming. At a rest stop, I watched a small group of prairie dogs, then picked a handful of sage to smudge my new home. My goal was to reach Laramie or Cheyenne before midnight. In the morning, after seven hours of sleep and a cup of oatmeal with cranberries, I loaded the station wagon for what I thought would be the final day of the trip. I was still in high desert, but after an hour, descended into the Great Plains.

My grandmother's station wagon, a blue Plymouth and one of my prized possessions, broke down outside a small town in Nebraska. For the past two days, I hadn't been paying attention to my emotions, so the car did it for me. First, the heater stopped working. By the time I saw smoke wafting out of the hood, I knew I was in big trouble.

I got out of the car and backed away. After about twenty minutes, a farmer in a pickup truck pulled over and asked if I needed help. He drove me to a diner, where I called AAA, and he waited with me until the tow truck came. The rest of the day was a blur. Two salt-of-the-earth mechanics informed me the water pump was broken and the cylinder head had cracked. They wished I had noticed before it was too late. Considering the age of the Plymouth and the level of damage, they could either rebuild the engine or junk the car.

I asked one of the mechanics, "What would you do if the car belonged to your wife?"

He said, "Junk it."

I told him, "I'll sleep on this tonight and let you know in the morning."

The mechanics drove me to a cheap motel close to their shop and helped carry my boxes into the room. That night I dreamed I was in a San Francisco garden, surrounded by sculptures. Like many of the gardens in the Noe Valley neighborhood, my dream garden had several varieties of deadly nightshades. My visions were laced in belladonna.

Before I left San Francisco, my father had sent me one thousand dollars in Travelers Cheques in an overnight Fed-Ex envelope, to be used in the event of an emergency. This was prophetic. Before this trip, I hadn't realized the extent of my father's intuitive abilities or how much he loved me. With the help of the mechanic, I found a red Toyota pickup truck with a shell over the truck bed for $990. There was a bit of rust behind the mudflaps but the tape player worked, which felt like a good omen. Closing the deal took most of the day, but the mechanic checked the engine and told me the truck was good.

The next morning, I loaded my suitcases, boxes and sculptures into the truck and continued driving east – past cows, horses, sheep and tributaries of the North Platte River. In the afternoon, I stopped by the side of the road to eat a burrito and watched two farm boys with straw-colored hair paddle a silver canoe. Before sunset, I crossed the Missouri River, then pulled over to watch the moon rise over gently rolling hills. I felt a gentleness in the land, something deeply spiritual but hidden. Close to midnight, I pulled into Mt. Pleasant and found the house a faculty artist had rented for me. I unloaded my boxes into the front room, climbed the stairs, pulled out my camping pads, pillow and sleeping bag, and went to sleep with a waning moon bleeding through the window.

Chapter 28:

Too Close to the Tracks

Mt. Pleasant is a classic midwestern town, with a town square, two cafés, a tractor and farm supply store, a greenhouse, one Chinese restaurant, and a Civil War era hotel. The university nests on the north side of the train tracks, and my house, built in 1872, was close to campus. At first I was so delighted to have a full-time teaching job that I didn't pay attention to where I was living. My students and the art faculty became my new family, and I enjoyed the attention I received during student and faculty shows. But soon, I began to notice something odd – snare drums, trains and thunder in my dreams.

My house was too close to the tracks, and trains roared through at regular intervals all night. This was before Quiet Zone legislation passed the Iowa Senate. My colleagues said I'd get used to it in time, but I wasn't sure. Every time I thought about planting a garden, I worried that hourly decibels of train track thunder would kill the flowers.

Early in December, my father came to visit during a snowstorm. He flew to Chicago, then transferred to the California Zephyr train, which travels through Iowa on the way to the West Coast. Because of ice on the tracks, the train was several hours late. Even though I fell asleep with the phone next to my futon, my father never called. When he walked through my door in the morning, I was slicing bananas into a bowl of granola for breakfast. We shared a pot of Constant Comment tea as he told his story.

"When I called my travel agent and asked how to get to Mt. Pleasant, Iowa, her answer was, 'It ain't easy! I'll book you a flight to Chicago, but you'll have to take a train the rest of the way.' The plane was late getting into O'Hare, and I had to rush like hell to get downtown to the railroad station. The train was supposed to leave at six p.m., but because they couldn't find a working engine, it was more like 10:00 when we finally pulled out.

"I arrived at Mt. Pleasant about 2:30 in the morning and got off the train in the middle of a rail yard with no station in sight. I asked where the station was, and someone pointed to a little dark building. It was locked, but there was a pay phone outside. In desperation, I called the local police, explained my problem, and the cop said, 'Stay put, I'll come get you.' A few minutes later he picked me up and took me to the hotel.

"The hotel was right out of Gunsmoke, with lots of gingerbread and an open balcony. It was built by the family of Mary Todd Lincoln. The grandfather clock in the lobby had separate hour and minute hands. A bronze plaque announced this was the first clock west of the Mississippi, and farmers still came in on weekends to set their pocket watches.

"I walked into the hotel lobby at 3:00 a.m., woke the clerk and asked for a room. I stood there with my two pieces of luggage, and he asked if I wanted a room with or without a bath. I said 'with.' He looked me up and down, assessing my not-from-around-here face and beard for a long minute, and said, 'The room is twelve dollars, payable in advance.'

"My room had flowered wallpaper, a flowered spread, an antique table lamp, and old gaslight pipes on the walls and ceiling. Through a very tall window, I watched the snow descend and pile into drifts on silent streets. Then I fell into a peaceful sleep. When I came down for breakfast, two gentlemen were playing checkers in the lobby. The breakfast, all you could eat, cost $2.50."

As soon as I finished my granola, my father wanted to see the campus and my studio. He insisted on a library tour to see if it met his standards, then commented on a few missing books. I, of course, quipped that Iowa was not the place for most of what he carried in his bookstore in the West Village, still a gathering place for poets and politicos from Manhattan. At the same time, I felt something underneath his words, and I knew he would reveal it later.

Despite the stark beauty of the Iowa winter, walking around the campus was challenging. The wind started in the Rockies and had nothing to stop it until the Appalachian Mountains. For the next few days, we had wonderful conversations, listened to music, and lit a fire every night. I fed him my favorite veggie treats, and although this was not his favorite way to eat, he managed to survive. The last night of his visit, I spent a few hours drawing him from several angles illuminated by fire light. I wasn't sure if I'd use these drawings for sculpture or if they were just for my own peace of mind.

Since we weren't sure if my truck would start in the sub-zero early morning, my Dad decided to go back to the hotel to sleep and catch the 7:00 a.m. train back to Chicago. Even though it would be bitter cold, he could walk to the depot from there. Before he left, we sat by the fire and talked for a little while. When it came to advice, my father was not a man of many words, but when they came, they were important. He opened by asking, "How do you feel about living in Iowa in the middle of the winter?"

I told him, "I'm not sure yet. Sometimes I have to get into the bathtub to warm up, and I'm still in the process of finding my friends."

"If this is a mistake, you can go back home."

To which I replied, "I need to try this for a while. In any case, I'm not sure where home is right now."

Snowdrifts ranged from knee to waist-high on our walk to the hotel. We trekked under moon and stars, wrapped and layered, in a wasteland of silent beauty. In the lobby of the hotel, my Dad showed me the grandfather clock, and then we said goodbye. Before he went to sleep, my father asked the desk clerk if he could call the depot to see if the train was on time before waking him in the morning. In the spirit of midwestern salt-of-the-earth hospitality, the clerk agreed. This was a good thing because it snowed again that evening, and the train was late.

My father described his return journey like this: "The train got into Mt. Pleasant about 11:00 a.m., and on the way back to Chicago, we passed the westbound train, which had lost power and had been sitting in the cold for a number of hours. My flight home was scheduled for 6:00 p.m. and I got to the train station at 5:00. No cabs were available, so I took the bus to O'Hare and walked in at 5:45. The check-in line was long, so I asked the lady in front of me if I could move up, as my plane was about to leave. Her answer was, 'You can wait, as I did.' Fortunately, someone else heard me and let me move to the head of another line.

"After I got my boarding pass, I ran down the pod with my two suitcases and saw the stewardess waving me on as she was about to close the door. I huffed and puffed into my seat. The pilot then announced that the baggage loading equipment was frozen, and there would be a slight delay. Finally, the plane took off. Two hours later, we arrived at Newark Airport, where I discovered that the bags I had checked at the gate never got on the plane. I took a cab home after asking the baggage claim folk to deliver my suitcases in the morning."

As my father was flying east, I thought about my suitcases in the attic and wondered where I would be taking them next. Just before he returned home, I had a dream about three empty boxes – slit perfectly, everything gone, scattered in a field of frozen wildflowers. I woke up longing for touch, longing for friends, longing for sunflowers.

Chapter 29:

The Week of the Bloom

Despite the challenges of my migration to the midwest, the contours of the land provided new artistic inspiration. I spent the winter marveling at the shapes of winter trees, ice sculptures rippled with sunlight, and the hush of new snow. I was astounded by the infinity of the landscape. Evenings brought gorgeous sunsets, like an ocean of sky.

In the spring, I discovered the crossover day, when the air miraculously became warm again. It was sudden and unexpected. One day I was bundled in scarves and a long black coat; the next day my arms were bare in the April sun. Hyacinths, irises and tiger lilies pushed up from the earth. Soft green leaves pushed out from the skeletons of trees and crescendoed into the week of the bloom. The single note of winter expanded into a symphony of redbuds, dogwoods and tulip trees.

My garden was full of surprises. The previous tenants had planted hidden gifts that kept revealing themselves. As squawking geese shadows flew across the moon, a wave of oriental poppies opened. Daffodils collided with tulips. Blackberries twisted their branches around rose petals like a dancer who has stretched so far beyond her natural shape that the form has to break. I danced in the garden at night with pink lace climbing my ankles.

Wave by wave, the flowers revealed themselves. Columbines surprising the lattices on the porch, shasta daisies with double rows of petals wild as ostrich feathers, sunflowers spreading huge blossoms in the humid heat. Summer came in a flood, but the wind was still breathing with dahlias curling their leaves toward unknown colors.

In my dreams, I was flooded with petals, embraced by a dance partner who lifted me above the blackberry vines. Someone invisible kept reaching for me in the dark. Someone I kept trying to remember. I wanted to love him in the garden, with peonies bent to the ground by thunderstorms. I wanted to dance in a gallery of angels surrounded by wildflowers in a pasture of goats and sheep. Every day I discovered a new flower, like the petaled surprise of love. Every day the magenta blood of wild berries stained my fingers and my cheeks.

Chapter 30:

Twenty Miles to the West

Autumn came and I was back in the studio again, working my visions in clay and mentoring artists. My students loved that I was from San Francisco, a place of intense permission. In my classes they could give shape to anything in their soul – no rules, no boundaries. I offered a seminar in Japanese ceramics, featuring techniques I learned from the raku potters of Japan during a six month residency in Kyoto. It was wildly popular. But as the cold weather descended, I was caught in a chill that went deeper than my bones. I felt trapped inside a geographic flatness, and my emotions lived too close to the tracks.

After a year in Mt. Pleasant, the landscape wasn't doing much for my art, and my social life was nearly as flat as the surrounding wheat fields. After some initial exploration, I decided to move twenty miles west to Fairfield, Iowa – a new age community in farm houses. The people who lived there were interesting and unusual. Around the town square, Fairfield had a colorful assortment of antique shops and art galleries, with an Art Walk the first Friday of every month. There were health food stores with organic vegetables trucked out from California, even though a pound of tomatoes cost almost a dollar more than what I was used to at farmers markets in San Francisco. Fairfield had three Indian restaurants, two Thai cafes, an elegant French restaurant, a Mexican diner, a Chinese buffet run by expatriate meditation teachers, an angel store, an Ayurvedic herb shop, a new age bookstore called Revelations, and a coffeehouse called Café Paradiso. The town was full of artists, writers and musicians, and they had group meditations every morning and evening in two huge geodesic domes. It wasn't San Francisco, but I felt that I could live there.

The tap water in Fairfield was polluted with pesticide runoff from local farms. A few families had water filters in their homes. The rest of us gathered to fill five gallon jugs at the triple osmosis machines at Easter's and Hy-Vee. This was the Iowa version of the village well.

In April, I moved into a farmhouse on the far edge of town, converted the barn into a studio, and planted an organic vegetable garden with zucchini, arugula, kale, asparagus, cucumbers, heirloom tomatoes, cabbage, white corn, basil, oregano, peppermint, dill and strawberries. I planted flower gardens on three sides of the house, carefully layering roses and bulbs to bloom through three seasons. At the edge of my field, I planted apple, pear and cherry trees. Then, with the help of my neighbors, I got in on the first wave of the sustainable agriculture movement in southeast Iowa. I read Wendell Berry and became an avid composter, returning to the earth everything that could re-enter the wheel of life. A ring of hair clippings, feathers and mulch protected my fruit trees. This served to deter the deer, who don't like the smell of anything human.

It was easier to find friends in Fairfield than in Mt. Pleasant, and this could happen anywhere – at the post office, on the town square, by the village well, or during the First Friday Art Walk, where people gathered from all over the state. The Art Walk was a huge party, regardless of the weather, which tended to run harsh from late October to April. In May I exhibited at the ICON Gallery and started to find my friends.

In farmhouses in the southeast rural district, I learned shape note singing, and on Sunday mornings, I played early music with a chamber quartet. The musicians were unpretentious and played beautifully on violin, cello and harpsichord. With the addition of my flute, we expanded our repertoire to include music by Telemann,

Bach and Vivaldi. At the suggestion of the cellist, I went to my first contra dance on a Friday night at Morningstar Studios. This was the beginning of something larger than I could understand.

Chapter 31:

Circles and Stars on the Dance Floor

ontra dancing is a very friendly, community-based form of American folk dancing. One of the great things about contra is that once you get into a dance, the patterns take you to all the dancers on the floor. Men and women are equally free to ask each other to dance. After you've done a few dances, it becomes very easy to ask other people to dance because you've already danced with them! So in addition to having a lot of fun, contra is a flirtatious, playful venue for meeting people.

I'm always a bit unsure what to say when someone who is completely unfamiliar with contra dancing asks me to describe it. A physical description of the moves and figures doesn't convey the feeling of joy it brings. For a newcomer, I like to say that it is a highly accessible form of very social dancing which almost anyone can learn quickly and easily. It's a traditional community dance in which dancers stand across from their partners in long lines. Most people change partners every dance, so you don't need to come with a partner. There's always live music featuring fiddle tunes, along with a mix of guitar, banjo, stand up bass, piano and anything else you'd like to throw into the soup. Each contra band has its distinctive flavor and style, with names like Nightingale, Wild Asparagus, Lift Ticket, Uncle Gizmo, the Hillbillies from Mars, Airdance, Flapjack, StringFire, the Groovemongers, Notorious, and the Latter Day Lizards, who add saxophone, penny whistle, and flute to otherwise traditional instruments. The dances have names like Amy's Harmonium, Pigtown Petronella, Breakup Breakdown, The Enchanted Forest, Flying Flamingos, Shame on Shane, Chuck the Budgie, and Flirting with Love Again.

Each dance consists of simple figures like those in square dancing, such as circle left, right-hand star, forward and back, do-si-do, and of course, swing your partner. But unlike square dancing, you dance with a whole succession of people as you work your way up and down a line of couples. Each dance sequence exactly fits the length of one fiddle tune. Then you repeat the movements with the next couple in line, until you have danced with everyone. And here's the best part – you get to hold a different person of the opposite gender in your arms every thirty seconds – or someone of the same gender if that is your preference.

A caller teaches each dance in a walk through, then prompts each figure once the music starts. A typical dance evening also includes a few couple dances, such as a polka, two or three waltzes, and a Scandinavian dance called the hambo. I should probably mention that changing partners without commitment after each dance is attractive to many single people. At the same time, the ability to have a dozen different dance partners in an evening creates a sense of community.

But really defining contra dancing is elusive and difficult – a bit like describing making love. Too few words, and you rob the activity of its value and meaning. Too many words, and you risk smothering the life out of it with distracting details. One popular T-shirt from New England reads: "CONTRA DANCING: The most fun you can have with your clothes on!"

Contra dancers make eye contact with an astounding level of intimacy. This enhances the feeling of connection with your partner and helps reduce dizziness, especially during the swing. You could be swept off your feet that way, but remember: they're gazing into your eyes because they want to connect without getting dizzy. I found the intensity of the gazing confusing at first, but delightful. I loved being the perfect partner of the moment, before moving on to the next perfect partner. And with the change of partners, by the end of the evening, you are likely to have danced with everyone in the room.

A contra dance is like an amusement park ride, a tilt-a-whirl, a ferris wheel of strangers who become familiar. No classes are required, although many communities offer a free fifteen to thirty minute introduction to teach the basic moves before the dance. You do not wear costumes, except for the Halloween party, but people show up to dances in colorful clothes. A perfect dance skirt is colorful and dramatic. It can be short or long, but what is essential is the billowy swirl as you spin and turn. Some of the best skirts are handmade or come from thrift stores, and hunting for new threads in thrift stores is part of the fun.

As one of my friends described it, "The skirt must swirl as if my hips owned the universe."

Another dancer added, "The length depends on my mood – long is more dramatic and elegant, above the knee is playful and bold. I like tiered ruffles. I'm a sucker for a swirly skirt!"

Her favorite dance partner quickly agreed. "A great skirt not only lifts a little when it twirls but flows in circular waves around the beautiful woman who happens to be in my arms."

My favorite part was the swooshing and the satisfying wrap of a full skirt when you stop suddenly. On men, I liked a touchable shirt, maybe silk or Hawaiian, always dramatic and bold. Many men liked to accessorize with colorful bandanas and headbands. Some men even liked to dance in their own twirly skirts.

As someone who had started with ballet, learning to contra dance was easy. After getting the basics down, I found plenty of room for improvisation. I loved the flow and connection with everyone on the floor. As I began to dance outside of Fairfield, first in other cities and then in other states, I discovered that many contra dancers have distinctive styles. They also have distinctive names, like Flirty Paul, Mary from Madison, Amy from Atlanta, Tom the Dog, Tom the Cat, Tom the Lech, and Bernie from Bakersfield. I found myself gravitating towards men with dance training and a distinctive style, with extra spins, dips and flourishes at the end of a dance.

At contra weekends, my partners amped up the flirtation volume. Much to my delight, I noticed that outside of Iowa, men were attracted to me. I had partners who liked to swing in hug position instead of ballroom style, and partners who, after noticing my small size and ballet training, liked to lift me, dip me, and turn me upside down. Some of my partners liked to swing dance at the end of the line instead of waiting out. After a while, if I had to define contra dance to a non-dancing friend, I would say, "It's sort of like square dancing in lines, but really flirty – not like you did in fourth grade." Over time, this progressed to Ted Sannella's definition of contra dance as "a horizontal fantasy acted out vertically." The best part was, the joy I felt dancing added an extra layer of magic to my life.

Chapter 32:

The Reincarnation of Fishface

As time skidded over icy streets, I slid into a pattern of spending too much time alone, except when I went to contra dances. For a while, I dated a poet from Iowa City, but being a bi-coastal transplant was not an easy life in Iowa. My world view was from New York and San Francisco. I didn't think of myself as unusual, but when I said things that would have been fine in San Francisco, I shocked people in Iowa. Clearly, the laws of nature here were governed by an invisible gravity field I didn't understand.

After three years in my new home, my most trusted and constant companion was my midwife friend, Robin. She was ethnically exotic – a combination of Filipina, Chinese, and Native American with tiny genetic additions from several other nationalities. She dressed in sarongs from Bali, wore her grandmother's silver earrings, and her long black hair fell in a waterfall to her knees. Like me, Robin had a clearly not-from-here aura announcing her presence when she walked into a room. Unlike me, Robin had seven children, a husband who adored her, and a grandchild. Inviting me to dinner once a week was her strategy for adopting me into this huge, unwieldy family.

To keep my sanity, I traveled to dances out of state with Tom and George, two of my favorite dance partners, every four to six weeks. This was my entry into the dance gypsy community, a subculture of contra dancers who will travel five, eight, or even fourteen hours to go to a contra dance weekend. At these events, local dancers host out of town guests in their homes – anywhere a sleeping bag can fit. Tom and George had friends all over the midwest, the south, and as far east as Pennsylvania. Our dance weekends sparkled my creative spirit before returning to the deep freeze of the midwestern winter.

Two weeks before she went back to Bali, Robin handed me her betta fish, a lovely male with orange and silver markings and a silver fantail. Without waiting for my thank you, she gave me instructions. "Three pellets of food every morning, change the water every five days, and spend time with him. He's a sensitive creature."

I watched the betta swim in slow circles in his goblet lined with cat's eye marbles. Before I had time to consider if I wanted him, Robin handed me a second bowl, a small globe lined with blue glass stones. "Let the water stand overnight before changing it. The tiny quartz crystal in each bowl will bring you good luck." At that point Robin was in such a hurry to finish packing that she neglected to tell me his name.

In the way of anonymous neighborhood animals, whom I affectionately called Dogface, Catface, Moo, and Birdface, I named this lovely creature Fishface in honor of his predecessor in San Francisco. This coincided with my growing belief in reincarnation. Since I didn't want him to be lonely in the cold Iowa winter, I made plans to mate him with two female bettas, Lulu and Lola, who belonged to one of my students. I knew that betta fish, otherwise known as Siamese fighting fish, cannot be in the same bowl with another betta. But since Fishface and I had glass between us, we slowly became friends. When I'd come back from my studio in the evening, Fishface would swim in circles and blow bubbles. As I suspected, Fishface thought that I was another fish, but somehow impossibly large and unreachable.

Chapter 33:

Chicken Adobo, Tamari and Ginger

When spring came, as it does so suddenly in the midwest, I walked around the town square and felt claustrophobic. I hiked around the reservoir in the late afternoon, with the light pushing towards rose pink, but the wildflowers didn't speak to me. With the prospect of Robin leaving Fairfield in a few days, I was looking for exit strategies. At the same time, I wasn't ready to quit my job and travel west. I thought about it, but I was waiting for a signal that hadn't come in my intuition or my dreams.

For three days before Robin and her family left Fairfield, her harem of friends came over to finish cleaning the house, help pack, and say goodbye. I folded four loads of laundry, arranged them into travel boxes, then scraped a few lingering deposits of bird shit from the floor. Robin was not the kind of woman who kept her birds in cages. With a green parrot on her shoulder, Robin cooked huge pots of *Chicken Adobo, Gado-Gado*, and a stir-fry of mushrooms with sesame oil, tamari and ginger for her famous spinach shiitake salad. A whole house full of friends attended the last supper, and each one left with a gift – something exotic that hadn't fit into a suitcase. My gift was silver earrings from her grandmother's village and a sarong from Bali. The next morning, Robin and her family packed themselves and their suitcases into a van and drove to San Francisco. From there, they would board a plane to Bali, and I had no idea when I would see them again. As the van turned left onto Highway 1, I felt unspeakably sad.

Spring unfolded, but the transformation did not unfold inside me. The week of the bloom exploded its wave of color, scenting the air with an elderberry wind. Summer came, sweated, and left. By late September, it was getting cold again, and I could feel my emotions heading into the no-thaw zone with the north wind howling through the Great Plains, unhindered and unstopped from the Arctic Circle. By November, the wind was so cold I had to get into the bathtub to warm myself.

At the December contra dance at Morningstar, George told me that Rebecca, a stained glass artist who lived on a farm off Glasgow Road, had been traveling to weekend dances for several months now and had met a musician from Berea. They had fallen in love and she was planning to move to Kentucky in the spring. I was impressed! On the table by the door, I saw a flyer for the Jan-Jam, a dance weekend early in January in Champaign-Urbana.

I asked Tom and George if they were going, and Tom replied, "Yes, of course! Would you like to join us?"

I responded with my favorite word in the English language, "Yes!"

"Bring a sleeping bag, and we'll include you in our housing plans. One of my friends in Urbana has offered to host us any time we're in the area. I'll let her know you'll be joining us."

My hands reached for paint on trails through the Appalachian Mountains. Color returned to my world in short skirts that swirled to the cadence of Appalachian fiddle tunes. On backcountry roads, tiny treasures revealed themselves. Cottonwood trees, catfish cafes, and winding roads, even if covered with snow, were glazed with joy.

Contra dancing also changed my way of playing flute. I switched from a mostly classical repertoire to a more improvisational style. I began learning folk waltzes like *Two Rivers, Far Away, Ralph's Watch,* and *Star of County Down*. In the minor keys, hauntingly beautiful like the prayers of my childhood, I felt my heart open. As I followed the music of my joy, I became a dance gypsy.

Chapter 34:

The Crossover Point

To prepare for the Jan-Jam, I took out my collection of short, swirly skirts, wacky socks, and exotic earrings. It had to be a good omen to dance into the new year. Tom's friend invited us to stay at her farmhouse after the dance. More than twenty people would share guest rooms, a greenhouse porch, two sofas, Persian carpets and floors, followed by a huge brunch the next morning. Despite an early morning snowfall, Tom and George came to pick me up after lunch. By then the roads had been plowed, and not enough new snow was falling to interfere with our plans for a dance weekend. We drove to Champaign in the kind of magic snow creates.

The evening began with a potluck dinner followed by contras and squares with a local old-timey band. As the evening progressed, musicians from Stringdancer showed up on the dance floor, and after the break, took over the makeshift stage at the front of the room. The flirtation decibel level got higher as the evening progressed, but I was not prepared for what happened next. On the other side of the room, then closer, I saw someone who for a moment felt familiar. Since I was new to the dance gypsy community, I wondered if I was having a deja vu. A few minutes later, circling around me, then passing my left shoulder in a hey for four, there was Christopher! It was the first time I had seen him in twenty years.

We found each other close to midnight, danced a contra, then a waltz. His cornsilk blonde hair was embedded with silver, like the hay in a folk tale, but he still had farm boy muscles. His eyes were the same – they knew me.

Christopher and I stayed up most of the night talking. There was so much to remember – our hikes on the Appalachian Trail, his grandmother's cabin in the mountains, the house concerts in my living room, and the language of the birds. There was so much to discover – our lives as artists, the places we had lived, and where our lives had taken us for the last twenty years. It was an amazing coincidence that both of us were teaching art, although his primary genre was pencil and charcoal drawings and I mainly expressed myself through sculpture. Both of us painted from time to time, and we had similar ideas about living our lives as an art form.

Before the sun came up, we made plans to meet at the Valentine's Dance in Knoxville, Tennessee. Then we shared a long hug and fell asleep for a few hours, with snow falling gently on the other side of the window. At some point in my dreaming, I was fourteen years old again, in the Appalachian Mountains, hiking with Christopher, surrounded by birds.

In the morning, several of us took turns flipping buckwheat pancakes and making omelettes. Tom and George brought a crate of oranges and made juice for everyone while two other dancers prepared a huge fruit salad. Christopher and I continued to share memories. When I asked Tom and George about dancing in Knoxville, they were enthusiastic. It was only fourteen hours from Fairfield, and Tom had a friend with a huge house and an anytime invite to stay. Five weeks to paint and dream, and then I'd be sharing a weekend with Christopher!

Chapter 35:

My Year as a Dance Gypsy

When I began my year as a dance gypsy, Fishface went to a series of foster homes. He began living with Joel and Lisa, two artists on Pleasant Plain Road, but that ended abruptly after Joel, without warning, packed his car and drove to Sedona. Lisa went into a funk, and though she didn't stop feeding Fishface, she stopped cleaning his bowl. When I went to visit a week later, the water was green and I knew I had to rescue him.

Before I went to sleep that night, I filled the fish goblet with water. In the morning, I moved Fishface to clean water. He responded by swimming in circles and blowing bubbles. For three more weeks, I enjoyed the flamboyant company of Fishface, listened to him crunch his food pellets in the morning, and watched him flash his fins at me every time I entered the room. He offered sweeter company than most humans I knew.

However, as the second weekend in February approached, I knew I had to find a home for him. Since the morning after the Jan-Jam, I'd been eagerly awaiting the Valentine's Dance in Knoxville. As much as I hated to let go of my betta, I knew these dance weekends were hard on him. Even though I had someone feed him whenever I was away, Fishface was always upset when I came home and refused to eat for two or three days. I couldn't stand it when he did that.

My rescuing knight appeared in the form of Dennis, a helicopter pilot from Alaska. Dennis overheard me talking to a friend about my betta problem and came to our table in Revelations Café to introduce himself. Dennis had years of experience breeding betta fish and was intimately familiar with their habits. He offered to adopt Fishface for the six months he would be in Fairfield studying ayurvedic medicine and promised to find a reliable home for him when he returned to Alaska. Intuitively, it felt right, so we made a date for the adoption ceremony. I was sad but I knew my beloved betta would be happier in a stable home.

The night before I went to Knoxville, Fishface and I drove across town for the adoption ceremony. Dennis reassured me that he would provide a stable, happy home for my betta. He photographed us together, with me hugging the bowl and then waving my hair like seaweed. I stood beside the bowl as Dennis did a formal portrait, and then he got a close-up of Fishface swimming over the blue glass stones at the bottom of his bowl. He was elegant, flirtatious, showing off his silver fins.

As I was getting ready to leave, Dennis said, "Feed him! It will make you happy."

"But I usually feed him in the morning."

"It's ok. I feed my fish at night."

I dropped two tiny pellets in the water, put my ear over the bowl, and listened to the tiny crunch of his teeth.

Chapter 36:

Nightingale in Knoxville

During my year as a dance gypsy, Tom and George became my family. They were caring brothers and feisty dance partners. We traveled to dance weekends every few weeks and kept expanding our circle of friends. George drove a white van with a license plate that said *Brahman*, and Tom's iPod provided us with travel music. When conversation ran out, Tom had over ten thousand songs to share. Many of these were perfect for singing in harmony. These two gentle souls initiated me into the dance gypsy world. They took good care of me, made sure I was always included in their housing plans, and introduced me to their friends throughout the midwest and the south. During long conversations in the Brahman van, I discovered what made them happy and what they longed for.

George's dance weekend was not complete unless he fell in love with a beautiful woman – and preferably two or three beautiful women. This could take place in five minutes or in a fantasy that lasted for months and spanned several dance weekends. There was always a woman in George's heart and soul, whether she was aware of this or not. George was a teddy bear, with a spiritual innocence that few people in the dance world noticed or understood. But he hoped one day the woman of his dreams, whoever she was, would share his love of dance and meditation.

Tom was a lanky silver fox with a fondness for thin, muscular dance partners. He had a colorful collection of straw hats and

Hawaiian silk shirts that matched the colorful aspects of his personality. George described Tom as a silver-tongued devil, but I saw him sweet and caring in the way he became a brother to me. He had an intuitive sense of when I needed to talk and when I needed a hug on the dance floor. Tom was a good listener. We had conversations that wove through two or three hours while George was driving, and we could bare our hearts to one another.

The dance gypsy community convened every few weeks at a different location. Like most dance gypsies, I had my harem of dance partners. Simon, who was married to a fiddler in one of my favorite bands, would spin me, dip me, and flirt in such a bawdy, body way that I had to ask him about his marriage. He explained that he and his wife had an agreement: "I don't care where your appetite comes from, as long as you eat at home." Off the dance floor, Simon was well behaved and devoted to his family. Many contra couples, within the context of a stable, loving relationship, liked to share energy on the dance floor and then come home to make wild, passionate love. I was inspired by the open, friendly ways of the people I met – people living their lives with joy, in tune with the music of their souls. I met some amazing couples on the dance floor – partners who traveled together, danced together, and after many years were still best friends. Even those of us who were single got an entire weekend of flirty dancing and touching. For me, this made life beautiful.

I found soulful sisters in the dance community. Jo from Chicago was a wise woman I gravitated towards. Her hair was like a flock of goats bounding down Mt. Gilead. Jo had an astounding dance style, didn't care if she danced with men or women, and when we talked, she always had something so deep and important to say that I would think about it for the next few weeks. At any dance weekend, I always carved out a few minutes to connect with her and feed my soul. Jo's art form was silk-screening Dance-A-Runi tee shirts. These had various contra figures – such as petronella, lady's chain, and hey for four – illustrated by rune-like graphics. Since she didn't have a shirt my size at the Knoxville Weekend, I ordered a hot pink, french cut tee in size extra small. I was hoping for her petronella design, but my rune said "box the gnat," which made me wonder about subtext and hidden messages.

During meals, which included potlucks and group restaurant outings, I overheard revealing bits of conversations from both men and women.

"She doesn't have to be nice. She has cheekbones."

"He is my beauty and the beast fantasy."

"I had to take a cold shower after that dance."

My San Francisco friends, Beau and Tammy, traveled cross-country once a year on a dance gypsy odyssey and became famous for "Beau's Big Bang Beet Juice" at the potlucks. His Champion Juicer recipe included white peaches, Fuji apples, red bell peppers, carrots, beets, parsley, celery, spinach, pears, cucumbers, Merlot grapes, and Amazake Almond Shake. Beau was careful to make sure the produce was organically grown. His recipe sheet included notes on Einstein's theory of relativity and Hubble's expanding theory of the universe. Beau and Tammy traveled to dance weekends up and down the California coast. However, this wave subsided in favor of swing and ballroom dance after they got married, as they were not a share energy couple. At their wedding, which was an awesome music and dance event, they adopted me as their honorary sister-in-law. But this is background, a canvas ready for music, color and swirl.

Before sunrise on Friday morning, Tom, George and I left Fairfield to drive to Knoxville, Tennessee. I spent the first three hours of the trip curled up on the bench seat in the back of the van, finishing my dreams. But as the sun rose higher over the winter fields, Tom decided it was time to wake up. Tom, more of a morning person than I will ever be, started playing his favorite tunes from the latest Groovemongers CD. After a thermos of strong black tea, I enjoyed driving through places I had not seen before. Later that afternoon, as in my childhood, I fell in love with the Appalachian Mountains. Something about the land was speaking to me.

Tom could feel how excited I was about seeing Christopher, but he cautioned me to remember the rules of the contra community. Playing the ultimate big brother, he cautioned, "Everything that happens on the dance floor is dancing. The signal in this community for interest off the floor begins with the last waltz of the evening. The next signal is an invitation to do something alone somewhere else."

To which I answered, "Tom, I already know him. We grew up together, and I'm not sure if the usual rules apply."

"Katerina, you don't know him as an adult. He may have changed."

I was too excited to pay attention to anything that sounded like a warning, but I assured him I would keep this in mind. Tom was relentless. With a brotherly sense of protection, he continued. "At a contra dance, you can fall in love every five seconds. See what happens off the floor."

The Valentine's Dance in Knoxville was huge, with seven contra lines spreading back from the stage. Nightingale played for the contras and Stringdancer followed with waltzes. I didn't see Christopher during the first part of the dance and partnered for the first waltz with a sweet talking man from South Carolina. I loved the lilt in his accent and the way the cut of his shirt revealed muscular arms, which I, as a sculptor, thoroughly enjoyed.

Two dances after the break, during a corner spinoff, I whirled into Christopher's arms. We enjoyed a long gypsy, then a swing. Before he let me leave his arms, he asked for the next dance. Christopher had a gentle way of leading – creative, connected, in control. We whirled around the floor as Nightingale vibrated the walls with the minor keys of *Tam Lin*, then *Julia Delaney*, then *Time Will End*. He ended the dance with a hug and a kiss.

Christopher gave me all of the signals I could have hoped for that weekend, beginning with the last waltz on Friday night, when Stringdancer played *Two Rivers*. This was already one of my favorite waltzes, and by the end of the dance, its magic had amplified. After the music stopped, Christopher and I hugged for a long time. Then he told me, "In the morning, I'll be attending a workshop for callers. But if you wait for me at the end of the morning dance, I'd like to take you to lunch and catch up. I brought my portfolio so I can share some of my art with you." We hugged again and then I went off to find Tom and George.

Tom, George and I were hosted with six other dancers in a huge Victorian house two miles from the dance. Our host offered tea and blueberry muffins for a midnight snack, with Brahms' First Symphony floating in from the classical music station. After that, I enjoyed a soak in the lion's paw tub. By the time I fell asleep that night, I was ecstatic with anticipation.

Chapter 37:

Artists' Reunion at the Cleopatra Café

On Saturday morning I put on a long yellow dress from India with a scooped ballet neck, an exotic design, and a skirt with a billowy swirl. After sharing a breakfast of french toast and tea with our host, we got in the van and drove across town through a light winter rain.

The Saturday morning dance was full of alchemical magic. Despite the weather, I felt cocooned in southern-style friendliness. As someone who grew up in the north and came of age on the West Coast, I found the slow music of the southern accent exotic and enticing, but what had even more magic was knowing that in a few hours, I'd be dancing with Christopher. Toward the end of the morning, he found me in a contra line, and we shared a late morning waltz. Then we found our packs and, hand in hand, went wandering through the streets of Knoxville. Christopher suggested a middle eastern café on a side street close to the city center. As we held hands under my yellow duck umbrella, I enjoyed the familiarity and the newness of my childhood friend, who I was only beginning to know as a man.

Christopher taught art to middle school students in Lexington, Kentucky. Often he sketched his students while they were doing their art projects. In this way, he didn't keep himself apart from the young artists he mentored. After we ordered falafels, babaganoush, and a cucumber, mint and yogurt salad, Christopher showed me a sketchbook of drawings, photographs of his paintings, and recent print art from carved linoleum blocks. His art was process-oriented and full of energy. It was different enough from what I create to intrigue me.

As we ate our falafels and shared the salads, I thought about the unspoken but widely observed no garlic rule at contra dances. Oh well. Maybe the Egyptian mint tea we shared at the end of the meal would help. I hadn't brought a portfolio, but I told Christopher about my goddess sculptures and recent gallery shows. He was intrigued but told me he didn't exhibit much. He said, "I'm not ambitious that way."

Our conversation progressed to our recent relationship history, which was not much to report from my side. Christopher's story was different. He told me about a woman from Brattleboro, Vermont he had fallen in love with three years ago during the Dawn Dance. Suzanne was a French Canadian dance gypsy. They went back and forth with a lot of visits, broke up twice, then got back together again. They talked about commitment on many occasions, but neither of them could make up their mind – at least not at the same time. Last fall, even though he had lingering doubts, Christopher decided she might be the right woman for him. She continued to touch him in a way that other women did not, so he decided to move to New England and find out. He arranged a leave of absence from his teaching job for six months, to give him the freedom to return if it didn't work out. The move date was set for December, but just before Thanksgiving, Suzanne called and asked him not to come.

He got very quiet at that point, so I asked him, "How did you feel?"

"It's funny. I felt disappointed and relieved at the same time."

"Interesting... Are you still in contact?"

"Not right now. We decided not to see each other for a while. She's going through a career change, she just bought a house, and she needs her energy for other things."

Here we were, holding hands around a plate of falafels. Across the table was my childhood friend, who I knew and didn't know at the same time. He was so familiar that we were eating off each other's plates, but there was a huge part of him I didn't understand. I was at this contra weekend because Christopher asked me to meet him here. At the same time, I knew two months was not enough time to get over such a huge disappointment.

In the silence that followed, I studied his hands – clearly those of an artist. I looked into his eyes and saw beauty there. I looked out the window, looked back and studied his face. What I saw there was not entirely broken and not entirely whole.

In the presence of Christopher, I was an innocent fourteen-year-old girl inside the body of a woman. I felt my heart open to him, as it had long ago, but I had to know what was possible. In the tradition of our childhood agreement to speak without a filter, I asked him, "Do you think you and Suzanne will get back together, or are you available?"

He hesitated, thought about it for a while, then said, "I'm available. Suzanne and I have been back and forth too many times, and I need to move on."

Outside, it was still raining with the sharp needles of a February storm. We finished eating and split the bill. On the way back to the dance, we shared my umbrella and got tremendously muddy when we crossed a vacant lot instead of taking the street. Christopher apologized for the mud on my new shoes, as he had chosen the route.

I told him, "Don't worry about it. Last October, I walked around Italy with a group of student sculptors, and it rained almost every day for a month. My shoes were constantly wet but they survived."

We caught about half of the afternoon dance, including a waltz workshop. Then we joined a few of his friends for dinner at a Thai restaurant and almost didn't make it back to the dance. In the front seat of his pickup truck, Christopher and I discovered that we had amazing kiss chemistry. His kisses made me stop thinking. His kisses felt too good.

As we got closer to the dance, he asked me if I wanted to go back to his hotel room. None of the other dancers would be there until late at night. I knew I needed more time before getting close that way, so I said, "Let's go back to the dance. I love dancing with you."

He replied, "Okay then, let's do every other dance with each other. And of course, the last waltz."

When we re-entered the dance, we were lit up with each other in a way that people noticed. He improvised with a playful dance style and gave me room to respond with twirls, dips and flourishes from ballet. Christopher moved in a way I found totally sexy. When we wandered off to enjoy other dance partners, we always found our way back to each other, culminating with another midnight waltz.

Chapter 38:

Two Rivers

hristopher and I honored our "go slow" agreement that weekend. I returned to our host's house with my friends from Iowa, and Christopher slept on the floor of a motel room with seven other dancers from Lexington and Louisville. Unfortunately, they had a bomb scare at four o'clock in the morning, and none of them got much sleep.

As Tom, George and I drove across town in the midnight rain, Tom asked if I was in love, and he knew me well enough not to need an answer. When we returned to our host's large Victorian home, all of the dancers were in the kitchen, practicing newly acquired swing dance moves and enjoying a late night snack of strawberries and ice cream. At one o'clock in the morning, we listened to a radio concert of the Cincinnati Symphony Orchestra playing *Fantasy on a Hymn by Justin Morgan* by Thomas Canning. The music was gorgeous and mysterious as this night. As our conversation played out, Tom fell asleep on the sofa. I put my futon on the floor, and George slept in his van.

My dreams were saturated with memories weaving through hidden paths in the Appalachian Mountains. An old train bridge in Tennessee, someone invisible playing a mountain dulcimer, and Christopher with rivers of light in his hands. We swirled together with my yellow dress floating. I lost him, found him in stars and rings, with a bass old-timey rhythm vibrating the barn dance floor.

Below an ice-hazed moon, I waltzed with Christopher. In an open sky, the winter constellations moved around us in a slow circle. Everything blurred out of focus, except for his eyes.

Christopher was a wild pony, kissing me in the time zone where days begin and days are torn apart. Above us, the Pleiades, a swan moon, distant stars releasing. In the part of my vision where art is born, I saw a green donkey glueing tiny mirrors to pieces of a dream. This was a symbol I would not understand in the morning, but I often sculpted goddesses who held secrets to be revealed at a later time. Their secrets were my friends.

In the morning Christopher and I were two rivers who would soon go in separate directions, but our final dance was sweet. After the last waltz, he gave me a long sensual hug and a passionate kiss. He didn't care who was watching, and I was too caught up in the magic to care. He asked me to meet him in six weeks at the Pigtown Fling in Cincinnati, and I enthusiastically agreed.

There was a light dusting of snow on the way back to the van. Christopher walked out with us and hugged me for a long time. George, of course, was eager to get on the road, but the stop signs across the city were broadcasting my emotions. Tom must have felt this, as he let me pick the music for the next two hours.

While light was available, I enjoyed the beauty of the Appalachian Mountains. Everything was illuminated with the sweet light of new love. When evening came, we stopped at a greasy spoon and found a few things our mainly vegetarian diet let us eat. I had never tasted fried green tomatoes, so this was a must, along with a catfish fillet. George ordered poppers and cole slaw. Tom had a grilled cheese sandwich with an iceberg lettuce and tomato salad.

After dinner, the snow got heavier. George was an excellent driver, but the road was icy and full of unplowed snow. After watching a few cars skid into snow banks, Tom suggested that we find a motel and try again in the morning. George reluctantly pulled off at the next exit, but all of the motel rooms in the nearest town were taken. We could have stayed at a local church, but I was worried that they would try to convert us, which wouldn't be fun for three tired people from a new age community. My intuition was clear that if we kept going, we would make it back home, and just before dawn, we arrived in Fairfield.

Chapter 39:

Robin's Dream

Two weeks later, Robin called me from Bali. I had no idea she could afford international phone calls, but she was worried. "Last night, I had a dream about you. I'm not sure how to interpret what I saw, but I know you will understand. In the dream, you were dragging a pony behind your pickup truck. I don't feel good about the pony."

In her work as a midwife, Robin had access to a powerful shaman voice, and her dream was a trail of crumbs leading to Kentucky. I knew the dream was about Christopher – the symbols were too clear. Since the first Kentucky Derby, Lexington was the hub of a horse-centered universe, and the pony, as a symbol, pointed there. But in contrast to the magnificent racing steeds bred on bluegrass farms, the pony as a symbol was emotionally young.

Robin would not let up. "The dream came to me because your angels knew you wouldn't listen. You're not paying attention to your shit detector."

One of the things I love about Robin is that she doesn't have a filter. Whatever she feels comes tumbling out of her mouth. At the same time, I had to tell her, "Robin, I'm going to make my own decision."

Even though I had my own quiet misgivings, as Christopher's recent break-up had not passed the critical six month line, Robin didn't know Christopher. Since the summer we spent hiking in the

Appalachian Mountains, we shared an amazing closeness which I still felt, and I hadn't asked Robin for advice.

"Christopher was my childhood sweetheart. He's someone whose soul I know, and it feels like a miracle that we met again after so many years."

"The soul is one thing. How well do you know the man?"

Robin attempted to redirect my enthusiasm by asking about my sculptures and my students. We talked about art as a way of opening yourself to the edge of your emotions and not going insane. In her life experience, art was more important than love.

I told her, "I need both. I love the way the world speaks to me when my heart is open."

Robin continued to argue with me. "Love is an elephant, dead weight on the road." When I didn't agree, she argued with her quirky wisdom. "Thank the elephant by kicking him sometimes."

I put a sketch pad on my knee, picked up a piece of charcoal and started sketching the Hindu Elephant God, Ganesha. My students from India pray to Ganesha whenever they want to overcome an obstacle. If love is an elephant, I'm going to offer this elephant a prayer.

Robin picked up on my thoughts by telepathy. "Katarina, there's a surprise for you out there. You're not going to be alone for the rest of your life. I'm just not sure this man is the one."

"Robin, you haven't met him and you haven't seen us together. Christopher feels like a soulmate, and he's felt that way since I was fourteen years old."

"And that's why you've been together since then?"

I shook my head. "Robin, please understand. I have to find out." The promise of new love, even long distance, felt so delicious. Most dance gypsy relationships started that way.

Robin returned to her vision. "Love is impractical. In the dream, I saw you unhook the pony, let him float off without a cloud, singing, light of heart and load."

"Robin, this is your dream, not mine. In my dreams, we're hiking the Appalachian Trail next summer. We start in the Great Smoky Mountains and hike all the way to Maine, visiting all the places we discovered together earlier in our lives."

"Have you talked with him about this?"

"Not yet, but we'll be seeing each other again in a few weeks. As teachers, we both have long summer vacations. It would be amazing to enjoy that time together."

"You're on a cloud right now. Just see what happens, and pay attention to what you see. Tell me about your art."

I described the collages I had been building since the Knoxville weekend – anti-war posters embedded in images of nature. Dreams of the Pleiades, a Snow Moon over Mt. Fuji, distant stars releasing secrets. Tibetan mandalas, glitter circles inside an expanding universe. Even though she didn't want to know, I told Robin about Christopher's portfolio and our weekend in Knoxville. "Christopher's art is process-oriented, and his focus on the human figure intrigues me."

"What is his vision about love?"

"Right now, his vision is, 'go slow.'"

"And your vision?"

"Easy beginnings never get you anywhere. I see love as slow moving cinema etched with a charcoal pencil, slow dancing with the ending hidden by mist."

Robin interrupted me. "Don't put a horse trailer behind your Toyota."

That was the end of our conversation, and it was a lot to think about. I thought about how I felt when I was dancing with Christopher, and I thought about Robin's pony. Something was missing – an image I couldn't quite remember. I let the animals swirl – elephant, horse and pony. I dug into my clay and asked my fingers. My vision returned as my hands remembered the green donkey glueing tiny mirrors to pieces of my dream. And what were the mirrors reflecting? The animals swirled together like a kaleidoscope and defied interpretation. Maybe it would take time, but I would let my life reveal the answers.

Before I went to sleep, I lit a beeswax candle. Falling into a lucid dream, I saw glitter and paperwhites, as the nation prepared for a war we didn't want. I was dancing under the aurora borealis with the snow etched into the shape of an angel. I saw Christopher on a green donkey. He saw me dance in my yellow dress, swirling inside a snowstorm, cutting origami paper into snowflakes. I danced with him under northern skies splashed with the aurora. Across six hundred miles we breathed in lindy circles, the jagged steps of a swing dance.

The fantail of my betta fish swirled over blue stones in the kitchen. A cardinal on the elm told me to leap over the hills and kick the donkey. I was waiting for my pony, doing the elephant walk, inhaling the steam of eucalyptus.

Then I was fourteen years old, in the forest walking with Christopher. He spoke to me in the voices of the birds. We were sharing secrets in the Appalachian Mountains, on our backs in a bed of moss, watching the constellations on their slow trek through the sky. In light and shadow, my fingers were shaping the memory of his face.

Chapter 40:

Pigtown Fling

ometimes I wonder if love is an agreement between two souls or an obsessive-compulsive disorder. Christopher and I met again at the Pigtown Fling in Covington, Kentucky. It was a weekend of mixed messages, with Christopher claiming all of the last waltzes, broadcasting a message to the circling dolphins with his male pheromone claws, announcing, "this is mine." But something felt different I couldn't yet define.

On Saturday afternoon, we left the dance for a few hours, took a long walk, then sat down with a cup of chai in a bookstore café. Christopher showed me a new portfolio of his drawings and launched into a monologue about his artistic process – the way he gets into a drawing and gets lost there, often not knowing which way to continue the charcoal or the line.

"That must make it hard to finish a drawing sometimes."

"It's one of the things I struggle with in my art . . ."

I became silent and noticed the hairs on my arm standing on end.

"And speaking of unfinished lines . . . A few days ago, I decided to go to Brattleboro during my spring break. Unfinished business with my old girlfriend. Process lines not resolved."

I listened and caved inside. My spring break was the same week, and I had planned to invite him to visit me in Iowa.

At dinner in a Korean restaurant, I told him, "I think you're doing the right thing and I hope you find resolution one way or the other." Then we returned to casual conversation. A few minutes later, Christopher invited two dancers from St. Louis to share the booth with us. In between courses of exotic entrees, they took photographs of us across the table. Robin tells me that I have the ability to sparkle, even when my emotions feel like spider webs on oak leaves tearing apart. The photographs I saw two weeks after the Pigtown Fling proved her hypothesis.

After dinner, Christopher was all over me in his pickup truck. I guess his body was telling him something different than his words. Maybe there was a whisper, a shaman or a donkey, that didn't believe what he told me about Ms. Brattleboro. His place of quiet misgivings. After all, she dumped him last December. But Christopher felt he had to go to Vermont one more time to see if she was really done with him or if she would change her mind.

We steamed up the windows of his truck. Then we went to the dance, where Christopher proceeded to ignore me for the rest of the evening. If I walked toward him, he walked in the other direction. If I tried to catch his eyes, he looked away. After all, it was Saturday evening and more dance gypsies had arrived, close to two hundred people now. The hall was a sea of dancers, with so many goldfish to explore. Christopher knew he had the last waltz with me, and now he demanded the freedom to swim elsewhere.

In a quiet voice, the kind that comes from nowhere, I said to myself, "Katarina, this man is going to break your heart." I started walking off the dance floor. Then I said to myself, "Katarina, this is bullshit. Change your attitude!" That's when the dolphins started circling.

I climbed to the top of the bleachers to close my eyes, meditate, and get back in touch with the quiet place inside myself where I am strong and full of joy. About five minutes into my meditation, one of the dolphins came and sat next to me. When I didn't open my eyes, he decided to sit there and wait. Twenty minutes later he introduced himself and told me his name was Angelo. As in dolphin guardian angel. Then he asked me to dance.

I think that Angelo and Kevin, the other dolphin, detected a sinking ship. They'd been watching Christopher and his dance toward and away from me and sensed an opportunity. On the bleachers above the Pigtown Fling, I told Angelo about Christopher, how we had known each other since I was eight years old, and how we met again at a contra dance. I also let him know what had happened this weekend and how sad I felt.

Angelo had been watching my wave crash down. His observation, "Your friend looks edgy and confused." In a gentle way, he explained, "I'm not trying to gain an advantage. I'm just not sure if you want to be part of this man's struggle to find himself." He thought I deserved better and decided to do the manly thing – step in and take over.

After a few minutes of silence, Angelo escorted me back to the dance floor. His style was playful and flirtatious, with a menu of swing moves in between the contra figures. He was quiet but grounded, sweet and present. The other dolphin, Kevin, was more dramatic. With years of ballet training, he lifted me into positions I'd seen on stage at the San Francisco Ballet. Instead of a contra swing, he pulled me into a bear hug spin. When we waltzed, he slipped his hand up my back, on bare skin under my silk shirt. His hands made me shiver. It's what they call sleazy contra in this part of the world, and Kevin was an expert.

Despite my best intentions, I was dazzled and seduced by his ballet training. With a partner like this, making love can become an art form – especially if it stays on the dance floor. And as Tom continued to remind me, in the contra world nothing counts unless it happens off the floor. Everything on the dance floor is dancing. Just that afternoon, Christopher surprised me with a sleazy contra move. He carefully placed my hands around the back of his neck, then ducked down and came up between my arms, being careful to look at my eyes the whole time. He played the southern gentleman with a come hither look in his eyes, but Christopher's dance fantasy was playing out with someone else tonight.

During the break I sat on the top row of the bleachers with Angelo. He told me about his new job at an Air Force base in Ohio and about the problems with his last girlfriend. From my perspective of not knowing either one of them, I found the details hilarious. Especially his story about the night before they split up. They were having a serious conversation while spooning in the loft of his condo. Angelo curled around her, holding onto a thin thread of hope. Abruptly, she pulled his hand away from her breast and said, "This is mine!"

Later in the evening, Angelo confessed how he felt when we were dancing. "You're hot when you dance, which makes me want to jump your bones. I've also had a wave of fear. My sense is that you are someone capable of a deeper intimacy than most women I've met, and it may not always be comfortable."

I leaned away from him. "How do you know that's true? You just met me."

Angelo spoke with a quiet confidence. "Sometimes the runes give me visions, but in your case, I can see it in your eyes."

I wasn't sure what to do with this, as I had come to this dance to spend the weekend with Christopher. I wasn't the type of woman who fell easily for a man, but once I did, it wasn't going to change in an evening.

Back on the dance floor, Angelo and Kevin kept circling back to me, swimming in a sea of bodies, face to open face. I was the butterfly angel who danced in flame blue swallowtail wings, my eyes burning a soft trail of fire. The location was nowhere, everywhere, something exotic, foreign, something more musical than linguistic.

Angelo's presence was comforting. His eyes said, "Let me be a soft cocoon for you." He took me spinning through soft blue light. Kevin came to find me every fourth or fifth dance. By the end of the evening, I realized that Angelo and Kevin were treating me exactly the way I had expected Christopher to treat me that weekend. Further proof that expectations are deadly.

Christopher showed up as promised for the last waltz, but the magic had disappeared. At the after party in a huge Victorian house in Cincinnati, we shared a few minutes of edgy conversation. Then he excused himself to play tablas with the band. I went into another room to swing dance with Kevin. Kevin was a cad, but he was my feel better candy for the evening. When I left the party at three o'clock in the morning, Kevin was on the couch with his head in the lap of a buxom blonde, while a dark haired woman at the other end of the couch massaged his feet.

My shit detector kicked me, invoked the donkey, remembered the pony and whispered, "Pay attention to that."

Chapter 41:

The Honeysuckle Scent of Morning

It was hard to sleep that night, with my emotions pulled in so many different directions. Tom, George and I were hosted by a dance couple with a three-year-old daughter and a closet full of vintage dance costumes. We slept in a narrow attic, with Tom and George in a trundle bed towards the front of the room and me on a day bed by the rear window. Sleep came occasionally but not easily. Dreams washed over me in the geometric patterns of contra lines, but then a bee would sting me and I'd sit up in bed. It was good to discover that the bee was only a dream, but I was awake again.

Memories of the evening washed over me through the night. I felt my heart and my body pulled by my longing for Christopher, along with magnetic currents of Kevin and Angelo longing for me. High above us, a new rain covered the full moon. Morning came too quickly without a shield of dreams.

Our hosts made Belgian waffles for breakfast with sliced fresh strawberries on top. Tom gave a quick waltz lesson to their three-year-old daughter, and by ten o'clock in the morning, we were packed, in the van, and ready to catch an hour of waltzing before the closing dance. The air was full of a honeysuckle scent that was making my mind thick and lazy. Made me want to run outside and scoop up some of the warm and humid morning.

I had misgivings about coming back to the dance, and knew I had to distance myself from Christopher. I told myself, "no expectations," and shaved a layer of watermelon ice in front of my emotions.

Christopher responded by being attentive again. He asked me to dance a lot and reserved the last waltz before the end of the first contra dance. My apologies to the dolphins, but I'm sure Christopher could sense the competition.

After the last waltz, I went up to the bleachers, found my pack, and took off my dance shoes. Angelo came by for a hug and asked for my telephone number. A few minutes later, Kevin came by and kissed me, which I had to admit was sweet. Against my better judgment, I was attracted to him. Just before George was ready to leave, Christopher asked if he could speak with me for a few minutes. I found George and told him I needed a little bit of time before we left. Tom, of course, didn't mind because he was enjoying the after dance glow with his dance gypsy friends.

Christopher took my hand and led me to the top row of bleachers. He gave me a print of the Red River Gorge and a drawing that could have been a self portrait. He used a technique of keeping his charcoal pencil on the page and drawing in one continuous motion to give the figure the energy he felt. He rendered the same man from two different angles juxtaposed, and the drawing intrigued me. We were back in the artist-to-artist zone, in the state of communion that only two artists can share, and I remembered how much I adored him.

Christopher let me know, "I won't be going to Kimmswick this year. Next month, my teaching schedule is too intense to get away, but if you come to the Dance Trance, I'd love to show you around Lexington. I know that Tom and George stay on the horse farm with Lucinda, and I already have guests lined up at my place. If you can stay for a few days after the weekend, I'll show you where I live and we can go hiking in the Red River Gorge. It's one of my favorite places."

I didn't know what to say, so I was silent for a long time.

Maybe Christopher knew that his trip to Brattleboro was a long shot. Milkweed blowing in an early summer wind. I looked at my shoes and then looked up at him. Christopher had tears in his eyes. He took my hands and said, "Please don't give up on me!"

Chapter 42:

Rivers of Light

ove is a white rain, a meteor shower, a halo around the moon embedded with the memory of a face. An electric current through a mobius strip stretching to the other side of the universe. A war zone in a foreign country, a waterfall, a poem whispered in a haunted voice. Sometimes I wonder whether my muse is inaccessible to arouse a higher vision out of the echo of my longing. That's my dance with the *Yoga of the Impossible*.

Back in Iowa, redbuds and tulip trees unfolded against the backdrop of an international war. Magazines flooded the world with images I didn't want to see, and for the first time in my life, I could understand what Germans who were opposed to Hitler must have felt during the Second World War. My friend Kambiz, who was exiled from Iran when the Ayatollah took over, told me that during his country's war with Iraq, people his age responded by breaking sexual taboos. Young women came to parties with miniskirts under their burkas, and the rest of it usually came off before midnight. Nobody knew if they'd be shot or bombed before the sun came up.

Christopher called me every two weeks. He talked about taking me hiking in Kentucky but didn't say anything about his visit to Brattleboro. I felt intensely vulnerable. After our conversations, I dreamed about whitewater rivers and arches of rock, but my heart was limping in the question mark zone. My hiking boots were close to destroyed from trekking in the Himalayas. They were in a closet somewhere in San Francisco, so I went to Iowa City to find a new pair of boots. Christopher called again to explain he was at a point where the lines in his art were leading him to directions he couldn't see yet. To follow them with a charcoal pencil, I knew he would have to step into a war zone.

There was so much I didn't tell him. I wasn't getting the signal I needed to open myself to him that way. As the war expanded, I continued to make collages, which I displayed at ICON Gallery and on telephone poles around the town square. Inspired by Christopher, I followed my dreams with a charcoal pencil, and occasionally layered them with watercolor. Rivers of light flowed through my hands, streams of light and shadow.

Every night before I went to sleep, I said goodnight to Christopher, and I felt him around me in the morning. I hiked every weekend and found the places in Iowa that revealed their simple beauty. The vulnerability I felt made me realize why I had avoided love for so long, but love created an opening. I felt a sense of infinity in the Iowa landscape which, after three years in my new home, I finally let myself enjoy. I let the trees and the rivers speak to me, listened to dragonflies skimming ponds in a gently undulating landscape. Then in silent conversation, I spoke to Christopher – calligraphy in my journal, words that he would never see:

Rivers of light flow through your hands. This might be about memory or loss, or the imprint of molecules you gave me in your red pickup truck when you kissed me. My emotions fill with lavender the way music triggers memory, your artist arms circling around my heart, giving gyroscopic signals I can't interpret right now.

I want to tell you about the way blackberry vines are pushing up from my garden, how the sky is warmer now. I dream through the weekend, clearing leaves from my garden as early tulips and columbines unfold. I want you to see the way my hair gets curly and wild in the humid April heat. I'd like to ask you questions.

Around my pillow at night, the orbit of a humid empty space. And in the emptiness, the singing of a flute, a tremolo voice saying, "Love it. Hold the memory. Fill it with light and singing. Fill it with your face."

Your eyes change color to match the emerging leaves, the sky, the bark of an olive tree. They cannot see lavender. The lines that shape muscles are process oriented, stone bridges over the river, your hand slipping up the bare place on my spine.

My dreams fill with lavender – an echo, a flood, a space shuttle. What else can't you see? The future is hidden now inside the trajectory of asteroids, across the Plum Creek River, flowing by red rock arches under oak leaves.

Chapter 43:

The Dance Trance

The first Friday in June, I drove to Kentucky with very low expectations. Our local dance gypsy troupe drove in a caravan, so that Tom could help me drive my truck. Actually, he drove most of the way, except for an interlude when he wanted to close his eyes and meditate. Tom and I talked so much that we forgot to listen to music. As we got closer to Lexington, he teased me and kept asking if I was in love yet until I said, "Ok, Tom, I admit it. I don't have expectations, but I want to see him."

Tom looked back at me with a quizzical look on his face. "In love and no expectations? You expect me to believe that?"

"I don't have an answer for you or for myself, but I've learned that expectations are deadly. As they say, if you want God to laugh, make plans." Most of my life was working, but love was a Zen koan, and I was trying to navigate the enigma.

We arrived in Lexington with time for a dinner buffet at the India Palace before the first dance. I especially liked the idlis with coconut chutney, sambar and samosas. After dessert, we drove to the middle school gym that would house the Dance Trance for the weekend. As soon as I walked in, five people hugged me.

The Dance Trance starts on Friday evening and continues through the weekend. Christopher found me while I was changing into my dance shoes and asked for the first dance. It had already been claimed, so I gave him number two. After that, he kept track of where I was on the dance floor. Like the dolphins, he kept circling back to me, and after each waltz, he always kissed me.

Tom and I stayed on a horse farm with Lucinda and sixteen other dancers who camped in the bedrooms, the loft, and tents in her backyard. Lucinda's kitchen was full of potluck treats and several varieties of tea. In her livingroom I discovered one of Christopher's paintings – a still life of his studio in blues and greens, with an overstuffed sofa, a window and his bicycle. The painting provided an entry to a life I had not fully entered, and I felt magic there. Tom and I slept in a room with two thin beds and a river of moonlight pouring through the window. As Friday turned into Saturday in my dreams, I danced all night.

On Saturday morning, the dolphins showed up. I'm sure Christopher noticed the intensity of Kevin's attraction, as he gave me lots of attention, even on Saturday night, as the mountain music of Flapjack moved us into an altered state of consciousness. Angelo, of course, was eager to display his swing dance moves. He asked if I was going to Sugar Hill in August, hopefully without Christopher. Since I didn't know, he said he would keep in touch with me.

When I found Jo on the dance floor, I noticed a wedding band on her finger. She smiled and told me, "Yes, Jim and I got married two weeks ago." When she saw the surprise in my eyes, she continued. "Everyone is looking for love, but when you find it, you have to believe it. And then you have to let it in. The real thing is just amazing. I'm still amazed after two and a half years."

Somewhere inside, I knew that love was an opening to the deepest wisdom of the soul. My heart wasn't wired for casual encounters. Something deep inside me remembered a hologram, earlier times, an island or an eon, when no was never challenged, and yes was always a gift. A vision of the sacred sexual and clearly out of phase with the world I found.

On the gym floor of the Dance Trance, I saw people looking for love, people looking only to dance, and people searching for casual encounters. I saw dance gypsies gathered to commune with their friends and share three days of joy, then go their separate ways until the next reunion. I saw couples who enjoyed community, and lonely souls casting the net of their dreams, hoping to land the big one. People flew out of their ordinary lives and dressed like butterflies. Above us, a canopy of delicate colored lights sparkled the evening, whirling dreams stretched to the wall. Love was a gypsy moth, a weave of desire and fear. Balance and swing. Apart, together.

Christopher and I wove in and out of the contra quilt, danced with other partners, and found each other again. Bernie from Bakersfield lifted me over his head at the end of the line, then used the end of the phrase to dip me and turn me upside down. Kevin had his dance harem but kept orbiting back to me with slinky swing moves and a sensual dip at the end of the dance. I gravitated towards both planets, the Christopher planet, the Kevin planet, with Angelo keeping guard in an elliptical orbit. At the horse farm on Saturday night, dolphins swam through my dreams.

Late morning Sunday started with an hour of waltzes, then three hours of contra to Flapjack's driving mountain melodies, a banjo voice that would echo for weeks in my dreams. After three days of dancing, the connection I felt with more than two hundred dance gypsies was astounding. Christopher and I did the last waltz, and then he took me home.

Chapter 44:

Catalpa Trees and Guatemalan Bedspreads

Christopher's apartment was artistic but moderately trashy. He lived in the historic district of Lexington and his home was a living museum, the chronicle of an artistic soul – with drawings of nudes, black and white photographs of the Red River Gorge, paintings of women prone on a blanket and lovers entwined, Guatemalan bedspreads, and collages of wood and bone. In honor of my visit, he placed a bouquet of sunflowers in a blue vase on the kitchen table, a new addition to his ecosystem of art objects.

The front room had huge windows and bookshelves filled with art books; eastern philosophy; guides to birds, flowers, trees, and medicinal herbs; and myths from Central America. Around the room, scented candles, hanging plants, conga drums, paintings on easels, and stained glass. Mirrors everywhere and a soft moon trickling through a sky about to rain. It was the kind of place where I could spend hours just looking around, and I did.

I brought my camping mat because I had no idea whether I'd be sleeping on the floor or sleeping with him. I found out late at night when, after an impromptu swing dance in his kitchen, Christopher unzipped my dress. The first night was just for sleeping, to see how we would dream, with the moon dripping over our bare shoulders – the fulfillment of a fantasy I had carried since I was fourteen years old. In the morning, we enjoyed Lebanese fig jam and almond butter for breakfast, spooned onto a seeded foccacia over a linen tablecloth draped on a conga drum.

In the afternoon we hiked into the Red River Gorge. As he led me through the rain forest, I became convinced that Kentucky is one of the hidden wonders of this planet. Every moment was astounding, with red rock arches, hanging rocks, and natural stone bridges over the river. Like an artist combined with a middle school science teacher, Christopher explained the process of glaciers and erosion – the way this came to be.

The world was lit up with beauty – furrows in the creek bed, the silver fins of minnows, rhododendron blossoms snowing on mossy forest beds. We climbed over the waterfall arch, with Christopher pulling me up to footholds higher than my head. He told me he had a feeling of deja vu in this place. We sat and watched the water for a long time as the sun was falling lower and lower in the sky. The rest of the world disappeared, and it felt like a huge meditation but connected to the world and sensual.

On the hike back out, we saw a profusion of birds and butterflies. Two mating cardinals chasing each other from branch to branch, then over the edge of the stone bridge. Huge circling hawks above the gorge. From a precipice, we watched their slow circles against the blue sky. Christopher and I were enchanted by the wild beauty of the earth. A glitter of light trickled through the canopy of trees. Butterflies with exotic wing patterns appeared and disappeared. Now the early evening light was drizzling through a lacework of leaves, and we were clearly in the magic hour – the forest a profusion of night music. Later, a soft Kentucky moon, the sky about to rain, Christopher's face a mirror for the light. The flat rocks a coincidence, the underbelly of a dream.

Christopher had a blank canvas with a thin mirror over his double bed, a futon with a Guatemalan bedspread. Outside the window, catalpa trees with their orchid-like flowers newly blooming, the scent sticky sweet and intoxicating. Inside the window, I inhaled his art – paintings of naked men and women in shades of blue and green. Christopher inhaled my skin. After midnight, our last waltz curved into its logical conclusion under a thin mirror.

Chapter 45:

The Umbrella Magnolia

hat night, my dreams led me further inside the Kentucky rain forest. I was hiking with Christopher on a path in a gorge surrounded by mountains. As the full moon rose, we explored the banks of a river I had not seen before. I saw the moon through a lacework of trees, then higher. We were glowing in its lemony radiance as we walked to the river. Further down the path, we saw a rainbow of light spraying up from a waterfall. Christopher pointed to the rainbow and whispered, "You'll find fairies there." Then he dissolved into a nighthawk, a dream bird in flight, with visions across each long, pointed wing.

When I shared this with Christopher in the morning, he told me, "I think you dreamed about the moonbow at Cumberland Falls. It's visible for five days around the full moon."

"Have you ever seen it?"

"It's one of my favorite places. We just missed the full moon by a few days, but maybe the next time you visit Kentucky, I can take you there."

I was excited by the possibility. We had not yet spoken about a future visit, and this felt like a good omen. We shared a breakfast of tea and blueberry scones, then went back to the Red River Gorge with our sketchbooks. The trail to the Red River wove through a pink and green paradise of rhododendrons, mountain laurel, and ferns. As we hiked into the gorge, we were amazed by a profusion of butterflies – monarchs, viceroys, painted ladies, a zebra swallowtail, a tawny emperor, and a pair of great spangled fritillaries – more species than I had ever seen in a single afternoon. They appeared and disappeared all over the forest. On a stone bridge, we enjoyed a picnic of Jarlsberg cheese, marinated artichoke hearts, heirloom tomatoes and foccacia, then found a grove of pine trees, where we listened to bird calls with our legs intertwined on a hand-woven Guatemalan blanket.

In the late afternoon, we hiked out to catch a gallery opening. Butterflies hovered in the light above the trail. Phoebes, larks, plovers and kestrels called to each other through the forest. Then a nuthatch and a tanager. As the trail got steeper, we discovered a huge magnolia tree with gigantic leaves and an elusive blossom hovering over a precipice. We were both urgently curious about how it smelled, but not curious enough to climb on a thin branch over a gorge.

The gallery opening, an exhibit of paintings and sculpture by local artists, was nicely crowded. The art was specific to Kentucky, with an interesting mix of inner and outer world visions in local color, featuring painted and sculpted images of race horses, mythological horses, and dream horses. In an alcove, three walls were filled with impressionist renderings of the river gorge, migrating birds, and exotic butterflies. In the café next door, we watched a group of belly dancers weaving their hips under a rainbow of coin scarves. One of the dancers was so attentive to Christopher that I wondered if she had been his lover. Later that night, I forgot about my misgivings as he held me warm and close in the moonlight. With shadows of catalpa leaves weaving patterns on our bodies, we loved each other for hours that night.

The next morning, Christopher went hunting in his closet for a book to identify the elusive blossom we had discovered in the gorge. He called out his progress report. "Searching for photo essay entitled *Land of Arches* about the Red River Gorge... Well, apparently, I don't have that book anymore. But I did find another small book entitled, *Kentucky Forest Trees* with mention of the umbrella magnolia!

The description fits, though there is another blossom called the *big leaf magnolia*... I like *umbrella magnolia* much better."

I quickly agreed. The name seemed to fit the flower. It also fit my emotions, as in, love is a huge umbrella magnolia hanging over a precipice. Sweetly scented, exotic and dangerous.

In the evening, Christopher prepared a veggie and ginger stir fry while I sat on a wooden stool and played my flute. When the rice was steamed, he opened a bottle of sake and we ate by candlelight. This was my last night in Kentucky, at least for a while. With candles burning, we took out our sketchbooks and drew each other in a wash of soft light. Later, as Christopher held me inside a river of moonlight, he told me, "I am very inconsistent at being close to anyone, but I'm glad we've had this time together, Trina."

This was something I didn't want to hear as we embraced each other with light streaming on our arms and legs through the open window. I let his touch imprint like oak leaves. Bamboo over a koi pond, his eyes eggshell blue full of messages. A few minutes later, I looked directly into his eyes and said, "I'm open to other possibilities."

Christopher smiled and told me, "I am too, but you'll have to be patient with me."

I felt my body relax as he wrapped a blanket over my shoulders. I draped my arm over his chest and whispered, "You should come and see Iowa." But at this point, we were half dreaming.

In the morning, Christopher packed my travel bag with a blueberry cheese danish and an almond croissant from the bakery around the corner, along with two bottles of lemon iced tea and a map of the road from his street to I-64. For travel music, he gave me two cassettes, one with Larry Unger waltzes and the other with Flapjack fiddle tunes. We hugged each other for a long time. Then I got in my truck, put the Flapjack cassette into the tape deck, and headed out.

Christopher was waving, watching me. In my rearview mirror, his image faded into the shadow of a catalpa tree.

Chapter 46:

Driving Back from Kentucky

The drive back from Kentucky was a green odyssey of six hundred miles, powered by Larry Unger waltzes, Flapjack, and lemon iced tea. I listened to the music Christopher gave me, along with Peruvian and Israeli folk songs I brought from San Francisco. I enjoyed the delicious treats he packed with sweet memories of our time together, and wondered when I would see him again. Christopher had talked about wanting to see Fairfield, but he didn't say when.

As I drove on winding country roads, the land stunned me with its beauty. A few miles before St. Louis, I passed through a sun shower with a huge double rainbow. Then the arch and the bridge over the Mississippi River. Later that evening, a rain of milkweed and fireflies.

I came back to Iowa to find close to two hundred roses blooming in my yard and the first tiger lilies of the season by my bedroom window. The flowers were speaking to me again – snapdragons, columbines, lilies with henna constellations on the petals falling out to an edge of original light. Later that week I attended a kathak dance performance at Morningstar, then caught the end of a birthday concert at Café Paradiso. On Sunday morning, I played Telemann and Scarlatti with my friends – a palm reader on violin, a homeopath on harpsichord, a poet on cello, and my flute. All of us in town on the same Sunday morning was close to a miracle.

When Christopher and I spoke on the phone a few days later, he talked about the summer in Lexington. "Wonderful gentle breezes moving through light cool air. Between that and some unexpected sunshine, it has been an absolutely beautiful late afternoon! I've been so busy that I've hardly spent any time in the garden I planted, so today I was able to catch up with it a bit. I watched two chipmunks wrestling and playing between the summer squash and the tomatoes, and I've been listening to a chorus of bird voices – a phoebe, a lark, a nuthatch and a tanager."

I thought about Christopher's eyes, how they were deep and beautiful in a way that made me fall into them, especially when we danced. In the Red River Gorge, I watched them reflect the earth, the sky and the trees. He asked me about the history of my farmhouse and I described it to him – how it was built by Amish carpenters and what was growing in my gardens. Six hundred miles away, I could feel him light up when I described the oriental poppies and the week of the bloom.

Christopher quickly replied, "I would love to see them."

"They won't bloom again until next April, but I'll paint them for you. It's an astounding color, and the petals have delicate shapes. I love the way the early morning sunlight illuminates the petals, as though from inside."

For almost an hour, we talked about art and the local dances, but the conversation didn't lead into an invitation for another visit. When we touched on that topic, he told me, "I need to go slowly and take time with these things."

I hesitated, then told him, "I think it takes a long time to really know another human being. It was sweet to share your home and learn more about your life. Maybe the future will bring another opportunity." I was worried about saying too much, but I wanted to keep my heart open.

He ended the conversation by saying, "Let's stay open to the possibility."

In the humid air under the moonlight, I danced with my memories. Fireflies flickered as a meteor streaked across the sky. Then a tiny shower, with starlight playing on raindrops. In the tension between who I was and who I wished to be, Christopher was an enigma, a comet streaking a blue path into the dark night. I opened my sketchbook to the candlelight drawings from our last evening in Lexington and studied his face, his eyes, his hands, the shape of his muscles. I knew my hands would find his form in clay.

I thought about our love nights, Christopher telling me, "You have very soft skin and an amazingly beautiful body." During my time in San Francisco, I had gotten too hard. Too many broken promises. Too much deadly nightshade in the gardens. Too many unfinished dreams. Christopher made my edges softer. As I thought about how we waltzed in his kitchen the night before I left, my body went into an altered state of consciousness.

That night in a dream, I heard a canon for four voices and a cello. The music was hauntingly beautiful, but I didn't have a way to access my vision in the morning. I could still hear echoes of the voices, but I couldn't repeat it clearly or write it down. Now I had to find my way to cope with living in Iowa again. As much as I loved teaching, I was having increasing doubts about the midwest as my future.

Chapter 47:

Last Day of August

A thunderstorm drifted over Fairfield's meditation domes during an evening meditation at the end of August. First thunder, then rain, then hailstones the size of cat's eye marbles bouncing on the dome and rolling down. Sky the color of a bruise. We had the doors open, and all the time, the scent of rain. Too much water music to settle in for a while. Later, when it passed, a huge silence. A tornado almost touched down but moved off in a different direction.

After the Dance Trance, Angelo started calling twice a week and wanted to come and visit me in Fairfield. I wasn't sure about it. I knew Angelo was a great guy, solid and sweet, but the timing was wrong. I liked his machismo, but it troubled me that he worked for the Air Force and would probably be annoyed by my anti-war posters. Angelo was intuitive – he threw runes and had a keen sensitivity to my emotions. Was he a paradox, or was there something larger at play I didn't understand? Angelo was handsome in a way that appealed to me, with olive skin, warm brown eyes, and a Mediterranean charisma, especially in his hips when he danced. I just wasn't sure I could fall in love with him if I had to conceal parts of myself. To complicate matters further, my heart was still hitched to a pony in Kentucky. Communication with Christopher had drifted into silence, but something inside me knew we weren't done yet.

I was trying to listen to my soul inside the percussion of my emotions – the artist, the dance gypsy, and the vulnerable woman.

Sun and ice, drive to Chicago or Wisconsin in the George-mobile, dance for three days, balance and swing. Drive to Iowa City through a hail storm to get an AIDS test, the pre-mating ritual of single people in the twenty-first century. I drove there with a group of artists making a political statement that people in Iowa should be more careful about their sexual health. My conclusion, right after this: I should probably move back to San Francisco.

When I walked into Café Paradiso that night, my silk dress dripping with rain, my married friends asked me where I'd been.

"I just drove back from Iowa City."

"Oh my God! Through this thunderstorm? You poor thing."

"I only had to pull over once when the hail was too thick to see the road."

"Didn't you hear the tornado siren?"

"Actually, no. Nobody said anything about tornados at the Free Clinic. You'd think they would have told us before we got our AIDS test results."

Silence.

"Don't worry. I'm okay. It's negative."

Silence.

"When you get the test, they scrape a Q-tip on the inside of your cheek, and it leaves a bad taste in your mouth. When it's done, they give you a butterscotch mint and two condoms. You have to come again in a week to get the results, just in case it's positive. They won't tell you anything over the phone. At the clinic, you follow the medic up two flights of stairs. He holds your eyes for a long rhetorical pause before he tells you because he wants you to think about it."

Silence.

That was when I realized that being married in Iowa, they probably didn't know that HIV negative means I'm okay. It wasn't my place to tell them that their children would have to do this one day. People in Iowa took chances San Franciscans would never take. I needed a hug, not because of the AIDS test, which I wasn't worried about, but because of driving through hail and thunder, with shafts of lightning too low in the sky, then grounding in the surrounding

176

cornfields. A San Franciscan wouldn't understand that, except from a movie, but in San Francisco I'd get my hug instead of this weird, judgmental silence.

At the clinic, you had to talk about your plan for staying healthy. My plan – what I truly wanted anyway – an exclusive relationship with someone who loves me and has been tested, or else condoms. Is that okay? And don't roll anyone from Iowa.

Later that night before I fell asleep, it came to me, what I really wanted at Café Paradiso. Besides the hug, perhaps concern. "Are you worried about anyone?" "How is it going with Christopher?" But this was a seemingly impossible act of communication.

The next afternoon, after more than twenty years of silence, I got a phone call from Jonathan, who was now on his second wife. Jonathan, who had disqualified me for having long dark hair. In a radio rant, he told me about an award winning show he created with his best friend, his divorce four years ago, a flurry of polyamorous lovers, and then finally meeting the woman of his dreams. At this point I had two choices – hang up or ask him to tell me about her. I chose option #2.

Option #3, which wasn't offered: To tell me how, many years after his graduation from Cornell University, perhaps at a 12-step meeting, he had a flash of memory about a young woman who played the flute and loved him, and how he threw her heart away. Maybe no regret that he did it, but perhaps about the way he did it. Option #4, to apologize. But this would be a seemingly impossible act of communication.

Jonathan went on to describe an enigmatic woman he met through the radio call-in line. She was born again, had escaped an abusive childhood, had lived in the street for a while, but over time let Jonathan soften her rough edges. She wasn't educated but had an innate wisdom, and Jonathan trained her to be his assistant at the radio station. The process of reconciling their differences opened new areas of his soul, and he didn't have to walk on eggs, as he did with his first wife.

"No eggs? I guess that's a good sign."

"It's one of many omens that have continued to unfold since I met her."

Leaning against the wall of my farmhouse, I listened to his radio voice, disembodied, far away, and listened to the summer rain outside my window. I could hang up or congratulate him. As his voice droned on, I chose option #2. "Elli made a good choice, and I hope you are happy."

He said, "You should call her and tell her too, especially about her good choice in a husband. Her phone number is . . ."

What? You want me to spend my money on an international phone call for that? You live in another country now in so many ways, sweet talking on the radio and Sufi chanting above the northern border. I changed the subject and told him about Christopher. "I've been seeing a man who lives in Kentucky, six hundred miles away, but we meet at dance gypsy gatherings every four to six weeks. We dance for three days, maybe go out for falafel or sushi. Play kissy-face in the truck. He might be all over me in a city between Iowa and Kentucky, or he might ignore me to dance with other women for the rest of the night. This is making me crazy."

Jonathan, immediately changing the subject back to himself, told me, "I've become a therapist. I pitched it on the radio, and now I have a lot of clients. The only problem is that I'm getting lost in other people's auras."

"It's better than losing your voice."

I offered to fly to Toronto and teach him Chi Gong. "It's a great way to clear your aura, and then you can have your own dreams at night. I do it every Tuesday night, after I teach my sculpture workshop, so I can feel the shape of my own visions again. If I fly to Toronto, I could meet Elli and spend some time with the Pre-Columbian Art exhibit at the Gardiner Museum. But you'd have to let me sleep on your couch. Do you think Elli could handle that?"

"Can you tell me how to do Chi Gong over the phone?"

I started to describe the process, but Jonathan interrupted me. Evidently, this was too much for someone who had stopped dancing years ago.

"You know, it's a little weird with women from the past who have been important to me."

Aha! I've been important to him! I remembered his problem with my dark eyes, my ethnic hair, and the fact that I wanted to spend my life with him. This, of course, would have required a commitment, and we were both very young.

When I tuned in again, Jonathan was saying, "I have to be careful about emotional infidelity." Then he started giving me advice about how to find a husband and told me about a book I didn't want to read. Jonathan, my ex-boyfriend, appearing like lightning through a time warp, had suddenly become my big brother. "Seventy-five percent of it is having someone work with your issues and not get plugged in."

Not get plugged in? Right! My emotions whirled around Christopher again. Our waltz had detoured into a question mark, and I lost my appetite for a week every time I saw him. Artistically, Christopher inspired me and profoundly influenced my sculptures and my book of dreams. But really, I wanted more than that. Maybe Christopher was a gift from the Muse and not for my heart.

I faded back into Jonathan's voice, saying, "Trina, it's possible to find what has always eluded you. I did it. I found it. I'm happy." Goodbye. Click. Silence. Another seemingly impossible act of communication.

Before I fell asleep that night, I had a fantasy about meeting Jonathan again, after his next divorce. We'd be reintroduced by a mutual friend who would let me know he hadn't become an axe murderer. It would start on my answering machine. He'd call when I wasn't there and say, "Hello, this is Mr. Destiny." He'd go on to explain he hoped it wasn't strange that he wanted so badly to see me.

I'd call back and say, "Hello, this is Aphrodite." The next evening he'd call back, and radio style, we would fall in love over the telephone for the next month, to the tune of a huge international phone bill. He would try to fake me out with the offer of a plane ticket, but I'd say, "When?" His only condition would be that I had to stay for ten days, even if we couldn't stand each other. "Whatever comes up," he'd say, "we have to work through it."

With all the years that had passed, I'd be shocked when I saw Jonathan at the Toronto airport. Visually, he would not be handsome anymore, but every human face is a reflection of God. You just have to pay attention and look deeper. In the ten days we would spend together, in Toronto, Montreal and his farmhouse in between, I would grow to love that face.

The Iowa thunder interfered with my ability to sleep that night – lightning splitting cottonwood trees, weaving through my dreams and my memories. Sweaty nights, wandering through the Montreal Jazz Festival. The house where we stayed with its balcony over the music, his face lit by candles. We had wild conversations. Jonathan isolated seven artistic subpersonalities – the sculptor, the geisha, the dancer, the Egyptian priestess, the poet, the court jester, and the vulnerable woman. He had conversations with each of them separately. There were times I didn't know if he was a genius or totally out of his mind. What I knew was that I loved him.

Elli would not approve of these memories. Humid afternoons, slices of watermelon, chasing each other through a field of sunflowers. My hair drenched with rain, and the way he loved me. Especially that night in his lion's paw tub, with the room lit by candles. The night I shaved his face and photographed him both ways for a sculpture. A gift I gave him that Elli now admires.

Now I have his voice, saying, "Trina, don't give up. It's possible." Wisdom that echoes against the floating voice of an Indian astrologer, who tells me, "You are very skilled in relationships, but you have difficult karma from past lives."

I need to be with a man who thoroughly believes in me. A man who loves me so much he can pull me through this karma. Guide me through the hail storm. Drive my car through lightning. Steady me in the middle of this shattering thunder.

Chapter 48:
The Six Hundred Mile Deja Vu

utumn brought three waves of Indian summer before the first frost. Strong winds sweeping across the Great Plains carried a wave of restlessness. In clay pots around my garden, marigolds, dahlias and peppermint were still blooming. By the fence, a final wave of roses, tomatoes still heavy on the vine, and stems of chrysanthemums under my bedroom window. As the cold season approached, my dreams were more interesting than my life. Many mornings I'd wake up thinking, *I've got to get out of here.*

My communication with Christopher took the form of occasional phone calls and postcards we painted and drew for one another. We talked about meeting at the Leaf Festival, but his truck broke down and the car pool he tried to arrange fell through. I decided to go anyway to see my dance gypsy friends, but a note of my inner chord was missing. We thought about meeting at Breaking Up Thanksgiving until his family asked him to fly back to Saddle River for the holiday weekend. Christopher's postcards were filled with images of Kentucky, observations about his inner world and stories about his students, but never the words I was waiting for. Nothing even hinting at "I miss you" or "When can I see you?" The artist in me loved every detail of what he shared, but the vulnerable woman crumbled inside. And from what I'd learned of American men, I knew I had to let him lead this dance.

The snow came early, making it even more difficult to cope

with living in Iowa. Salt and sand from the roads were rusting the bottom of my truck. Artistically, I had already expressed what I had to say about this place, and I felt a vacancy in the growing cold. My hands were frozen. The only way I could release them was to go deeper into my inner world, where visions came in the form of dreams, desire and memory.

Since Christopher had inspired me so deeply in the spring, I went back to my notebooks from that time. In anticipation of my visit to Lexington, I had observed and sketched horses, and on the first of May, had watched the Kentucky Derby. It was fascinating to hear stories of the people who bred and trained these magnificent steeds. When interviewed, these accidental visionaries quietly revealed their wisdom, especially the owner of a favored horse who said, "Great expectation brings great disappointment," and the jockey who told the sports announcer, "The best horse doesn't always win this race."

In the late afternoon light, I studied the shapes of the horses. In charcoal, I sketched proud heads, magnificent muscles, the powerful sway of a back. These horses were stunning, nothing like your Iowa barnyard nag, and had mythological names – Andromeda's Chariot, Sun King, High Fly, Spanish Chestnut and Sea Hero. Memories of the Kentucky Derby rippled into my longing for Christopher. I had no idea when I would see him again. Our love was an unpredictable horse. But even months later, these horses continued to inspire me.

Once again, my hands were hungry for clay. Goddesses emerged from ice ponds, rode on meteor showers across the sky. Even in my sleep, I was filled with visions of rolling hills and prairie fields, as the colors of the day condensed into oddly shaped leaves and flowers. The contours of the world spoke to my fingers, my hands found the form, and all of it spoke to my emotions. It brought happiness to find expression for something so deep within me. I was searching for a new vision, my personal relationship to everything I'd seen. It was urgent – I was finding my place in the universe.

Twice a week I walked through the snow and read novel chapters to Emma, my neighbor, an old woman in a wheelchair. One afternoon, she asked to see some of my sculptures and offered to pose for me. Her hands looked like someone had dipped them into chocolate. Her fingers were fused together, and I could see the ridge of the bones. I was terrified by her deformities, but they fascinated me. For an instant, I just let go and let her touch my hands, then my sculptures, even though I was afraid that she might break them. That night, I dreamed about her hands.

I spent the next few weeks sculpting mythological horses, then preparing them for the foundry – making the plaster mold, then pouring layers of casting wax to create a hollow egg with the shape of the sculpture inside. During my breaks, I'd walk across the snowy field to Emma, who was fascinated by the whole process of bronze casting. "The next step," I explained, "is the investment mold and the sprue system, attached to the piece in key areas to give access to the sculpture. During casting, the sprue system melts away to create channels to the hollow cavity. This creates a structure to protect the wax during the casting process, with tunnels to the outer surface of the piece, so the molten bronze can be poured in."

Emma, at eighty-five, had a body that was broken, but her mind was clear as the sunlight pouring through her kitchen window. Her sense of design was evident in the cut of her shaker chairs, the antique rose pattern of her china, and the way she arranged pears in the depression glass bowl on her kitchen table. Like many women of Amish descent, she used to weave and sew, and she cooked with herbs she grew in her garden, which her children still tended with loving care. Her house was full of treasures from thrift stores and yard sales by the Mississippi River, but her keen intellect was limping for good company, which I was happy to provide.

Emma was fascinated by the wax eggs I showed her. As I tied ribbons in her long white braids, I explained how the sprue system is connected to a v-shaped cup, like a pyramid. "Usually, sculptures are cast upside down, like monkeys hanging out of a tree, or a space ship that gets wider at the bottom. The wax egg creates a hollow space for bronze, like a miniature universe waiting to be created. In the foundry, I am the goddess of the underworld, where everything that flows from my hands becomes real.

"In the foundry, you hear the roaring of the blowers, low and hollow. It's an industrial roar, a hidden world where sculptors hold their visions in wax before the alchemical transformation. I melt the bronze in a furnace, the door to the underworld, Persephone and Pluto heated 2500 degrees. The bronze has to be preheated outside of the crucible. You can see it sweat, dripping out of the ingots. I get so used to the roar of the blowers that the silence is shocking when it stops. It's a dramatic, unexpected silence. You can hear the wind outside. You again hear people talking as they gather to watch the pour."

Emma's eyes were wide as she told me, "This is something I would like to see and hear."

"Right now, I'm not sure I could get your wheelchair through the snow, but maybe in the spring."

"My grandsons could help you with that. They're twins, fourteen years old now, and one of them likes to paint."

"I'm sure that watching a pour would inspire them. It looks like you're pouring a river of light. At first, the bronze is glowing as it fills the mold and solidifies. Within minutes, it cools to an increasingly duller glow. As you watch, you can see the fire diminishing."

"It sounds beautiful and mysterious, like campfires late at night by the Cedar River. When I was a girl, I liked to build fires with my friends and then watch them burning. Our parents would tell stories and sometimes we'd sing, but most of all, I loved the fires. I loved to watch them blaze, change shape, and later disappear into the reflection of the river."

"When I was a girl, we built fires by the shores of Lake Hopatcong. I used to go there every summer with my family, and later with my friends."

Emma closed her eyes. "My family had picnics at Lacey Keosaqua. Sometimes late at night, I think about time traveling around the world – and what that looks like to a bird, or a cloud, or someone from a distant star. Thousands of lakes and rivers, lighting up our planet like a jewel. Sunlight sparkling on the water. Then, night travels like a wave around the planet, with people lighting fires, sipping tea, heating stones, cooking their evening meal, and letting the shape of the flames fill them with magic."

"That's why night is my favorite time for pouring bronze. People are mesmerized by the melting of the bronze and the roar, dramatic in the semidark."

Emma looked at me. "And then you finally see the result?"

"Not yet. I'm urgently curious to see my sculpture, but I always wait until the next morning. The cooling takes several hours, and my hands are important to me. After a pour, the world lights up the way objects intensify after walking through a museum. The ride home late at night is stunning, with moonlight etching patterns on the snow through winter branches and perhaps a deer running across a snowy field.

"My dreams are always interesting that night. They are wild and glowing. The next morning, I crack the investment mold with a hammer. It shatters like glass. Then, I clean off the shards and remove the sprue system with a cutting torch. After that, I grind down the pouring channels to reveal the surface of the piece. It's sand blasted to remove the rest of the investment mold and the fire scale, and finally you can see the surface of the metal.

"The noise and the equipment, the industrial nightmare you need to make a sculpture is overwhelming. It's a messy, grimy, dirty process, although you would never know this in a gallery or a museum. Once the piece is smooth enough, you chase the metal, which is preparing the surface of the metal with a hammer and a cold chisel. The sprue is like a scar. Chasing makes the scar look like the surrounding metal and hides the imperfections. You pound away until you have the desired texture.

"Then, you take it to the patina area of the foundry. The patina artist creates the look of the piece – the color and the reflectiveness. He heats up the sculpture with a large torch, brushing or spraying on chemicals which oxidize the metal to the desired color. After the patina is done, the sculpture is cooled and waxed. Then I finally get to see what I have done."

Emma made me promise to bring my sculptures to her kitchen before they went off to a gallery.

"Yes, of course. We'll put them all around the room as a setting for the next chapter of *Sense and Sensibility*." With a promise to visit again in two days, I walked out into the cold, crossed the snowy field, and went back to my studio.

My horses were large and mythological. I liked to reach into the hollow areas to get a contour. I loved the undefined places – the mounds and the bulbs. I'd start at the shoulder and run the tool all the way down to the leg. Then run it down to the knee and the foot, a sensual journey of shape shifting. After that, I'd follow with my fingers. At that instant, everything would transform into another dimension, where the visible meets the invisible.

I could never plan a sculpture in advance – I had to discover it as I worked the clay. Sculpture, like life, wasn't a tool for working with hard edges. And what was it about my life that I was trying so hard to understand? What was my sculpture trying to teach me? And why wasn't I getting it?

At this point, I didn't know what to think about Christopher. We had our postcards flying from state to state, but I hadn't seen him since his last visit to Brattleboro. Occasionally, I accepted a date with a dancer from Fairfield or an artist from Iowa City, but nobody inspired me. At the Café Paradiso swing dance, I danced with a man who was very passionate, but not devoted. My intuition gave me clear signals to stay away from him. At the Farmer's Market, I met a man who was devoted but not passionate. Okay then, we could be friends. I went to contra dances, but most of the dancers in Iowa were coupled. When it came time for the last waltz, I walked off the dance floor, changed my shoes and went home.

At one of the dances, I had a deja vu. I think it was triggered by a banjo playing "Clinch Mountain Backstep." The rhythm of that tune carried me over two rivers to Kentucky. I was hiking over stone bridges at Red River Gorge. I was dancing with Christopher, sculpting his face.

As much as I tried to forget him, I knew that Christopher and I weren't done yet. For that reason, the phone call early in November from Brent, a patron of the Cross Gate Gallery in Lexington, was not a surprise. Brent was a folk musician and art collector from Kentucky. I had played flute with his band during a late night music jam at the Dance Trance, and he had called a few times to talk about art. He was always fascinated to hear about my sculptures, especially the mythological horses. Sometimes, he'd call late at night and play his banjo for a few minutes, then wish me sweet dreams. Now, he was making arrangements with the owner of the gallery to feature my mythological horses.

Brent asked if I was available early in December to visit Lexington for about two weeks to set up the show, attend the opening, and spend time with patrons of the gallery. When I expressed my enthusiasm, he offered to arrange housing for me in Lexington. I said I'd let him know, since I had a friend there who might want to host me. I liked the idea of putting up a show just before the December holidays, and the gallery opening would create an opportunity to visit Christopher. An interesting coincidence, or perhaps my universe set it up that way.

When I called Christopher to tell him about the show, he invited me to stay with him, as I had hoped. Without any hesitation, he said he was happy about the opportunity to spend time together again, and I started having fantasies of taking what we had begun to the next level. I was a little bit worried that two weeks might be too long, as Christopher was accustomed to spending most of his time alone. But when I asked him about this, he told me, "I'm sure it will be fine, since we're both so comfortable around each other."

Since Iowa weather was unpredictable in December, often treacherous with the risk of ice storms, I asked George to drive my bronze horses to Lexington on the way to a barn dance in Berea. He was planning to dance in Kentucky a few weeks before my gallery opening, and he had enough room for my sculptures in his van. George had fallen in love with a woman in Berea and was planning to propose before Thanksgiving. Tom and I tried to get him to date her first. With the sculptures traveling early, I found a good deal on a circle ticket, starting from Cedar Rapids to Lexington early in December. After the show, I would fly to San Francisco. The return flight on the ticket was open. I asked for a six month sabbatical from teaching in Mt. Pleasant, and one of my students agreed to rent my house and take care of the gardens. I missed the redwood trees and I ached to be back home – a place where I could be myself without asking permission or shocking people.

Chapter 49:

Lexington, Kentucky

I flew into Lexington, Kentucky in a small Mesaba turboprop, my window under the wing. From the sky, I watched the lights and looked for patterns – lights in the shape of a question mark, then a saxophone, then a heart. The evening felt like deja vu, and the oracles were in the lights. As we began to lose altitude, I felt it in my ears. Beyond my window, a half moon rippled on a curve of the Kentucky River. A few minutes later, the city lights of Lexington, amber and green, glittered through a stream of the contrail.

Christopher was waiting at the baggage claim. The kiss he gave me was friendly but not passionate. He lifted my bags, which were heavy, into the back of his pickup truck, and we headed toward the historic district of Lexington. In his kitchen, two sand dollars I gave him from Taraval Beach in San Francisco were leaning together in an alcove, but the photograph where I was standing inside a redwood tree was gone.

We ate dinner at home and shared a pot of ginger tea. Christopher opened a small box of baklava for dessert, then told me he had plans to visit Brattleboro over the Christmas vacation. He wanted to visit Suzanne to continue their discussion about moving to Vermont. I tumbled into myself, thinking I would want this for him if it could be possible. I wouldn't want to be with a man who desired to be somewhere else. But in the part of me that knows things without knowing how or why, I got a no. It was clear to me that for the third time, Suzanne would say no but keep him dangling – their version of the *Yoga of the Impossible*. Since Christopher had to find out one more time, and it's bad form to offer advice when it isn't asked for, I was silent.

Christopher told me he still felt possibilities for a life with Suzanne down the road. He looked at me and said, "Sorry, Trina. I didn't know about this until a week ago."

I didn't tell him what I was thinking, which was, "Right, Christopher. She might marry you in three to five years, if the next twenty men she sleeps with don't work out. You're her insurance policy."

I didn't know if Christopher had a clue what I was feeling, but it must have been transparent from my face. He put his arm around me and said, "Don't worry, Trina. I'm glad you're here and we're going to enjoy our time together. You've always been like a sister to me. When I was home for Thanksgiving, Mom made me promise to bake you blueberry muffins. She would have made them herself but didn't think they would last until your visit."

A blueberry muffin wasn't going to resolve what I was feeling. Cocooned in my own world now, I was flooded with images of our visit in June. In the periphery of my awareness, Christopher chatted about a papercut project he was doing with his middle school students – a gift for the winter holidays. In the bedroom, his ceiling was patterned with a collage of papercut snowflakes, with echoes of the way I loved him resonating against the walls. I watched through a kaleidoscope of memory as Christopher gave me his futon to sleep on. Silently, he took out his dance gypsy gear, camping pads and a boy scout sleeping bag to make a bed for himself by the radiator. To be faithful to the woman who in three weeks he would again discover he could not have, he slept on the floor.

Simultaneously, six hundred miles away, one of the men in my dance troupe decided he would propose to me if I didn't find my soulmate in the next two years. His version of the *Yoga of the Impossible*. He saw his omen in the aurora borealis, which he had never seen until I took him driving on a November country road. But he wasn't listening to himself. Or to me.

That night I dreamed I was back in California, hiking above

Muir Woods in the redwood forest, singing to the trees. Higher on the trail, I found one of my favorite trees – a giant beauty with a hollow inside the trunk large enough to sit in. Even though these hollows were carved from the scar of a burn, it felt like a cathedral or a pyramid inside. I sat inside the hollow and closed my eyes. In the huge woody silence, I saw a path open up, with the trail leading higher up the mountain and sunlight streaming through the leaves. Above me, a blue heron flew into the light. Following the bird, I hiked to a glen by a brook with eucalyptus trees surrounded by wild orchids. It felt so peaceful. Tiny pebbles sparkled like jewels at a river crossing. I was full of joy, not for any reason other than the beauty of the mountain and the simple pleasure of being there. But at three o'clock in the morning, I woke up in Lexington, Kentucky with Christopher dreaming on the other side of the room. As I leaned against my pillow, he let out a soft sigh.

In the morning I unpacked two goddess sculptures and placed them on the table with our breakfast – the granola I brought from Everybody's health food store in Fairfield with raspberries and cream from the Good Foods Co-op in Lexington. In the early afternoon, Christopher cycled to a gallery across town to teach a drawing class. This gave me several hours with my sketchbook and my own thoughts. I thought about the way lovers develop a personal language – a language of the body and soul that only the two of you share. Then you dismantle it, like pulling bread apart.

While we were making dinner that night, Christopher told me about a woman who had never taken an art class before. She came to his studio with a bouquet of sunflowers in a Chinese vase and a determination to try.

I listened as I stir-fried shiitake mushrooms, snow peas and tofu in his wok. "Well, how did she do?"

"Not bad for a first attempt. It looked like a drawing from an eight-year-old, but something about it spoke to me. When I told her what I liked about her lines, she was surprised. She told me about a grade school teacher who convinced her she didn't have a gift for art. It took her forty years to try again."

"I'm glad you encouraged her."

"Most people can draw if they take the time to learn how to see. But people are too impatient. They want the finished drawing before they start. And their ideas are so strong about what the finished drawing will look like, they don't give it the time to come into being and find its own shape."

I told him, "It's the same with sculpture," and he smiled. "But there's an extra dimension you have to feel with your hands. Most people who sculpt can draw, but not always vice versa."

We continued to talk about our students over brown rice, shiitake mushrooms, and stir fry, anointed with two cups of ginger beer. I could tell he was deeply happy to talk about these things with a kindred soul. We were beyond time, inside the communion of souls, and could have been anywhere on the planet – in an art salon in Paris, under a waterfall, inside a redwood tree. We talked about the way a painting or a sculpture comes into being and the need to let it take its own time and find its own way.

And without a filter, these words came out of my mouth: "Loving is that way."

Christopher was silent. He was out of his comfort zone, dancing away from the steaming rice, flying over the moon. After some time, Christopher broke the silence and talked about art again. He said, "I'm more process oriented than anything else. I'd rather get lost in the process than finish a drawing too early."

I could see this in his drawings and in his life. A lot of what I saw on his walls seemed partially painted, partially undone. I wondered if Christopher would ever choose a woman or finish anything.

Chapter 50:

Black Holes and the Bridge
over the Kanawha River

As the romance with Christopher continued unraveling, we became dance gypsies again. We sat at opposite ends of the bench seat in his rusty pickup truck, speeding to West Virginia. In the late afternoon, we crossed the Mud River, then the steel cantilever bridge over the Kanawha River. Except for the scale, it looked like the Erector Set bridges my brother used to build when he was a boy. I studied the reflection of light in the water. No messages.

From what I have learned about love, what you see on the outside doesn't tell the story. Something deep inside says yes or no. If whatever that is says yes, it doesn't matter about compatibility, geography or differences. You work it out, even if it makes you crazy. If the coin flips, you're gone. Last spring after the Dance Trance, the coin said yes for me. Six months later, the coin had flipped to the other side.

As the sun was setting, we looked out separate windows. A huge flock of birds, maybe grackles or red-winged blackbirds, converged in a circular pattern, then disappeared to roost for the night. Christopher was captivated for a few moments. He told me, "I like to watch the shape of them, how they form patterns, split off and merge." I watched the birds, feeling empty.

On the radio, we listened to a replay of an interview with RFK, Jr. on *Fresh Air*. Commenting on our times, he confessed, "I feel like I'm living in a lunatic asylum." Then his voice faded out of range.

Dark comes early in December. In silence Christopher and I watched the early winter constellations. Then without warning, he started talking about black holes. Christopher, the science teacher. Before that moment, I hadn't realized there are billions of black holes in our own galaxy! Maybe there was a black hole inside this pickup truck.

I wanted to tell Christopher that I'm not just a mystery to be superficially explored. Maybe I was too open or too vulnerable. Slowly, I drifted back to the conversation. Black holes, galaxies, constellations, mysteries of the universe. The world is alive with magic, and why am I making everything about love? My version of the *Yoga of the Impossible*.

Love is a black hole, an intense gravitational void, a distant star collapsing. The body is a magnetic field, a celestial gravity, a star that is dying. A black hole is a collision of atoms and molecules collapsing to almost nothingness, perhaps the size of a fingernail. You could cover the moon with that finger.

I thought about the unfinished paintings on Christopher's walls in Lexington. In his bedroom, two women sunbathing on a blanket, facing each other in a garden of teal and blue. On the opposite wall, an outline of a bed, unpainted. I thought about black holes and how they can pull a whole star into themselves. But where does the star go? Into a universe of anti-matter? Into a more subtle layer of creation?

Christopher pointed at the moon through miles of mist. I had stopped listening. In the echo of my silence, he put on a cassette of mountain music.

In West Virginia, Christopher called a contra dance. Listening to his Kentucky cadence weaving around the room was seductive. The band was hot, and we savored the last waltz together, spinning through constellations of whirling dancers. Our waltz was steamy, and as we whirled around each other, Christopher remembered what initially drew him to me. When the music stopped, he pulled me close and started to kiss me, then suddenly pulled back. After that, he created even more distance.

Chapter 51:

Disembodied Voices

ometimes, late at night, when I dream in my own silence, I feel like my heart is dying. After the gallery opening, which was a joyous event, I stayed up listening to late night radio, where a disembodied voice was telling the night sky, "Think of your life as a spiritual detective novel. Each aspect of your life, especially the really quirky, maverick parts, are clues." The voice was familiar from KPFA in Berkeley. In two seconds, I realized I was listening to Caroline Casey!

Christopher was asleep in the bedroom while I sat at his kitchen table. My life was certainly quirky right now, not unfolding according to any plan I would have written. But was there a deeper blueprint inside, a hologram waiting for me to discover the clues and the hidden message? In a parallel universe, Grandma Helen was whispering, "Let go, Katarina. It's time. Let go now." I studied one of Christopher's paintings and wondered what he was dreaming. I started to envision a sculpture and wondered what normal people think when they are sad. Should I walk away in the morning? Or, using the fact that I would be in Lexington for another week as a clue, might there be another layer to unfold?

I could see Grandma Helen at her kitchen table, with her shepherd pups by her ankles and a tall glass of Coca Cola in her hand. Halfway between awake and dreaming, I could feel the ice against the glass. I had been living on hope for months now. Hope could function as a tremendous catalyst for creativity, and I let my unresolved visions find their fulfillment in my art. Somehow, I needed to bring the power of my art to the other half of my world. Yes, I was a highly respected artist, but I was also a woman who wanted to live without a shield around my heart.

My life was woven inside a double helix of public and private worlds, the visionary artist and the vulnerable woman. The artist was fearless and lusted for experience. As a woman, the gift I longed to share had not found its expression in the world. Somewhere inside, I knew that I needed to let the vulnerable woman make more of my decisions. I needed to carry my dream visions into daylight, for myself even more than for my art. I thought of Grandma Helen again, and felt her smiling at me from the Spirit World.

My attention wandered back to the disembodied radio voice, then to Grandma Helen. I could hear her whispering, "Usually people are worth a lot more than they think they are." A hummingbird flew to her hand. As Caroline Casey continued to banter about private and public voices, I left the radio world and entered the dream world, where the minotaur maze of my life unfolded in a series of late night images – a trail of shooting stars, a weave into the geometry of longing. At some point I walked from the kitchen table to the futon. Life was an amethyst bead in a necklace of riddles, a mandala that concealed its secret. My dreams were a maze of symbols I could not interpret in the morning.

The new day entered through the branches of a catalpa tree. I sketched the images from my dream, then drank jasmine tea from a cup with Christopher's name pressed into the clay. I did what I could to be a good guest, bringing groceries into the house, washing dishes, and keeping the trail of long dark hairs in Christopher's bathroom to a minimum. In the afternoon, I walked to the Cross Gate Gallery. Brent, who had helped me set up this show, purchased one of my mythological horses, a large brass sculpture of Pegasus. He told me he was deeply inspired by the sensuality of the image and hoped it would whisper to him as a musical muse. Since he knew Christopher from the folk music community, he was curious about how things were going. I'd been giving him a daily weather report about my situation, and he offered me a way out – an invitation to stay in his guestroom.

A few hours later, when I asked Christopher if he wanted me to stay somewhere else, he said no. In fact, he was especially sweet that night. As I cooked an Italian dinner, he opened a bottle of Pinot Noir and lit candles on the table. After dessert we waltzed in the kitchen to Bare Necessities playing "Gypsy Round." By the end of the waltz, I knew he wanted to kiss me, but Christopher controlled himself.

As our dreams crossed between the futon and the floor, I traveled back in time to the forest where we slept as teenagers. Moonlight poured through the trees and I felt his arm around me. I heard music floating from the leaves, and it was disappointing to wake up in the morning. Christopher, seemingly unaware that anything odd was floating between us, woke up, took my hand, pulled me into the kitchen, and pointed to the full moon on the calendar. With a charcoal pencil, he wrote *Moonbow at Cumberland Falls*. He was thinking about my dream when he told me, "The moon will be full in two days. If you don't mind staying up late and getting wet for a few hours, I'd love to take you there."

I was elated! Even if the dream I most desired had turned into vapor, something new and beautiful was presenting itself.

Christopher continued, "It will be cold. We'll need to wear two pairs of socks and layer ourselves, but you wouldn't want to miss it."

"I packed my new hiking boots and the socks I wore to trek over Thorong La in Nepal. The altitude is much lower here, so I'm sure I'll be fine."

"That sounds perfect, and I have an extra rain parka you can put over your coat to add another layer."

Christopher loved to share his wealth of information about the natural world, as he did when he was a teenage boy and I was twelve years old. He told me, "The moonbow is one of the hidden wonders of Kentucky. During the full moon cycle, if the sky is clear and the mist is just right, a delicate arc of color reveals itself. There are only a few moonbows in the world – Victoria Falls in Africa, Bridal Veil Falls in Yosemite, a water cascade in a remote part of the Himalayas, and Cumberland Falls in Kentucky. It's only two and a half hours from Lexington!"

We brewed chai and ate pepper cheese scones from Magee's Bakery; then we looked at the calendar again. Christopher penciled in an arc of light where the moon would be full in two days.

Chapter 52:

The Moonbow at Cumberland Falls

On the evening of the full moon, we followed the Moonbow Trail, a boulder-strewn gorge by the Cumberland River. We hiked to Cumberland Falls, with echoes of "Gypsy Round" reaching from the trees to the water. The air was full of muffled December night sounds, the skitter of perhaps an animal, wind in the trees, and then the electric air of approaching water. I thought about John Muir saying, "The clearest way into the universe is through a forest wilderness." I was far away from the redwood trees I love, but the trees on the way to the river were speaking to me. I felt their power.

The wheel of the year had turned halfway since Christopher and I first became lovers. We had bloomed, scented the night air with exotic mountain flowers, and faded the way petals fall apart. We were a trickle of light shining down from the highest trees in the forest, the echo of an abandoned dream.

Hiking with Christopher in the Appalachian Mountains brought memories of a warmer season – three bird orchids, crested coral root, camellias, huckleberries and wild azalea. The love that had bloomed and faded sang to me in the wind that burned my face, in the voices of endangered species – brook saxifrage, river-weed and snakeroot. In the mountains, evening fell early, descended in shades of blue. Stars trickled into vision like the canopy of light at the Dance Trance, revealing the winter wheel of the constellations.

Night uncovered memories of two children with a secret language to communicate with the birds.

It was still two hours before the moonrise, so we went back to the truck to warm ourselves. We turned on the heat, pulled blankets over our legs, and shared a car picnic of salad, lasagna and walnuts. We scat sang, then listened to Kitka and Hotpoint. Just before the moonrise, we walked back to the falls, past a long row of lanterns and more people than I would have imagined on a night this cold, all hoping that the moon, the night and the river would reveal their secret. I was amazed by the unexpected crowd in the shivering, shimmering cold, waiting for the moonrise with its delicate arc of ephemeral beauty.

We walked into the veil of mist at the edge of the boulders and waited. As it got closer to the moonrise, I could feel the excitement growing. I watched the changing shape of the waterfall and saw a veil of fireflies. I remembered my grandmother telling me that one in a thousand fireflies is always a fairy. I listened to the music of the water and heard a cacophony of tree frogs, the calling of a wood-thrush, old Chinese coins in a jar of hand-rolled glass. In the water I heard the trilling of a flute. I saw visions in the cloud of mist, the cadence of love's music tumbling over rocks.

Everyone was watching the sky. We stood in the cold with a sculptor as she gathered driftwood from the river, flood art. By the shelter, a group of musicians entertained the crowd with banjo and fiddle music. I put my flute together and added ascending notes to the night harmony. Two sweaters, a down jacket, and Christopher's parka kept me warm and dry inside the rain of mist. Then the moon rose over the mountains.

The moonbow appeared as a fuzzy arc of light in the moonlit mist. Ephemeral as love, it formed near the base of the falls, then arced downstream. It lifted into the sky like a bridge of fairies, a parade of unfinished dreams banding together in soft colors to form a lunar rainbow. Above us, a bright moon pouring its nectar through a cloudless night, over the mountains, into the river gorge. Around us, mist rising from the waterfall. Sometimes the colors were barely perceptible and sometimes they were bright. You viewed it from a slant in the eye, at an oblique angle, sometimes clear, sometimes an afterimage. Like love, showing up was not a guarantee that you would receive the gift.

Christopher and I held each other under an arc of astounding beauty. I was stunned by the delicate radiance spilling out of the water. Christopher was inspired. He opened his sketchbook and rendered shapes on paper to serve as memory. These lines in charcoal and graphite formed an artistic door, a portal he would walk through over and over again. He drew in the dark with his eyes closed, then opened to waterfall, trees, mountains, moon and sky. His charcoal revealed the moonbow and something inside it that was mysterious even to him. He let the forms reveal themselves and guide him to their own expression – bird, mountain, river, what he knew so deep inside, and what he refused to feel before.

The world was full of beauty – the gorge, the sky, the river, wet stones lit by the full moon light. Tiny droplets of water filled my body with color and light where voices were invisible. My emotions bled into the voices of owls, where a small wind echoed through Cumberland pines like a banjo.

Chapter 53:

The Two Week Pajama Party

During the two weeks we spent together, Christopher and I did everything lovers do, except for making love. We cooked together, danced, watched movies, hiked, visited friends, and stayed up talking until two o'clock in the morning. We dirtied every pot and dish in the house. Most nights, he washed the dishes while I rinsed and placed the plates and cups on the wood rack. I later described this time to one of my girlfriends as the two week pajama party.

I brought a dozen yellow roses into the bedroom, given to me by a secret admirer at the Cross Gate Gallery. He left the flowers, a hand-blown glass Pegasus, and a note at the feet of one of my mythical horses. Christopher was annoyed by the roses; perhaps they drifted through his sleep. I wondered if the glass craftsman in Kentucky had been the mentor of the glass blower in Ghirardelli Square in San Francisco. Both of these men had shop windows full of unicorns and flying horses in a similar style.

As December progressed, Christopher filled his apartment with tiny colored lights, blinking on and off slowly. We watched them through a glass kaleidoscope, where the colors formed geometric patterns, then distorted, changed and blurred. Whatever would or would not be between us, he was artist to the core.

Whether Christopher was in the apartment or out somewhere, the paintings on his wall nourished me. I took clay out of the bucket in his kitchen and created tiny animals – frogs, salamanders, seahorses, seagulls and a snow leopard you could hold in your hand. I chanted while I was thinking with my fingers, in the body-centered way I lead myself into my inner world. *Isis, Astarte, Diana, Hecate, Demeter, Kali, Inanna.* I was the Spider Goddess, spinning the world out of my belly. I was the clay maiden, creating the shape of the world with my hands. But with Christopher, I was careful not to spin stories.

I thought about what Christopher told me, long ago, after swimming back from the light. While he was under the lake, he had a review of his life with a Being of Light. He told me she looked like an angel, and as they observed his life like a movie, he saw that all of the situations he had agonized about, things that happened in school and with friends that felt wrong to him, were in truth the way they were supposed to be. It's funny – I hadn't remembered our conversation until now. He was fourteen years old at the time and I was twelve, but this was the wisdom I needed now.

During the nights that followed, we became addicted to a British soap opera called *The Grand*, with an occasional detour into a pint of Soy Delicious Cherry Nirvana. The only nudes in the apartment were behind the closet doors, on sketch pads, in charcoal. Every day, when I went to the gallery, Brent was waiting for me. He'd feed me chocolate truffles and ask for a weather report. I'd give him the Christopher update, and he'd say, "How can you stand it?"

This time I told him, "Really, it's okay. I only have a few more days now, and there's something I need to figure out."

Brent looked at me. "Don't you think it's already totally clear?"

"Well, yes and no. There's one missing piece of the puzzle."

"Can't you just leave it alone? I don't like seeing you so upset."

"It will be more upsetting if I have to leave without what I came here to find."

As Brent turned away, he grumbled, "Katarina, I don't understand you!"

How could I explain something I didn't fully understand myself? There was something I needed to remember, something I needed to touch inside myself, and for some reason I couldn't fathom, I had to do it here. I was on the trail of something I could not see, and I knew I was close. A trail of silver stones was shining in the moonlight.

Brent told me stories about the people who bought my sculptures. I'd think about mythical horses entering those universes and wondered if they would change the lives of the people living inside them. Always, the conversation wandered back to Christopher. Brent kept inviting me to stay in his guest room. He had two guitars, a banjo, a lot of musical friends, and maybe he had some fantasies.

I replied, "I am where I need to be right now."

"Katarina, you should meet my friends. I can invite them over tomorrow night, and we can jam for a few hours. They know some tunes from the mountains you would love."

"Invite them to the gallery, and I'll bring my flute."

Brent retreated into an alcove, while I sat in the middle of the gallery sketching a charcoal horse with Pegasus wings. I began with a charcoal rendering of a stallion, then let my lines lead me into images that had been appearing in my dreams. The wings were inspired by the Pegasus myth, with Pegasus as a symbol of the muse. I patterned the dream images from my sketchbook on his wings.

When I got back home that night, Christopher asked me how things were going at the gallery. I showed him my Pegasus drawing, and he admired the blend of myth and rendering. He told me what he liked about the lines and shared a drawing from his sketchbook of the Kentucky Derby. I knew he did this drawing during the two minutes of the race, and I felt the energy of the thoroughbred horses racing to the finish line. When I told him about Brent, he told me, "I've known Brent for a long time, and I don't trust him. Trina, the gallery is fine, but don't go home with him."

I nodded and started cutting shiitake mushrooms, parsnips, red peppers and broccoli for our dinner.

Chapter 54:

At the Scheherazade Café

We danced on Friday night in Lexington with Cary Ravitz calling his geometrically complex and perfect dance symmetry. On Saturday morning, Christopher and I became dance gypsies again, speeding north to a dance in Cleveland. Since Christopher and I had discovered each other again at a dance weekend, it was fitting that we would be ending our relationship this way. We followed directions from our Dance Gypsy Manual: Bake banana walnut bread the night before you leave and eat it in the car. Bring camping mats, your pillow, and sleeping bags. If the driving distance is more than two hours, make arrangements to stay overnight with a fellow dance gypsy.

After six hours in the pickup truck, munching on chocolate-covered raisins, sharp cheddar cheese and banana walnut bread, and scat singing counterpoint to contra bands, we arrived in Cleveland. At a coffeehouse near the dance, we met up with a dance gypsy named Michael, who was also an architect and a painter. A new layer of snow began to fall. We drank chai to warm up; then Michael took us on a walking tour of the city, an unpredictable mix of gritty and gorgeous. Snow drifted across the sidewalks as the two men talked nuances of urban architecture. We then proceeded to the Scheherazade Café, a vegan eatery in an artsy part of the city.

At the Scheherazade Café, I was privy to a conversation women don't ordinarily hear. It was one of those rare man-to-man conversations, with Christopher and Michael baring their souls to one another. I listened quietly as the evening revealed its magic feather. We warmed our hands over a pot of ginger tea and shared a salad as the two of them talked about their long distance relationships, their ambivalence, their fears, and not knowing whether they made a mistake or not during the initial break-up. Then they asked for my opinion!

I thought about it for a while, then asked Michael, "Can you let a real woman into your life, with her flaws and her gifts, or are your standards so high that nobody can meet them?"

Michael became quiet, then replied, "I don't know."

I ate a falafel while Christopher and Michael shared a spinach tofu pie. Michael talked about going to New Orleans in January, maybe moving there. Again, he asked for my opinion.

I took another bite of my falafel, studied him for a while, then said, "If you tell her you know that she is the right one for you, she will be thrilled to her core if she loves you. If she hesitates and tells you she doesn't want you to move right now, something about you isn't right for her. A woman with integrity wouldn't want you to uproot your life and then break up with you. When you put your cards on the table and make your move, listen carefully to what she says. And don't pretend it isn't true."

The two men continued to share stories, during which time I found out that Michael was the one who broke up with Ms. New Orleans two years ago. But now he was wondering if he had made the wrong decision. Then the mysterious secret came out. Christopher told Michael that he had broken up with Ms. Brattleboro at the six month point, but then changed his mind. No wonder she didn't trust him!

I asked Michael, "Was the problem just the distance or something more?"

"Something more, and those issues might still be a problem."

The three of us shared a large slice of tofu cheesecake. Christopher ate in silence. At least I was able to say what I felt to his friend, and as fate would have it, Christopher was at the table. We finished the tofu cheesecake, emptied the pot of ginger tea, and then the three of us walked to the contra dance.

Chapter 55:

In the Shivering Cold

uring the second half of the contra dance, a man so handsome he made me shiver walked onto the dance floor. His face told a story. You could see it in his eyes – the kindness and vision of a fallen hero. I felt the kind of visceral pull you sometimes do with strangers and hoped I'd have the opportunity to dance with him. Although it did not happen, we shared several corner swings and a long gypsy. After the last waltz, Christopher walked over to chat with him. I joined them, found out his name was Stefan, and discovered he was our host for the evening.

Christopher followed Stefan's Volvo to a neighborhood of large Victorian houses up a winding hill, then up a narrow driveway covered with a light dusting of snow. We entered the house through a mud room, took off our boots, then walked into a large kitchen with an antique stove. A few minutes later, Zoe, another dance gypsy, walked into the kitchen. She untied a box of French pastries, found a Japanese plate in the hutch, and added an assortment of eclairs, puff pastries, and strawberry tarts to the table. Stefan brewed tea and set out Chinese lacquered bowls filled with pecans, almonds and dried apricots. His house was in mid-stages of remodeling – the topic of a long discussion. The first floor was close to finished, with an elegant brick fireplace and hardwood floors, but upstairs, an Indian bedspread marked the future site of a bathroom door.

Zoe looked at Stefan with longing in her eyes. During the week she worked as a physician at a women's health care center in Cincinnati but drove to Cleveland for contra dances on weekends. She had electric blue eyes, chestnut hair to her waist, and wore one of those flower dresses popular with women from the midwest. She and Stefan teased each other in the unspoken language of lovers, but something for them this night was not connecting. Abruptly, after a second cup of tea, she put on her coat and walked out, leaving the kitchen full of the subtext of unfinished stories.

Christopher and Stefan continued their discussion about the nuances of remodeling, combined with the vision of Christopher's dream house – the one he might build or remodel if his heart would ever settle down. Then, since Christopher and I were not lovers, Stefan gave us separate rooms. My bedroom was large and cold. From my second floor window, I watched snow swirling under a street lamp. Worried that I might be cold, Stefan came back with two handmade quilts, heirlooms from his grandmother. I lit a candle for a while, then fell asleep inside the quilt cocoon.

Perhaps it came from the freedom of being away from him, but at some point that night, I dreamed about Christopher. In the early morning light, I walked around the corner to a house next to a field of tiger lilies. Christopher opened the door. He was not expecting me.

It's amazing the way a man gets larger than life. How you enter his house in a dream. His surprise, the way he opens his arms to you and remembers the place in his heart you occupy. For a moment we both remembered everything. Dragonflies circled his hands, and the way we embraced had no barriers.

A woman in fishnet stockings descended like a spider from a trapeze dangling through a hole in the ceiling. Her red hair in an expensive cut fell just below her shoulders. She took Christopher's hand and pulled him out of the room. I walked out of the door flooded with premonition, into the tiger lily morning light, knowing how much I loved him, knowing that it would never be, knowing that it was impossible.

In a field of tiger lilies, I took out my flute and played a song for him. My lips trembling, I poured my feelings into the music, let the tremolo of the highest notes spiral into the light. Somehow, inside the echo of my music, I found myself again.

Chapter 56:

The Last Waltz

It was a difficult weekend. At times, it was snowing so hard that I lost my sense of direction, inside and out. Christopher and I shared an astoundingly deep connection on the dance floor. His fingers felt like fireflies, giving me energy, sparkle and light. I saw a warmth in his eyes, a sky-colored magic that asked me to love him. At Christopher's request, we always did the last waltz, and he hugged me, long and tight. But like the firefly, it was an on off thing.

Sometimes after people fall asleep, they are more honest. I wondered if Christopher dreamed about his upcoming visit to Brattleboro or dreamed about me. Possibly both. I would never know, and in two days, it wouldn't matter. But my questions, along with the cold in that big empty house, kept me awake for hours. I lit a beeswax candle and watched the snow falling on the other side of a century-old window. I watched the shape of the wind under the wrought iron street lamp. And at some point, like the snow, I drifted into a light sleep.

In the morning we left early to give ourselves extra time to drive to a barn dance in Kentucky. The snow had stopped before the morning light, and when we hit the freeway, the road had already been plowed. In Kentucky, the snow started falling again, but lightly. The barn dance was off a rural road in the Appalachian foothills. Our travel omen was twenty blackbirds.

To go to a dance like this, in weather like this, is a sign of a seriously addicted dance gypsy. In the barn we were joined by dance gypsies from around the state. The owner of the farm had a fire burning and fed us soup – split pea with carrots and onions for the vegetarians, and a chicken vegetable soup for everyone else. Then we danced to the music of the Evil Twins. Christopher called the dance until we melted into the last waltz. An outside observer might have detected a soulmate connection, but I had given up. In the waltz, however, I surrendered to the moment.

I know that Christopher loved me, but it was a brother-sister love, the kind we shared when we were children. I, on the other hand, loved him the way a woman loves a man. We returned to Lexington in the early evening, and I packed. I gathered my dance gypsy clothes, wrapped my goddess sculptures into my carry-on, and packed my memories.

Just before midnight, Christopher fell asleep. Christopher always fell asleep quickly, and I listened to the rhythmic exhale of his breathing. I was ready to leave. After a year inside a question mark, the yes no yes no thing with Christopher was totally driving me crazy. There were moments I wished I could memorize every nuance of our visit after the Dance Trance, when we made love morning and night. I wished to replay those memories, frame by frame, like a movie in slow motion whenever I wanted to love him. Then maybe it wouldn't pull at me so hard to be sleeping on the futon while he was sleeping on the floor.

Perhaps I was suffering from pheromone addiction. But sleeping a few feet away from where he was dreaming, having our dreams cross and signal like fireflies in the middle of the night, was not the way to get over it.

Chapter 57:

Into the Light

A̧t four o'clock in the morning, I woke up with the moon in my eyes. I thought about our lives – where the lines connected and where our stories flowed apart like currents in two different rivers. I thought about Christopher's voice and how easily we harmonized as we traveled hundreds of miles in his truck to dances. We came so close to the happiness I longed for but never completely crossed the boundary.

As a fourteen-year-old, Christopher had so much promise. He lived with his soul open and revealed himself to me. He lived with a passionate reverence for nature. When we hiked in the Appalachian Mountains, he lifted a veil that most people never see beyond. He was the one who taught me how to draw, to listen to the language of birds, and to see things that to others are invisible. We were so close we could communicate by telepathy. So how did he grow into the man sleeping in this room – someone who kept himself apart from people? Christopher had depth and vision – I could see that in his art and in his soul. Why did my friends think he was shallow?

And how did I grow into a woman who kept herself apart from people? I was mysterious even to myself. Suddenly, I thought about the tunnel. I saw myself swimming with Christopher inside the light. I wondered if Christopher and I had unknowingly left a piece of ourselves on the other side, and I knew we had to go back and find out. Maybe we couldn't find the way to love each other, but we had to go back into the light. Maybe we would discover a wrong decision as we swam back to the world. Or in the moments after we found ourselves on the shore of Lake Hopatcong. Maybe we could free each other one more time, even if that gift would ultimately go to someone else.

Maybe, like some of my friends in Fairfield said, our love was ill-fated due to my astrological sign. Or maybe my timing was impeccably wrong. Christopher and I had come full circle back to the brother-sister love we shared when we were teenagers. Maybe that was the truth about our love. Or maybe he was one of those men who always had to be free to explore the next mystery. In the core of my atoms, I knew that Christopher and I had to talk in the morning. I also knew this sharing – and not love – might be the reason we had come back together.

When I saw Christopher stirring in the morning, I brought him a glass of pomegranate juice. He received it as a gift, got up to brush his teeth, then came back and hugged me without holding back for the first time in two weeks. We hugged for a long time, embracing each other on the futon, and then we started talking. The veil lifted and our telepathy was back. It didn't matter who was talking, as we both could have said the same thing.

In the hours that followed, we compared notes about the tunnel of light, what we saw there, and the challenges of coming back. We talked about our lives, our visions, and our art, perhaps for the first time finding the language.

"You know what other people call God? For me, it's the being I met inside the light."

"For me, it's a flow of love and guidance."

"That's how it is for me too, but I never talked about it before."

"I still feel the love and guidance every time I remember."

"And remember the light? How bright it was?"

"Brighter than the sun, but soft and loving."

"What I saw inside the light is more beautiful than anything in this world, which is funny, because I love the world."

"Especially the birds and the forest."

"But there was something in the light – a warmth, a sweetness, an embrace – a knowing lit up from inside."

"It's at the center of everything I draw and paint."

"And everything I sculpt and teach my students."

"It's in every cell of my body."

"In everything I see."

"And everything I know in this world."

"It's given me a strength, but kept me apart from people."

"I know what you mean."

"Sometimes I go back there in my dreams."

"Always in the middle of the night."

"There were so many times I had to forget what I saw there to keep on living."

The whole time we were talking, we were wrapped around each other. A light rain brushed the window, and in the distance I heard an oboe, probably one of the neighbors playing a concerto by Albinoni. Christopher's stomach growled and we both laughed. "Clearly time for breakfast." We helped each other up and headed for the kitchen, where Christopher grilled mung bean and potato pancakes.

Christopher took my hand and led me to the window. We saw two kestrels mating on a telephone wire. It had just stopped raining, which seemed to be an omen, and I knew there must be a rainbow somewhere.

Chapter 58:

The Gift

A few hours later, Christopher drove me to the airport and I boarded a plane to San Francisco. Two days ago, I would have said the flight was seven days too late, if I were making the rules, but I had a non-refundable ticket. This morning I knew the timing was impeccable.

Because of the guidance I received that morning, I let go of Christopher completely and I was able to bless him. He blessed me as well, and I knew it was a gift I would carry through my life. On Thursday, Christopher would drive to Brattleboro. By intuition and observation, I knew he wouldn't find love there, but I knew he needed to find out one more time. I also knew he would find the way to free himself.

On the airplane I thought about our journey back from the light and Christopher's quirky wisdom when he was fourteen years old. As I drew in my sketchbook, I thought about our two week pajama party. I thought of the little goddesses I made in Christopher's kitchen, the feeling of Kentucky clay in my hands. I was bringing these goddesses back to San Francisco, and yes, those two weeks had been a tremendous blessing.

When Christopher came back to his kitchen later that afternoon, he would discover a box with two sand dollars and the goddess sculpture he loved the most. When I unpacked my suitcase, I would find a drawing of two lovers on a stone bridge over the Red River Gorge.

I didn't realize I was moving back to San Francisco until I got there. On the way back from the airport, the night was clear and cool. I watched the reflection of the moon on the Pacific Ocean and felt deliciously happy.

Part III

The Yoga of the Impossible

Chapter 59:

Orchid Backlit in Saturated Light

he photograph I most wanted was blurred. Hands were placed on my head in a gesture of blessing, but his face was out of focus. My emotions were swirling between the Sahara Desert and the South Pole, with a magnetic shift oscillating in the ionosphere.

He shows up to dance with broken angel wings, searching below seven shields of beauty for a familiar face. We spend the weekend sewing costumes – silk, velvet, ribbons of lace, lilacs on shaded backgrounds – to move ourselves backward through time. In the late afternoon, we stitch ourselves into Renaissance ballrooms. Then we dance, connecting our fingers across the rose satin of American Prairie ball gowns and Romeo shirts.

It's confusing when you dance – eye to eye, so close. As your hands connect, you feel the trajectory of the circle you move through leaning back into time. You feel like you've danced this way for thousands of years with the same eyes in different bodies. Suddenly, you're in love. For a moment, the colors and countries bleed through tinted leaves. Twigs of rhododendron forests break under your bare feet, but it doesn't mean you have a future.

The angels say sleep on the ground so you can feel the wetness of sunflower fields around your heart. Let the moisture in the earth seep into the quilt you've been stitching for seven years. Even though the moon is a sliver now, it will send its silver light into your dreams. They keep the future hidden so you can learn, but the guidance comes from inside, like a melody you heard from the flowers when you were three years old but forgot to tell anyone.

A group of traveling musicians discovered a tree in India with the pattern of everyone's life printed on the leaves. The flute player said it was in a courtyard on the way to Shangri-La. You know the place by the silk draped over the goddess with six arms. You can visit her there, in the scented garden of her secret flowers, or wait for a message in a dream. She is a wild orchid flying across the moon, and what you have forgotten is drowning.

Sometimes when I look at photographs, I feel like I'm looking at ghosts – people who have disappeared into other lives. Sometimes, when I look in the mirror, my face is far away, but I remember footsteps between the tiger lilies behind the empty lot at the corner. The music in the mud under the orchids is pulling me to the earth, planting roots there. I am the woman under the veil. This is what I am dreaming.

Chapter 60:

The Pacific Time Zone

On Tuesday morning, I woke up in the Pacific time zone. I had arranged to share a house with a friend in the Outer Sunset, a few blocks from the edge of the continent. In my first night of dreams, I walked through a forest blooming with wild orchids, with light filtering through the branches of redwood trees. As the dream faded, I opened my eyes to a studio flooded with early morning light. French doors opened to a garden, with birds of paradise and calla lilies blooming in the yard, unfurling their waxy petals. The rainy season had started, making the Pacific flora green again, alternating five and six day storms with a few days of clear skies and crisp air. Today, the sky was blue as an egg shell. I could feel every cell in my body saying, "Yes! This is where I want to be."

Jenna, my housemate, was a graphic designer during the week and a dance gypsy most weekends. When we shared a meal, she was easy to talk to. I set up my part of the house as a live-in studio, with large plants, a work table, sculptures from my time in Iowa, two betta fish, and a sleeping loft. It was isolated enough from Jenna's rooms to give me a lot of privacy. The hidden gift of this house was the skylight. Late at night when the trickle of traffic diminished, I could open the skylight and hear the ocean.

On the night of the winter solstice, I walked to the ocean to let the waves clean my mind. She answered with two perfectly formed sand dollars as the moon's silver light rippled on the waves. From that time on, when I wanted exercise, I crossed the Great Highway and went to the beach.

As the days gathered toward the end of the year, I gathered my rhythm of making sculpture. I worked in clay and formed the shapes of my dreams. Once or twice a week, I went to the zoo with a bucket of clay and observed the animals, shaping what they revealed to me, tenderly working the flow of their muscles with my fingers. Then I brought the sculptures to my studio and visioned what they might see in their dreams. All of this I layered into the sculptures.

As the wheel of the year turned, I made a collage of holiday cards from friends and a few men who had been my lovers. I let their voices weave through my fingers, opened myself to the feelings these memories evoked, and released the tide of emotions into the clay. Sometimes my art took the shape of a human figure; other times it went totally abstract.

Since I hadn't lived in the Outer Sunset before, I took long walks to explore the neighborhood. After living in Iowa, it felt like a miracle to see flowers blooming through the winter – camellias, lavender, and calla lilies. The warmth of the sunlight soothed my skin. Over time, I became acquainted with the dogs and cats in the neighborhood. At the beach, I watched the cycles of high and low tides. I learned the names of the birds who flew over coastal waters. I smiled at old Chinese women taking walks with their grandchildren. In the unspoken language of our blue and green jewel of a planet, they smiled back.

During my walks, I gathered the urban landscape to my eyes. By the ocean, I noticed a different quality of light than in the midwest. Maybe it was the reflected sunlight on the water, but in a subtle way, the air felt different here. The light inspired visions that called for the subtle tones of watercolor, a sensibility I shared with artists who had lived both places. I loved riding over bridges as the sun was setting and watching the colors fade and ripple on the water.

Even though I missed the astounding sunsets over the Great Plains, the beauty of the ocean more than made up for it. Hummingbirds flew to the flowers in our yard, a green whirring of wings.

Passion flowers grew up the fence. California poppies, trilliums and iceplant bloomed in the wildflower garden. On mornings when it didn't rain, sunlight streamed through the crystal hanging from my window and projected rainbows on my ceiling. This reminded me of the colors in my dreams.

Something I noticed about this time – I was perfectly happy. I didn't need anything outside myself. Night flooded me with pastel images of joy in the moonlight. When the light came in the morning, I shaped the joy with my fingers.

Chapter 61:

Fiddling Frog and The Latter Day Lizards

After my year as a dance gypsy, I was eager to meet the contra dancers on the West Coast and find my friends. I always followed my intuition about which dances to attend and when to stay home. Jenna gave me tips about the best dances and the best local bands. When the Hillbillies from Mars, Flashpoint, or StringFire played a dance, I was there. I went with Jenna to contra dances in Santa Cruz, San Francisco, and San Rafael, where I would dance, flirt, and forget myself for a few hours. If I felt restless, I'd borrow Jenna's car, drive north, and find a redwood forest or spend an afternoon painting in a field full of cows.

Early in March, at the recommendation of Bernie from Bakersfield, Jenna and I packed a few colorful skirts with matching socks, leotards and earrings, and went to Fiddling Frog, a contra dance weekend in Pasadena. All of Jenna's outfits were color coordinated with her curly red hair. I traveled with the echo of Rob Brezsny's *Free Will Astrology* as my oracle and his latest prediction from the *San Francisco Weekly*: "The months ahead will provide you with the best opportunity ever to come home to your body, to inhabit it with robust awareness and gratitude." His advice for the transition: "Put on music that moves you and dance yourself all the way back into your body."

Since Jenna already knew people up and down the coast, she included me in her housing plans. Her friends in Pasadena had a hot tub, which they generously shared with their dance gypsy guests. In

Jenna's world, the best way to cap off a dance weekend was soaking in a hot spring, in the sage brush at dusk, watching the stars appear. If a hot spring wasn't available, a hot tub in a night-blooming garden would be the chosen oasis. Jenna liked to trade foot massages in the hot tub, and she never had any problem finding a willing partner. When I shared my stories about Tom and George, she decided to fly to St. Louis for Kimmswick in May. I knew George would offer to pick her up at the airport.

Jenna and I gave ourselves a whole day for the drive south, favoring country roads instead of freeways. In the Central Valley, we stopped for lunch at a fruit stand surrounded by blossoming almond trees. Along the road, egrets waded in irrigated fields, sparrows gathered on telephone wires, and hawks circled the early spring sky. We listened to music by Nightingale, Lift Ticket, and the Latter Day Lizards, who would be playing at the weekend. Within a few hours, I rediscovered the pleasure of being a new woman on the dance floor. The Lizards' alchemical music magic rippled through five lines of contra dancers. Their wacky virtuosity inspired waves of improvisational joy. Before the end of the evening, Bernie led me around the dance floor in a last waltz with intricate variations, waterfall dips and inventive twirls. At the end of the waltz, he dipped me to the floor and turned me upside down.

After a soak in the hot tub, my dreams went wild that night. I was on the floor with my foot extended to Cassiopeia, my toe pointing to the Pole Star. I was twirling into the birth of a new galaxy, as swirling gasses condensed into the choreography of my left arm. The music pulled me into the salty water of a lunar sea, where life, against all odds, was finding its first form. I was the heartbeat of a feather, finding the species and genus of a bird that was ready to fly into the dance of fingers. The dance whirled into the shape of a star, a dream inside of an egg, etched with the wisdom of an exploding universe.

I heard the chanting of an ocean, as it discovered the shape of a heartbeat and remembered how to dance, the breath of the buffalo running across a primal plain of first light. I was the writing on the wall of the cave, where the ocean echoes into the curve of a silver moon. An invisible partner dipped me into the Milky Way, my back arcing into the flute's high descant, singing the memory of the future, where the secret of species is revealed in the chord of the whir of grasshoppers, on a blue and emerald jewel in the shape of a double helix. The music revealed white fire in the belt of Orion, an arrow through time. I was dreaming the beauty of the Pleiades, the temple dancer, her silver bells, her back a sequence of vectors across oceans, across time.

All of this dissolved into sunlight in the morning, and in a few hours, I was back on the dance floor, feeling radiant and inspired. Sometimes it was delightful and at other times wrenching to be at a dance weekend again. At times, I was flooded with memories of Kentucky, but after a long gypsy, I'd find myself in the arms of a new dance partner. I gave myself to the magic of the moment, and the beauty of contra dancing is that the moment does not require more.

On Saturday evening, Jenna's friends invited me to a group dinner at Bua Na Thai, a family-owned eatery with an Asian fusion menu. As we walked in, I was drawn to a large bronze Buddha on a lotus altar by a bouquet of pink chrysanthemums. Bright yellow walls displayed a gallery of Thai art and photography, and each table was adorned with a red dahlia and persimmon colored napkins folded like birds. At the request of Jenna's friend, the waitress led us through a walkway of red bricks and palm trees so we could sit outside on the patio. We ordered several dishes to share, as the dance gypsies at Fiddling Frog told me about their cycle of dance weekends on the West Coast wheel of the year – Contra Carnivale, Dance Awakening, Monte Toyon, Faultline Frolic, Dance in the Desert, Balance the Bay, Harvest Moon, and the No Snow Ball.

After dinner, one of the dancers staying at a nearby motel let everyone use his shower before changing, since Saturday night was a dress up affair. As we entered the ballroom, I saw an ocean of glitter, sparkle and swirl – the best of thrift store *haute couture* from up and down the coast. Anyone who wanted to decorate themselves could choose from an assortment of temporary tattoos, and the dancing was ecstatic, culminating in a gorgeous last waltz. Later, after a soak in the hot tub, I fell into a peaceful sleep.

During times of intense transition, there are bridges the intuition cannot see. I was walking a high wire between the midwest and the Pacific time zone, floating between two languages. Like a hummingbird in an almond tree, my emotions were breathing, hidden behind a flower. Before I woke up on Sunday morning, I dreamed about Christopher, dreamed we were making love, and woke up full of longing. Images of his face filtered through the day like tule fog over a meadow. I wanted the echo of Christopher to fade the way a dream does, but it would take time. Invoking the quirky wisdom of Rob Brezsny, I gave myself to the music. With the Latter Day Lizards on stage and a room full of two hundred dancers, I danced and forgot my memories for a while.

Chapter 62:

Not on a White Horse

My inner life was a collage of quiet strength and intense vulnerability, with edges so open the beauty and pain of the world were constantly speaking to me. My art was a fusion of real world images and wild abstraction, a personal universe finding its form. At night I sometimes heard music and played it on my flute. Melodies came from I don't know where, woven with intricate harmonies. For the first time in my life, I was able to play and remember these pieces. I wrote them on rice paper, and they rippled through my art.

I had no desire to exhibit my art – only to create it. Dancing was my connection with the rest of the human race, and perhaps the only intimacy I could stand. A reel or a jig full circle on the contra floor. Maybe a last waltz. I needed my hands for shaping sculpture – they did not want to touch anyone. But as the season changed, dragonflies rippled through my dreams and I became restless.

I listened to late night radio with clay in my hands. On KPFA, Caroline Casey told the airwaves, "Entertain the possibility that you are an undercover agent parachuting down to this beautiful planet in its time of need. Astrology is a language that catalyzes your memory of your mission." I started wondering about my mission and whether my art would be pure expression or if I would return to teaching. Caroline Casey, who I would later meet at a solstice ritual in Petaluma, already felt like a friend from my inner circle.

Her vision put me in touch with the core of my being. Toward the end of her program, she quoted Martin Luther King: "I am convinced that the universe is under the control of a loving purpose. Behind the harsh appearance of the world, there is a benign power." I felt goosebumps traveling up my arms, one of my signals when something is true.

Something about her words forced me to be honest with myself. I opened the skylight and listened to the ocean. Then I filled the tub with an herbal bath. Naked in the water, I relaxed into my intuition and asked if I had a soulmate. The voice of the water rippled with a quiet "yes!" I remembered that yes from hikes in the coastal mountains, my favorite place for deja vu. Even though there had not been a whisper for many years, I remembered my Grandma Helen's promise. On the outside, there was no sign of a soulmate, but inside, I felt that someone was looking for me. As I sat in the bath with rose petals floating in the water, I had to listen to what my inner voice was telling me.

A few days later, since I needed to come to terms with something I could not see, I signed up for a weekend seminar recommended by friends in Marin County. At the "Yes to Success" workshop, I embarrassed myself by getting up in front of a room full of people and telling everyone, "I know I have a soulmate."

At the break, a woman came up to me and said, "You're going to meet him. I saw a rainbow bridge connecting his heart to yours."

The man standing with her agreed. "I saw it too. The man is going to come, but not on a white horse."

The woman who led the workshop was powerful and inspiring. After the break she told me, "God doesn't give you a strong desire unless you're meant to fulfill it. It's a signal from your soul." I thought about my soulmate and knew I hadn't met him yet. Or if I had, we had not recognized each other. A memory flashed through me, almost like a dream, but I didn't know if the vision I saw connected to the past or the future.

After the seminar, I was even more convinced that my future would unfold on the West Coast. A few weeks later, I flew to Iowa so I could drive my truck back to California. In my farmhouse, I carefully chose what to bring west – a few paintings, some of my sculptures, raku bowls, heirloom seeds, my wok, beeswax candles, and my grandmother's silver candlesticks. My trip coincided with a First Friday Art Walk so I could visit with friends, but by Tuesday I was ready to head west again. The student renting my house was happy to continue living there. She loved using my studio and assured me she would take good care of the gardens. I asked her to walk across the field to visit Emma once or twice a week, since I didn't know when I'd be coming back.

Emma and I had breakfast together my last morning in Iowa. I brought a tin of blueberry muffins into her kitchen to share. Emma had a small bowl of eggs on her table, and I scrambled them with mushrooms, onions and goat cheese from the farmers market.

Emma asked a lot of questions about my life in San Francisco and was especially happy to hear about the farmers markets all around the city. She was curious about what had been missing for me in Iowa, so I did my best to explain how I always felt like a stranger in the heartland. Emma was quiet for a while, then replied, "You know I'm going to miss you, but I understand. When you get to be my age, it's better to look back at your life and know you listened to the quiet whisper of your soul. But is there anything you're going to miss about Iowa?"

I thought about it for a few minutes, then told her, "One of the things I love about Iowa is the harmony with the land. While I was living here, I became more deeply attuned with the cycle of the seasons. I loved growing my own food – walking outside in the summer to pick an apple when I was hungry. I loved the tiger lilies blooming by my bedroom window, and the way the landscape reaches out to an infinite sky. Sometimes, I miss the intensity of the thunderstorms. Rain in an urban setting is annoying. In the heartland, you know when the fields are thirsty."

Emma smiled and said, "I know what you mean. We grew up that way."

"The beauty of San Francisco is very dramatic. The city is built on fourteen hills, surrounded by water, and everything is connected by bridges. Watching the sunset over the ocean is amazing, and the ocean has many moods. I can drive across the Golden Gate Bridge to hike in a redwood forest or take a streetcar to the heart of the city. Iowa has a simple beauty, a quiet beauty I grew to appreciate. The problem was that my heart needed something I wasn't able to find here."

Emma was thoughtful, her face illuminated by the early morning sunlight. I looked out the window and saw a tiny rabbit hopping across the yard. I smiled and continued, "You know, Emma, sometimes I miss my neighbor's horses, the cows, the goats, and of course, the bunnies, but living in San Francisco has other gifts. It's amazing to see flowers blooming through the winter. I love the ballet, the symphony, and the art museums. But the best part for me is that I can simply be who I am without causing a ruckus."

"Yes, and sometimes you created a ruckus here, I know."

"San Francisco is a place where I can more easily create my life in tune with my soul. I don't know what's going to happen yet, but I love the possibilities."

"Well, all the best to you, Katarina. Paint me a postcard once in a while."

"I'll do that. And yes, I'm going to miss you."

After breakfast, I brushed and braided Emma's hair, washed her dishes, and held her hands for a long time. Then I got into my truck and headed west.

Chapter 63:

Moving Pigments on a Multi-Dimensional Canvas

kept in touch with Christopher for a while, but then it faded the way touch does with distance and time. The last time I wrote him, I said: *"Greetings from the Pacific Ocean! It's taken a while to set up my studio, but I'm happy to say that I'm getting settled in my new home, close to the edge of the continent. I feel more comfortable here than I did in Iowa. Yesterday, the San Francisco Ballet gave a free performance at Stern Grove. It was a huge city picnic surrounded by eucalyptus trees. Our blanket was close to the stage and full of contra dancers. The pas de deux from Swan Lake was gorgeous – the passion in their dancing took my breath away.*

This morning, I walked at the beach, with seagulls flying overhead. So far, I've been able to resist the temptation to run into a seagull convention and scatter them. After my visit to Iowa, I enjoyed driving from the plains to the mountains. It was beautiful to watch the landscape change, with images as moving pigments on a vast, dimensional canvas. There are times I miss my farm, but my studio is large and full of light. After a very private time, I find myself getting more social again.

A few days ago, I discovered a distant cousin to the umbrella magnolia. It is smaller than the amazing flower we discovered in Kentucky, but larger than the tulip trees in Iowa, and with a scent that is completely intoxicating. I discovered the tree on a walk through my old neighborhood in Noe Valley, with a branch low enough I could jump up and pull it down to my nose. One of the most astounding scents I've encountered – the blossom totally filled me.

Sometimes, when I drive north to hike or see cows, I listen to the cassettes you gave me of Flapjack and Larry Unger. The music makes me remember dancing with you in Kentucky as I drive by redwoods and eucalyptus trees."

As I dropped the letter in the mailbox, I felt Christopher's presence as part of my history. He had painted on the multi-dimensional canvas that had become my life, but the colors were changing now. On separate sides of the continent, Christopher and I, like two rivers, flowed in our own directions. In San Francisco, the coastal fog melted into the heat of an Indian summer. Winter brought rain but not the bitter cold of the midwest.

Early in January, a friend called to tell me it was five degrees below zero in Iowa. I walked out to my yard to find calla lilies, birds of paradise, and passion flowers blooming. I thought about winter in Iowa, shoveling snow, and all of the times I had to get into the bathtub to stay warm. No, I didn't miss Iowa. A few days later, I went to the DMV and put California plates on my truck. Then I walked to the beach, where a flock of seagulls was gathering around a pile of kelp, their voices somewhere between an insistence and a lament. As I walked closer, they took to the air, flying in slow circles. In the distance, I saw a silver line of light, rippling on the water. Clearly, I was on the bridge to something in my life I had not discovered. Like the hummingbird, it was fluttering in my dreams.

Chapter 64:

The Sea Biscuit Café

I am not a person whose life progresses in straight lines. Visions, like new souls entering this world, are not easily born. For the rest of the winter, my romance was with my art. However, when spring brought warmer winds, it inspired a subtle change in my emotions. Maybe it was a different slant of light, but something like a flower wanted to open inside of me. With the encouragement of my housemate, who was not enthusiastic about long distance relationships, I decided to start meeting men in California. Reflecting back on my past few years, I thought the dance floor might not be the best way. On the first day in April, I got a new computer and signed up for eHarmony, Conscious Singles and JDate. After a barrage of e-mails, I started meeting strangers at the Sea Biscuit Café, among surfers and bare-midriffed women of the X-generation.

Even though I had walked by many times on the way to the beach, my on-line dating adventure led to my first afternoon inside the Sea Biscuit Café – the neighborhood java joint featuring music from local bands, retro glass bead curtains, a monthly poetry slam, and a huge mermaid mosaic on the wall. I had no idea what I was in for, and the mermaid should have warned me.

Tim was sitting two tables away from the glass bead curtain. As I walked in, he put down his copy of the *San Francisco Bay Guardian* and smiled at me. He had short blonde hair, blue eyes, wore a black leather jacket, and had an aura of calm assurance I found attractive. The motorcycle I had admired on the sidewalk in front of the

Sea Biscuit had been his chariot for a trek from Boston to San Francisco. I felt possibilities. Maybe I would ask him for a ride to see the evening lights from the top of Twin Peaks.

We ordered chai and started to talk with too loud techno music swirling around us from four speakers hanging from the ceiling. Tim was from New York and had migrated to the West Coast after graduate school. During the hippie years, he had traveled from Turkey through Afghanistan, India, Nepal, Thailand, Malaysia and Bali. Conversation was easy, and we discovered a mutual interest in foreign cinema. When he told me he wanted to learn swing dancing, I said, "I'll take the class with you. It's much easier to learn with someone who already knows how to do it."

After an hour of spirited conversation, trading stories about places we had traveled and foreign countries we wanted to see, I asked Tim if he wanted to join me for a screening of an experimental film at Yerba Buena Center for the Arts. Twenty minutes after I walked home, he called to let me know he had ordered tickets. "It's a small theatre," he explained, "and if we wait to get our tickets, we could get turned away." Even though I had been the one to ask him to see the film, he was happy about it. What a discovery! Now that I had left the midwest, I didn't have to pretend to be passive and wait for the man to make all the moves.

As I got to know Tim and a few other men, I began to figure out a few things about men in San Francisco. They'll take you to the symphony, but they won't drive you to the airport. A trade-off, perhaps, but far better than starting a tornado of gossip rolling through the Great Plains by accepting a date to the Co-Ed Theatre. After a sequence of swing dance lessons at the Metronome, I was not sure Tim would ever be a dancer, but wild attraction to dance partners had not gotten me anywhere. A slow burn courtship might be better than a bonfire that ends in the ashes. I was not wildly attracted to Tim, but perhaps I felt a spark.

Chapter 65:

Canoeing in Boundary Waters

That summer, something mysterious unfolded inside my music. It opened like a gardenia and revealed its petals. I woke up hearing melodies almost every morning and played them on my flute. Maybe this was a displacement, as things weren't going well with my art. Plastic molds would crack, clay would shatter and break while drying, and something inside me felt dry. Late in September an earthquake shattered everything on my work table – an obvious signal from the clay gods that it was time to start over.

I never had this kind of trouble with my sculptures before, and I didn't know how to navigate around it. In a fit of desperation, I called one of my mentors from art school. Sculpture was my way of communicating with my soul, and now it was falling apart. She asked me to be patient with myself, then advised, "Disintegration always reveals a hidden door. Maybe stop sculpting for a while and use your visions to paint or draw." A few days later, I decided to stop seeing Tim. Neither of us had been motivated to move beyond the dating stage. Our connection was pleasant but not deep. Perhaps the best gift he gave me was his dentist's phone number.

Even though I was still alone, I felt a sweetness in my dreams. They were space-time portals to other dimensions. The visions I saw were astounding, and I'd fill my sketchbook with ideas that were impossible to sculpt. One of my dreams began as a river through a desert or an asteroid. But the river wandered off into a grasshopper, then a symphony, then a planet. Everything was constantly coming into being but never finding its form. How do you give shape to a timeless place that vanishes in the morning?

Occasionally, I'd answer e-mails from E-Harmony and meet strangers at the Sea Biscuit Café or on the steps of Davies Symphony Hall. One of these men claimed to love classical music the way I did, so we agreed to meet at Ananda Fuara before a concert. My first mistake. The second mistake, while we were eating, was saying, "We need to leave by 6:45 to make the pre-concert talk."

Daniel promptly informed me, "On a first date, there is no *we*. Only a *you* and an *I*." He then proceeded to lecture me about boundaries and about how it takes time to build a *we* from a *you* and an *I* – knowledge he had gleaned from a seminar for divorcing men three months ago. All of this made logical sense to me, but something underneath didn't feel right. A minor chord out of tune. A crosswire fence. A locked door.

Daniel's eyes grew suddenly cold as he continued talking. "You know, I never agreed to go to the pre-concert talk. In fact, I'm not wild about Shostakovich. I haven't bought my ticket yet, and at this point I feel ambivalent about going to the concert."

I thought about this for a minute, then replied, "Really? That's too bad. I played this symphony when I was nineteen years old, and it was a doorway to emotions I had never felt before. Shostakovich is like a religion to me. His music sends me into a rapture."

The conversation went downhill from there. At 6:45 I excused myself, walked to Davies Symphony Hall, and went to the concert alone.

Later that month, I went on a blind date with a psychiatrist. Jay looked handsome in his JDate photograph but was in fact twenty pounds heavier and ten years older than his photo. When he rang the doorbell, my housemate sat at the top of the stairs with her telephone in hand, just to make sure he wasn't an axe murderer. As soon as he walked in, he proceeded to tell me what a terrible day he had. At the top of the stairs, Jenna was shaking her head and thinking, "This one is not for Katarina!"

For dinner I suggested two restaurants in the neighborhood with two different price ranges. Jay selected the less expensive one, which I knew was a signal. When we had spoken earlier that day, he was very enthusiastic about Thanh Long, a Vietnamese seafood house with exotic decor and white tablecloths. But now, he felt our neighborhood sushi bar would be a better place to acquaint himself with a stranger. While I was attempting to eat a small order of sashimi and edamame, he told me about a terrible fight with his ex-girlfriend, just last night, followed by graphic descriptions of submerged memories from a psychiatric patient under the influence of hypnosis. Nothing I wanted to be thinking about later in the evening.

When I reached the point where I couldn't stand it for thirty seconds more, I interrupted him to say, "Jay, I'm not sure you should be telling me this." I felt so sorry for his patient. As her psychiatrist, Jay was supposed to be helping this woman, and clearly, he was violating her boundaries.

Jay looked up with a hurt and confused look in his eyes. In a huff, he told me, "I was hoping to meet a woman I could talk to!" He retreated into a stony silence.

The main thing I learned about Jay that evening was that I couldn't tell this man anything I wanted to keep private. He offered to walk me home, but I said, "No thanks. I like walking alone by the beach at night."

After I got back home, I felt relieved as I shut the door. Then I felt depressed. On the fire escape, I watched the moon through a thin layer of fog. I missed my gardens in Iowa and I missed my farmhouse. As I watered my jade plants, the amaryllis, and herbs in terra cotta pots, I longed for a late afternoon run through a field of Queen Anne's lace. I wanted to watch redwing blackbirds fly away from long rows of corn, to hike up gently sloping hills blooming with tiger lilies and black-eyed Susans. I wanted a huge sunset over a field of cows grazing on wildflowers.

Late at night I fell asleep and found myself canoeing in the rivers of the heart. A nighthawk was singing inside the branches of a redbud tree as the tree filled with fireflies. She told me it was really okay to want a man, and he would be an inspiration for my art. I just had to wait for the right time, which was clearly not now. I got back in the canoe as my heart became a river, close to the Canadian border. I jumped out of the canoe and found myself swimming in boundary waters. I got lost and the dream faded out.

Chapter 66:

The Mysterious Package

ix weeks before my last date with a stranger, I made a dangerous discovery. The fruit and vegetable market by the Sea Biscuit Café carried Soy Delicious Cherry Nirvana iced bean. I dug into my bowl of quarters, walked back to the store, and carried a pint of Cherry Nirvana home with a red rose. It was one of the special treats I had shared with Christopher. Then, I walked to Sloat Garden Center, across the street from the Zoo, and brought home four clusters of daffodils. When I lived in Iowa, my garden bloomed with daffodils every spring, if a late snow didn't freeze the flowers. The thunder blizzards could stay in Iowa, but evidently, I was pulling pieces of Iowa into my life in San Francisco.

As I was weaving sand dollars and pelican prints into a collage at the edge of the continent, Christopher, in Lexington, was carving linoleum blocks for prints based on all of the important women in his life. It was an act of letting go for him, of creating art out of his soul path. In one of the prints, his lover from Brattleboro was running through a forest of old growth pines. In another, I was doing a belly dance between two Egyptian urns. This carving across the miles was the closest he had come to the art that I do, ironically, after our lives had taken separate paths.

A few days later, I got an e-mail from Christopher: "I'm sending a CD of the folk singers we listened to when you were in Lexington. I'm sure you'll remember their beautiful weave of voices. Along with this, I'm sending a linoleum print, one in a series I have been creating, where you might find yourself. This gift for you is a small remembrance of Kentucky. Of course, I've been trying to get myself to the post office to mail it for a week!"

I became intensely curious about what might be in that package, and whether Christopher would actually send it. At the same time, I tried to tell myself it didn't matter. At the Sea Biscuit Café, I met William, Doug, Charles, James and Jeffrey. I dressed in high leather boots, a black sweater, a red silk miniskirt, and an aura of bohemian bravado. I searched their faces like sculpture, looking for a door to a new life. None of the doors were open.

Two and a half weeks later, the mysterious package arrived on my doorstep. Astoundingly beautiful music, the love songs we had listened to in Kentucky. A papercut snowflake on gold-flecked origami paper. A carved print of a belly dancer, where I recognized my body and my face. No letter. I looked into my yard, where California poppies and a slope of ice plants were blooming. I was in one of my moods, where an inner voice I couldn't hush was whispering, "Life is a papercut. A ring toss. A snowflake that is mysteriously beautiful and evaporates in your hand."

For a few more weeks, I continued to meet strangers at the Sea Biscuit Café, and later for variety, switched to the sushi bar on Judah Street. I met an engineer, an astronomer, an accountant, and a suicide prevention counselor from a local crisis line. I received e-mails from a painter in Paris, an army medic from Israel, and a snake charmer from Australia. In his photograph, he was holding a huge boa. I constantly reminded myself this was not a game – these were real people with intricate lives, emotions, joys and secrets. This fascinated me, but none of these men were soulmates.

Spring comes early to San Francisco. In our sandy yard, calla lilies unfurled their waxy blossoms. It was a long process I monitored day by day. A geometric progression from a tight cone that hesitates like a shy young woman, to a fractally expanding spiral of light. An organic farmer from the dance community informed me it was a good time to start planting tomatoes. He told me the best varieties to grow in the Outer Sunset and where to buy seeds. He suggested Siberia tomatoes and pointed me to Totally Tomatoes, a seed company dedicated to love apples. He also suggested the Seed Savers Exchange in Decorah, Iowa. I already knew about them from my midwestern dance gypsy days.

Farmer Dave, as the dance gypsies called him, explained that all tomatoes evolved from pea-sized, slightly tart fruits that grew in the Ecuadoran rain forest. As we walked on the beach, he told me, "People have been selecting and spreading progeny of their trials for more than two thousand years, so now you can find five-pound beefsteaks, rainbow-hued oxhearts, and black tomatoes in northern Russia which are so luscious you couldn't imagine shipping them even a hundred miles without their becoming tomato sauce." He showed me photographs of fist-sized yellow sweet and sour tomatoes from the Czech Republic that will keep bearing fruit, even when almost every leaf is seared with blight. Then he got on his soapbox: "Who needs genetic engineering when you have patient loving farmers herding genes a year at a time?"

Even in the coastal fog, I decided that planting tomatoes had a much higher probability of bearing fruit than meeting another stranger at the Sea Biscuit Café. Along with heirloom tomatoes, I planted oregano, parsley, basil, dill weed, pink and yellow roses, and marigolds. In the center of the garden, I hung a feeder for hummingbirds with a stained glass mobile and a wind chime.

Over a period of four-and-a-half months, more than one hundred men had viewed my profile on the Internet. I had reached the point where I could not bear to meet another anonymous 48-year-old, finally ready to love, Stud Muffin and decided to go back to dancing. I sprinkled this with a generous amount of gallery openings, performance art, the Marin Astronomy Club, and poetry readings at coffeehouses in Half Moon Bay, San Francisco and San Rafael. As an act of completion, I made a collage based on the Sea Biscuit Café and the odd collection of souls I encountered there. I called it "Lies and Mysteries."

Chapter 67:

Farewell to Conscious Singles, eHarmony and Jdate

Just for the record, here is what I wrote about myself on the Internet: "I am a sculptor who desires to share my life with an artistic, loving man. I offer depth and mystery, intelligent conversation, and a simple, loving heart with the wiring correct. Some of my favorite things... dancing, hiking, playing the flute, the SF Symphony, ballet, foreign films, and sweet evenings with a loving man. I am slender, with long dark hair and dark eyes. You consider yourself a good catch – your life is working and you'd like to share it with a woman who loves you."

That was probably too straightforward. In any case, it didn't work. I thought about the *Yoga of the Impossible*. Over the past months, I had been gathering ideas to relate my life experience to this ancient discipline. So far, these were fragments of leaves I inscribed with sepia ink on rice paper. Maybe it was quirky wisdom from nowhere, but I knew I had to stop doubting myself. I picked up a handful of rice paper leaves, my version of fortune cookies, and turned over three of them. *Always remember that you are a goddess. Happiness comes from within. Stop thinking – live in the moment.*

As I deleted my profile from Conscious Singles, eHarmony and Jdate, I thought about the way art has been consistent in my life. *I like to think with my hands, and sculpture is easy. Clay gods and goddesses spin out of my fingers in a flood, a tide pool. An elbow, an ankle, a dream. The dance I do with men disappoints me.* In Iowa, my friends had decided it would take an act of God to get me into a committed relationship. Ok then, acts of God happen every day. *And don't we all have one wing caught in the other world?*

Above me, the San Francisco sky was hazed in a light rain. I ran outside to see a wide double rainbow covering half the sky. The arc was shimmering, almost imperceptible, but the colors spoke to me.

In a quiet way, I started to question my decision to move back to San Francisco. My life was art-centered when I was living and teaching in Iowa, and as much as I hated to admit it, a part of me was shaded in midwestern farm girl hues. I liked the small acts of chivalry there and the way you always knew the man would pay for the movie. This wasn't about the five dollars to get into the Co-Ed Theatre. It was a signal from a man to show you he cared. In San Francisco, men were afraid to open the door for you. In the midwest, they showed up with roses. Yes, I admit it, I wanted those roses again.

And what did I really want? A simple meal on a candle-lit table. A hiking partner, a hand to hold in the movies. A foot rub, a back rub, intelligent conversation. A long-stemmed yellow rose. A dance partner and a man who deeply loves me in my bed. Peppermint, dill weed and sweet basil growing in the garden. A scattering of tomato plants blooming in my yard, then giving fruit. What I wanted was simple, and it seemed impossible.

Chapter 68:

The Yoga of the Impossible

The next morning I took a streetcar to Chinatown and found a sketchbook covered in red silk with gold letters in Chinese calligraphy. I probably could have asked anyone on the street to translate the encrypted message, but perhaps it was better to leave it mysterious. It would follow life that way. On the first page, I drew the design for a new goddess sculpture, with legs emerging from a sea of lavender irises. Her body swayed in a belly dance. Next to the charcoal lines, I wrote, "Precepts of the Yoga of the Impossible." This is what I have figured out so far:

Precepts of the Yoga of the Impossible.

Precept 1: We are animals, and as such, need to take care of our animal needs.

Precept 2: Don't give in to your animal needs if it isn't in tune with your spirit.

Precept 3: With a lover from another country, the exotic clashes against a language barrier. When you can't fully understand each other, the animal takes over.

Precept 4: If you want a relationship, give it time and attention.

Precept 5: Love finds you when you're not looking.

Precept 6: Be radically honest. Stand barefoot in front of your beloved.

Precept 7: Tell the truth, but don't put all your cards on the table.

Precept 8: Get an AIDS test, regardless of whether this is a serious relationship or a dance gypsy fling. This will slow you down and make you talk, which is always a good thing.

Precept 9: Be clear with the universe about what you want in a man. Don't go out on a third date with a man you wouldn't marry.

Precept 10: Live in the moment. Enlightenment takes place in the present tense.

Precept 11: If you are a woman, let the man lead the dance. As you do this, stay rooted in the center of your feminine power. Remember, you are a flower.

Precept 12: Don't act like you're desperate. If you feel that way inside, fake it and act watermelon cool. Don't need a man. Enjoy him.

Precept 13: Live life one day at a time – until something better comes along.

Precept 14: A loving relationship is a path to enlightenment. It is also the place where we are most fully human.

Precept 15: The human soul needs love to be properly nourished and grow.

Precept 16: Always remember you are a goddess.

Precept 17: Happiness comes from within.

Precept 18: Stop thinking. Stop looking. The miracle is the moment.

And what is it like to be a woman? Watch the man you love chase women he can't have or marry his next girlfriend. Memorize the shape of his muscles and the fine lines of his cheekbones. Shape your tears into sculpture, but be certain the tears are invisible.

How much you love has nothing to do with it. Passion has nothing to do with it. How much you have in common has nothing to do with it. There's a mysterious switch inside every human being. The switch says yes or no. If it's yes, you work out the differences. If it's no, you're gone. And if the switch, as in Christopher, goes on a yes no yes no loop, it will drive you crazy.

So here is the bottom line: As a goddess in the world, go back into the world. Enjoy the gifts of every day. This is enlightenment. This may be all that life gives you.

That night I dreamed about a holy woman from India. She was wrapped in a white sari and had a diamond in her nose. Her heart embraced the planet – people, animals, oceans, redwood trees. I saw her walking in the mountains – dark skin, bare feet, bright eyes smiling. She hugged me and whispered, "Real contentment comes from within." Her eyes were a river, warm and laughing.

She held me close and spoke softly. "Don't be impatient for the bud to become a rose. It happens in its own time. Try to be content with what you have, and do your best to make others happy. When you see the smile of happiness on their faces, you will be happy too."

Then she whispered something in a language I didn't understand, but I could feel it. Her blessing penetrated my skin as she told me, "Wake up every morning where the dragonfly whispers secrets. Listen to the river. Be open to the gift."

Chapter 69:

Dionysus' Birthday Party

When you live your life as an art form, the story has many possible endings. One of these is to continue dancing, creating art, enjoying each day, and knowing that life is perfect exactly the way it is. But life is a river, a dragon kite, a cantankerous crab who never approaches anything in a linear direction.

On Friday night, I went to a party in San Rafael to celebrate the birthday of a friend who had recently moved to California. To honor the new life he had chosen, he changed his name to Dionysus, a fitting name to celebrate his love of beautiful women and fine wine. As he explained it to me, "Dionysus is the god of parties and festivals, madness, drunkenness and pleasure, forever young." The night we talked, he was setting up a scalar wave chamber, with the energetic frequencies of dolphins, whales, the rainforest, universal light, divine healing and divine love.

His house on the San Rafael Canal was decorated with goddess statues in the style of the early Italian Renaissance. They were not like mine, where the legs rippled into other dimensions, but lovely in a classical way. The ceiling was draped with white silk, like sails from a pirate ship or the inner sanctum of a harem. On the deck, a king-size bed was littered with balloons over a gold silk spread. Herons and egrets drifted in slow circles over the canal, where two regatta teams rowed long boats toward the sunset. It looked like they were rowing to Atlantis.

The women in his harem were dressed in feathers and batik, and most of the men wore silk Hawaiian shirts. In the bedroom, a small circle of friends inhaled smoke from a red glass water pipe. Another group gathered to watch the sunset on the back deck. In the kitchen, people sipped Shiraz around a circular blue glass table filled with expensive potluck treats – marinated artichoke hearts with three different kinds of mushrooms, potato dill bread, sushi, edamame, a salmon casserole, an heirloom tomato salad, chocolate covered strawberries and two birthday cakes.

A yin yang sun was setting over the hot tub, shimmering out to a sunset like the galaxy swirling before the planets were formed. I felt like an unintentional character in an erotic tattoo, and as the night progressed, the ink stretched further than anything I could imagine after living in Iowa. A woman I knew from the San Francisco contra dance walked in with glitter make-up, silver mascara, and thick black fishnet stockings. Obviously, a harem-worthy tantrika. A duo of new age musicians invited us to chant and Sufi dance. I joined the weave of harmonies, leaning against a tall man from Hawaii. His voice played against mine until two dancers pulled him into a hug.

A woman dressed in feathers and lace asked us to gather on pillows; then she honored the Iowa birthday boy with a burlesque strip dance, revealing a butterfly tattoo on her ankle, vines up her legs, and a Sanskrit *om* on her shoulder. At the end of her slink routine, after she stripped down to a g-string, she reached up to the heavens and began to channel Isis. She chanted a naked message about life and love.

As the music continued, the crowd got up to dance. They were tantric, polyamorous, and most of them danced like they already knew each other. The tall man from Hawaii pulled me into a hug that gently swayed into a dance. When the music stopped, we walked over to the punch bowl in the kitchen and Jonah introduced himself. He lifted the ladle to his nose and sniffed it, then smiled. "Good, the lemonade isn't spiked. Do you want some?"

I smiled and said, "Sure, I prefer it that way."

"Good to know. We're probably the only two people in the room who aren't high right now."

"You seem to know most of these people."

"Casually, yes. Deeply, no, except for the woman walking up the stairs. I spent a few years doing tantra workshops with this crowd, but it's not my scene anymore. And you?"

"I moved here from Iowa two years ago, and Dionysus used to live in the same town. A few days ago, he invited me to his party. He thought I might like to meet some of his friends."

"Interesting . . ."

"Hey, what's going on upstairs?"

"Trust me . . . You don't want to know."

The air filled with incense and music by Taipei Lounge. Jonah took my hand and we began dancing again. His shirt was electric blue silk, and I had to touch it. I thought about sculpting him, but he was too tall and too thin, with too many shields around his heart.

Jonah and I danced for a while. Then, we went outside to walk and watched the moon ripple over the canal. We began to trade stories, hugged for a while, then fell asleep on a sofa later that night. On the other side of the room, the magician healer massaged the breasts of his tantra teacher. He must have been doing this for hours, as it was the first thing we saw in the early morning light.

I leaned over to Jonah and whispered, "I'm not sure I want to watch the rest of the show."

He leaned back and whispered, "I don't either. Let's go."

On the way to the front door, I hoisted my pack over my shoulder, and Jonah helped himself to a stash of leftovers for a picnic. We drove to Mill Valley in my truck, parked it on a side street by Whole Foods, then drove up Mt. Tam in his white van. Jonah was a carpenter and showed me houses he worked on as we wove up the mountain. He pointed to elegant round windows, large redwood decks, and bent wood arbors he crafted for rich people while he slept in his van. I wondered if anything had changed since the Middle Ages.

Part way up the mountain, we stopped at a trail head and loaded our packs with leftovers from the birthday party. Something we ate wasn't digesting well, but that wasn't a reason not to climb a mountain. He said, "It was the salmon casserole."

I said, "For me, probably the chocolate raspberry cake. Or maybe I am allergic to love the way it is practiced in this part of the world." We vowed to eat only salad for a week. Salad and miso soup. This was a vow we would break in less than thirty minutes.

I followed him up the mountain. Higher on the trail, we walked through a meadow of tall grass, then spread out an Indian bedspread by a eucalyptus tree with a view of Sausalito, Angel Island, and the San Francisco Bay. Through the early morning mist, we watched boats drift on the water as he told me his story – an alcoholic father, a French Canadian mother who lit candles in church every morning, jumping a train out of New Orleans when he was sixteen years old, a litany of disappointing girlfriends, and a woman he deeply loved. When he was ready to ask her to marry him, she broke his heart – his version of the *Yoga of the Impossible*.

As he pulled me to the hollow below his shoulders, he told me, "I'm older than you." I already knew this from the river of lines on his face when I made him laugh. His voice grew soft as he said, "I'm sure you can feel how drawn I am to you, and I've been thinking we should be lovers before I go back to Hawaii. I have the sense that you've been wounded by something in your past, and we can heal each other."

"When are you going back to Hawaii?"

"Maybe two or three months. I work for six months each year doing carpentry and woodwork in Marin County. People put me up in their houses, or else I live in my van. The money's good, but I get tired of the people here and the way they live. Too many rich people. Too many redwood decks made of old growth trees. Too many rides on the polyamorous merry-go-round."

"And when you go back to Hawaii . . ."

"I have a sweet little house with a lanai, and my garden is full of flowers – jasmine, orchids, hibiscus, birds of paradise, passion flowers and plumeria. My yard has avocado, mango, orange and lemon trees – it's my own little paradise. I don't work in Hawaii. I like to hike in the rain forest and sit for a few hours by a waterfall. That's what I do for meditation."

"Do you live alone?"

"Well, not exactly." As he held me in his arms on the side of the mountain, he told me about an exotic woman named Megumi waiting for him on Maui. Her house was surrounded by mangoes and papayas, but a dragonfly told him she was not the right one. Then he told me about a few women he had lived with in Mill Valley, Fairfax and San Geronimo. They all had gifts for him, but not the right one.

"What's your intuition about me?"

He closed his eyes for a minute and then said, "You're not the right one long term, but my intuition says we have gifts to share as lovers." In the dappled sunlight, he weighed his options. "You've already gotten through three of my seven shields, and I know we can heal each other."

I assessed the possibility, then said, "I don't want to hurt your feelings, but it doesn't feel right to me."

"I've spent the past few years learning tantra. I could send you to heaven."

"Sorry, but I don't think so. I have girlfriends who like to hook up for a night or a weekend, but my heart doesn't work that way."

"I'm not going back to Maui for two or three months."

"Not enough time."

I couldn't tell if Jonah was relieved or disappointed. While he fell asleep in the sunlight, I put on my pack and walked back down the mountain. Two hours later, I found my truck and drove back to the canal. Quietly, I slipped through the sliding doors, found my dance shoes, and slipped them into my pack.

The party had circled into its second day, with a small group of women kneading bread and slicing cucumbers for a salad. The magician healer slid out of a green door. He gave me a sinewy hug, said, "You are beautiful to the core," and asked if he could give me a massage.

I said, "Thanks for offering, but no."

I walked to my truck and drove back over the Golden Gate Bridge. I was heading toward the downbeat of the 43rd and Judah contra dance. It was early evening, and the sun was falling into the Pacific. A burning ball of light.

Chapter 70:

Waiting for the Phoenix

I walked through the door of the contra dance with a red pashmina shawl draped around my shoulders. I put on my dance shoes and stepped into a river of Appalachian banjo music. I was a blue heron, lifting in sky ballet, to the tune of *Clinch Mountain Backstep*. I was on the dance floor again, doing my flame-thrower act.

My partner and I circled, starred, and gypsied down the line. We were dancing in the tantric temple in Varanasi, where Hindu gods and goddesses are perpetually making love, or was it the basketball floor of the gym at the contra dance in San Francisco? Under a floating summer night, I danced with friends and strangers, face to open face, my eyes burning a soft trail of fire. The banjo's tinny harmony weaving through the flute. At the end of the cadence, my partner led me into a waterfall dip, then lifted me through the Pacific Ocean moonlight.

I thought about the men I met at the party. Very handsome, all of them, but snowflakes. A delicate beauty, melting in my hand. Ephemeral art, invisible. Poof! Gone! Dancing was more reliable – eggshell blue notes, crazy happy, stolen time. A waltz with the whole room floating around in a 3/4 slow motion floor-gasm. Then a short walk home through salty air below a trickle of moonlight.

Back in my house at midnight, I thought about the Yoga of the Impossible. *Love is a dance of desire and fear, balance and swing, apart, together. Love is a waltz around a maze of sand dollars, a cliff dangling with hang gliders. Love is hiking up a mountain in Nepal, searching for a bridge to cross into the images of my dreams, through secret passageways, across a snowy river, to a waterfall of light. Love is an echo of burgundy satin, the shape of the ballgown I wore, a single violet fooled by the late summer's warmth into blooming, the room where we danced now empty except for the echo of a flute.*

Early in December a tidal wave swept the planet. Robin went out on a medical boat to Banda Aceh. I spent a month organizing artists in San Francisco, did a series of tsunami paintings, sold them to tourists, and sent the money to Robin. When I wasn't painting, I hiked up mountains in winter rain. Salamanders slithered across the stones, and the muse was a trickster running through the trees. I thought about Robin in Bali, inside a medical tent, delivering babies on the beach. I lit a candle.

On the night of the Winter Solstice, I walked to the beach for a ritual bonfire. Sixteen feathered drummers pounded the night language of a rain forest, in counterpoint to the rhythm of the waves. The beat was so sensual, I had to get up and dance. A bare-chested dancer cast a circle to create sacred space. Then she invoked a transformation in time, chanting, "Each moment awaits our invitation."

I was deeply present in my inner world, where I planted willingness, like sunflowers, in my garden. The Muse took my hand, and our spirits were whole. The solstice moon was blooming, and I was in the presence of love. Under the glow of the rising moon, everything was alive. I knew the future was full of possibilities. Like Scheherazade, we all were weaving stories. Inside my story, the goddess voice broke through.

Before the Phoenix bursts into flames and is reborn,
she sings a hauntingly beautiful song.
The whole creation listens.

At the edge of the continent, I saw visions in the flames:

I hear you singing in midnight language.
I swim in the echo of your collarbone.
I ache for you, even though I don't know your name.

I looked deeper into the fire:

With the tip of your paintbrush,
you reach across the distances through wind tunnels,
and the dreams you have been hiding
shape my face.

As I redreamed my future, the voice of the fire began to speak.

Let Venus be an offering, not an imposition.
By the power of fierce beauty, we transform war into art.
Follow the thread of light
until you feel it tug you into the future.

Chapter 71:

Zebulon's Lounge

t was a hot day close to the end of July in most of California, but a coastal fog was hovering over San Francisco to the west of Twin Peaks. A perfect day to drive over the Golden Gate Bridge and find the sun again. My excuse was an impromptu concert at Zebulon's Lounge, an intimate jazz venue in Petaluma. My friend Sharon, a bluesy soprano, was opening for the Manring Kassin Darter Trio. Sharon, a brassy blonde with a light Texas accent, wrote songs that were steamy. Scorpio, for the initiated only. Her set, from 5:00 to 7:00 p.m., hadn't been announced in Zebulon's schedule. She had five people in the audience, including the bartender.

After Sharon's first song, a man from the local neighborhood came to the door, scanned the room, and walked in. He was close to six feet tall, with green eyes, black curly hair, and defined muscles. He wore a lavender linen shirt, black pants with a loose fit, brown clogs, and had a sensual way of walking. The dancer in me had to notice that. It would have been easy to stare, but I kept him in my peripheral vision. He went directly to the bar, stood there for a while, then came to my table and asked, "Is it okay if I sit here?"

I was a little surprised, but since I was already intrigued by him, I said, "Sure, why not? Do you know Sharon?"

"I don't, but I heard her singing from the street and had to come in."

Sharon introduced her next song and started singing again. At least we had six people in the audience now.

After a few more songs, he leaned over to me and said, "Oh, I almost forgot... My name is Noah."

"I'm Katarina."

He looked over at me and almost did a double take. "Wait a minute. . . Were you at the opening at Gallery 16 a few weeks ago?"

"I was. Did I see you there?"

Noah studied my face. "There were more than two hundred people in the gallery that night, but I remember seeing you."

"Maybe this is unusual, but I was focused on the art more than the people. How about you? Do you go for the art or for the people, and did you enjoy what you saw?"

"I loved all of it, but especially the art. Huge painted snakes, mythological birds, and my favorite, an amazing mermaid sculpture holding a goblet with a betta fish. I was so intrigued by the mermaid, I wanted to take her home with me that night."

"You probably know that if a mermaid sings to you, she might enchant you. If you follow the cadence of her beautiful voice, you might not know what you are doing or where you're going."

"I'd love to be enchanted that way."

"I've always been fascinated by mermaids. Their ability to breathe under water is so mysterious. I'm sure they know the secrets of evolution and the ancient mysteries."

"And what did you think about the mermaid at Gallery 16?"

"She's a sweet one. I created her. Also the birds and the painted snakes."

Noah sat in a stunned silence as he let this revelation sink in. Then our eyes met for a long time. His eyes were warm and electric, a meteor shower in an open sky, a rain forest full of tropical birds. I was gazing into a green universe, a universe staring back at me in an intense state of curiosity.

After the next song, I leaned over to Noah and whispered, "The mermaid sang to me in a dream, a haunting melody, and I heard her voice while I was working the clay. Very mysterious, even to me."

Sharon started singing again. After her song, Noah leaned over and asked if I would share a small jar of sake with him.

"I only drink sake once or twice a year. In my universe, sake is only for celebration or a toast to a mermaid."

Noah put his hand on my shoulder and said, "I'll be right back."

While Sharon was singing *Temple*, the bartender came to our table with a heated ceramic sake jar and two small cups. They were beautifully crafted, in the style of the raku potters from Japan. Noah poured sake into both cups, and I sipped on mine while Sharon sang *Not Enough Love*.

I held the raku cup up to the light to admire the glaze. When I found the seal, I turned to Noah and said, "I thought so. These cups were made by a potter in a small village close to Kyoto."

"How do you know?"

"I apprenticed with that potter after graduate school. I can always tell his style by the unique color and texture."

"How long were you in Japan?"

"Six months, but really, it was timeless. The Zen potters of Kyoto gave a new direction to my art and helped me understand myself in a deeper way. It's a culture that celebrates beauty."

"Where did you live?"

"I stayed with a family in a small, traditional home in a quiet area of Kyoto close to a Shinto shrine. I remember my first night in Kyoto. They prepared my room like a work of art – a simple tatami mat, a futon, a raku bowl, and a stem of orchids. During the next week, they walked with me to several of Kyoto's Buddhist temples. I loved the gardens in the Buddhist temples – everywhere you look is a living work of art."

"You're making me want to visit Japan."

"I'd love to go back there. While I was in Kyoto, I became the protege of the master potter who crafted these cups. The raku *sensei* and I almost never spoke. He didn't know English and my Japanese vocabulary was not sophisticated enough for the nuances of what he was showing me. I learned by watching him."

I watched Noah as he turned his cup and then the jar to admire the pattern of glazes and the irregularity of the clay. As Noah held the cup in his hands, I traced the weave of the glaze with my finger. His eyes, a sea of green.

Sharon finished another song. Noah filled our cups again, then held his cup close to the candle. After a long silence, he whispered, "This blue is amazing. Like the eye of an Egyptian Pharoah."

"You should visit the Zen potters when you go to Kyoto. Every raku cup and bowl is a one-of-a-kind beauty, and they're crafted in a meditative silence. Raku firing is unpredictable and volatile, but produces exquisitely beautiful results. The intensity of the blue was generated in the glaze and given its sheen inside the fire."

"It must be amazing to see and I'd like to learn more about tea ceremony."

I'm afraid that Noah and I were a bit rude to Sharon during the rest of the concert. This was spontaneous and totally unintentional. I hadn't seen Sharon for more than a year and fully intended to listen to all of her new music, but Noah and I kept leaning together to talk. We touched shoulders while she sang and then leaned together between songs to trade stories.

Something about Noah was different from other people I'd met, but I couldn't define it yet. As we uncovered one coincidence after another, something inside me responded from the core of my atoms. He was intrigued when I told him I used to live in Iowa and still felt like Alice in Wonderland sometimes. I was intrigued when he told me he had traveled to Greece with the U.S. Olympic gymnastics team and spent most of his weekends playing fiddle with a Cajun band.

Between the necklace of our conversation, Sharon wove songs with provocative titles, *Holy Water* and *Work of Art*. Before the final set, I asked if she could play one of my favorites for an encore, a song called *Red*. She said, "I've almost forgotten that song, but I'll learn it again before my next West Coast tour."

After the concert we all stood up and gave her a standing ovation. Sharon and I already had plans for dinner with her band, but she invited Noah to join us. Everyone in the Zebulon's audience came with us, except for the bartender, who was still in the middle of her shift, and in any case, too busy sneaking out to the street to kiss her boyfriend. Sharon wanted sushi, which she felt she deserved after playing so passionately for such a small audience. Since Noah lived in Petaluma, he led our parade around the corner and down the street a few blocks to Hiro's. We passed a few street people who asked us for money. Sharon looked the young man in the eye and said, "Hey, I only made four dollars tonight."

At Hiro's I sat next to Sharon, but she was mostly bantering with the two other musicians and sharing chords for a new song. Noah and I were still leaning into each other, weaving a conversation, and feeling as though we had known each other forever. As I lifted a slice of pickled ginger from his plate, he reciprocated by spearing a tempura broccoli flower from mine, then insisted I try the *hamachi* and the herring. By the end of the evening, Noah and I were making plans to visit Japan, including a pilgrimage to the raku potters of Kyoto. He wanted to spend a few weeks in Japanese temples and Shinto shrines, and of course, see a dance performance in the geisha district. I suggested a theatre I knew in Gion, next year in April for the cherry blossom festival, during the week of the Kamo River dances.

Sharon and I turned to face each other at the same time. I used the opportunity to put a gift into her hands – a voluptuous music goddess, glazed blue, with a crescent moon over her shoulder. I wrapped her in yellow silk and whispered, "I hope this will be an amulet to help you find a lover." Sharon returned the gift with two CDs, *Live in Texas* and *Bootleg Bousquet*.

We shared the recent details of our lives before being swept back into other conversations – eddies in the river of the night. Through that small whirling window, I could see that Sharon's life had become even more complicated and impossible than mine. My life, on the other hand, seemed to be getting simpler.

Noah did not try to kiss me. He wrote down my telephone number and did not offer his. But as we were walking back to Zebulon's, he asked about my last experience with a man, who he was, how long it lasted, and what made it fall apart.

We sat down on the green wooden bench in front of Zebulon's. I looked up at him and asked, "Are you a frog or a prince?"

Chapter 72:

Noah's Ark

Noah and I got to know each other slowly. We didn't want to build a fire where the flames would consume themselves or burn the roof off the house before we knew what was inside. A further complication was Noah's commitment to his band, which played out of town many weekends. I was comfortable with our pace, actually relieved, although at times I wished he was free for a symphony concert or an evening at the San Francisco Ballet. Our connection was so immediately close that I kept wondering if I had met him before. Neither of us could come up with a time or a place, but being with him felt like remembering someone from a dream.

When we had time together, it was always special – a candle-lit dinner at his house, fourth row center seats to hear Joshua Bell play Tchaikovsky's violin concerto with the San Francisco Symphony, a picnic at Bolinas with foccacia, kasseri cheese, plum tomatoes, wine and marinated artichoke hearts. By the lake at Bolinas, I felt compelled to tell Noah about my experience at Lake Hopatcong when I was twelve years old – the light, the tunnel, my meeting with God underwater, then swimming back from the light. Noah was deeply moved by what I had shared with him.

We walked for hours that afternoon, often in silence. We hiked up to the redwood forest, then walked down the mountain to watch the waves roll in at the beach. Later that evening, we played music together, starting with folk waltzes, and then jigs and reels in minor keys – *Tam Lin, Old Woman of Galway, Blue Jig, and Cross-Eyed Cat*. He played violin, I played flute, and I felt my heart open with the music.

A few weeks later, Noah had a free weekend, so we took backpacks and a tent up to Tuolumne Meadows. It was the weekend of the omen. Late afternoon in the slanted sunlight, we were graced with the vision of a calliope hummingbird hovering over a purple lupine. She had peach-colored flanks, dark green spots on her throat, and iridescent green down on the upper part of her body. She fed on the nectar of that exotic flower, then became a tiny green acrobat, performing exotic dips and dives. Her voice was a high-pitched *tsew tsew*, and in that moment we knew we were in tune with something larger than ourselves.

That night, the stars were huge, with the Milky Way splashed across the sky. Under the open sky, Noah gave me a shiatsu massage. His touch was strong but very tender, full of feeling, and I felt my emotions relax along with my body. As the moon moved higher in the sky, Noah moved his hands slowly along my back and my arms before he kissed my neck. Then my face. Then my mouth.

Hours later, under an open sky, I fell asleep in a wave of joy and deep peace. The image I remember from my dreams was a wave of blue butterflies, then a message inside a nautilus shell. In the first morning light, Noah told me about a dream he had.

"It began with a rush of hummingbirds in the lucent awareness between waking and sleep. I thought I was awake, but I couldn't have been because you walked into my room, smiling. You were wearing a shimmering purple dress, the color of which was not so much bright as it was light. You positively glowed, and as you got closer, I realized that it wasn't even made of material. You were wearing a soft curtain of light. Its aura was like a purple neon bulb, a weave of violet and gold, a gorgeous hue that I associate with happy things like bright colored decorations in a jukebox at a well-chromed 1950's diner. In the music from the jukebox, I could feel people dancing. I marveled that you could be wearing a shimmering curtain of light and moving so gracefully inside it. A soft light emanated from your body, so that you even shimmered yourself. You never broke your smile, and I didn't want to break the spell by waking up. Then, just before dawn, I heard my guardian angels whispering, '*This is the one your soul has chosen.*'"

Noah and I sat in the meadow, watching the sunrise. What I saw in his eyes – a wildness and a vulnerability, something innocent as a child and something older than God. With the other men in my life, I had tried so hard to make it work. I had twisted myself into a pretzel to create a home for my heart that wasn't meant to endure. I had devoted myself, body and soul, to men who weren't devoted to me. With Noah, I wasn't trying to do anything. I was just being myself.

Chapter 73:

The Dreaming Room

uring the weeks that followed, dozens of long-stemmed roses appeared on my doorstep and in my dreams. I found roses inside the pyramids of Giza, as Noah anointed my feet with jasmine oil. Roses lit up in secret passageways, waiting to be discovered in the morning. Noah and I shared hundreds of stories. Soon, we were spending most of our time together, something I had not done before without hiding significant parts of myself. In his presence I felt a deep comfort, which was exciting and peaceful at the same time. We spoke openly, freely, without a filter. Even when we were sleeping, our dreams sent signals up and down the Pacific coast, with resonant images. A meteor shower, a ripple through time, a lotus with a thousand petals opening.

We hiked together in redwood forests and shared our love of music. Noah's passionate, improvisational style of playing the violin inspired me and opened new pathways in my music. He taught me a whole new repertoire of Cajun tunes, and I shared the contra waltzes, reels and jigs I had learned as a dance gypsy. Even with fiddle tunes I already knew and loved, Noah's wildly inventive style added fire and beauty. I liked to add descants and harmonies to his melodies with my flute.

I began sculpting a new series of mermaids, paired with paintings of underwater visions of sea horses, anemones, shimmering coral, and banded tropical fish. My dreams revealed fish with magical stripes – turquoise, orange, gold and silver. Dionysus commissioned seven bronze mermaids for his hot tub in Sonoma, where he had moved his tribe of silky tantrikas and dragon kites. When he arrived to meet the mermaids and transport them up the coast, he brought us a dinner picnic with a bottle of Hummingbird Pinot Noir. We shared this exotic treat in Noah's garden, surrounded by jasmine, passion flowers and birds of paradise.

We fell into a rhythm of spending weekends in Petaluma, where Noah had restored a Victorian house, a beautiful painted lady with hand-rolled glass windows and wood he had painted lavender, deep purple and lantern green. The living room had a fireplace and the furnishings were minimal – raku bowls on a small table, a rolled futon, two large silk pillows, and a Persian rug in front of the fireplace. Perfect for quiet nights, shiatsu massages and long conversations. The kitchen had the original built-in cabinets, a beautifully crafted table with two chairs, and an antique O'Keefe & Merritt stove with a custom copper exhaust vent. Perfect for sharing meals and baking bread. The bathroom had stained glass windows, a small table with floating candles, and an antique lion's paw tub. I loved the quiet elegance, perfect for bathing like a geisha.

A large room in the back of the house was completely empty, except for two turquoise silk pillows, a handcrafted cedar bookcase, and two stained glass dragonflies hanging from the window. Noah took my hand and led me to the window, where we saw a bird's nest view of a redwood tree. The room had a special feeling, something I could sense more than describe. When I asked Noah about it, he said, "This is my dreaming room. I was saving it for you."

Chapter 74:

The Mermaid in the Lotus

Noah liked to tell his friends that we had been introduced by a mermaid. Since the art opening at Gallery 16, when Noah was first drawn to me without knowing who I was or how he would meet me, he continued to be intrigued with the mermaid I had created. She often entered our conversations and our dreams. I surprised him one night with a note under his pillow: "When a mermaid sings to you, she will enchant you. She will whisper messages in your dreams."

Noah responded with a note by the candle next to the lion's paw tub: "I love to be enchanted that way." The whispering came in the form of music, which became a waltz he called "Mermaid's Dream."

I left another note in his car with a drawing of a mermaid: "If you follow the cadence of her beautiful voice, you might not know what you are doing or where you're going." He responded with a slinky tune he called "The Enchantment."

It was becoming clear to me that the mermaid, following my lead, was feeling powerfully drawn to the north. On a Friday night when Noah's band was playing in Cotati, I lifted the bronze mermaid into the back of my truck, drove her across the Golden Gate Bridge, and invited her to live on a blue silk scarf in Noah's living room. When Noah returned, he surrounded her with candles and gardenias, and we spent the night on the futon. It was beautiful and mysterious to feel Noah holding me, rocking me in a sea of shooting stars, a doorway of grace into a sky of infinite possibilities.

Since we were spending most of our time together now, Noah invited me to move my sculpture studio into the dreaming room at the back of his house. That way, when I woke up with an image in the morning, I could continue finding its form in clay. Since both of us enjoyed touch as our primary love language, Noah began teaching me the subtleties of shiatsu massage. At times we would practice for hours on the futon, warmed by the fire we kept burning.

I wasn't sure what to think about his car, an ancient blue Rambler with a white roof, a bit of a rust bucket, and not a chariot fit for a prince. When I asked him about it, Noah explained, "This house is really important to me. During the ten years I was fine-tuning my home, I put most of my resources into the house remodel, which left my automotive project languishing. Living so close to Kentucky Street, it wasn't a high priority. I usually travel to gigs with my band, and Petaluma is the kind of town where you can get most of what you need by walking.

"Actually, the Rambler is reliable, and it doesn't rattle or squeak. My grandfather took great pride in this car and kept it clean and tuned. Driving in his car gets me thinking of our family vacations in Bodega Bay and Jenner when I was a boy. Grandpa always kept a complete set of tools in the trunk, but I only remember one roadside repair. I inherited his tools along with his chariot. As you can see, they're still in mint condition."

"And his repair manual?"

"I keep it in the trunk with his tools. The Rambler is mechanically straightforward, easy to repair. Even the leak in the heater will be easy to fix – I just haven't gotten around to it yet.

"My grandpa bought the Rambler new in 1960. At that time, a smaller family car without fins was quite a novelty. It's built of solid metal, as opposed to plastic, even the dashboard. Built when things were made to last, which is better than so many things today that are made to be used up and thrown away. When I have the time to restore the chrome and give it a new paint job, it might be worth some money, but of course, I'm going to keep it. For me, the Rambler is reminiscent of a simpler time, something I like to get back to when I can."

"Clearly, you love this car."

"When you drive a car like this, you turn every head in town. At stoplights, people talk to you. . . . 'Hey, my uncle used to own a car like that.' Or I'll see a little girl on a bicycle, madly waving. Yes, it's still a project, but fun to drive."

"What about fuel economy?"

"Almost as good as your Toyota, thanks to the overdrive transmission. I don't know why they can't build solid, simple cars like this today. And look here... crank windows, which I like so much better than power windows. I still have Grandpa's floating compass on the dashboard. When I was a boy, it fascinated me to drive with him and watch the directions change. I love the chrome rings around the headlights, the chrome mesh grill, and the hood ornament. The wheel covers are a work of art. An elegant design, with so much less that can go wrong. It gives me a tremendous sense of freedom."

As a sculptor, this was something I could appreciate and understand. I smiled at Noah and told him, "I'm not the kind of woman who judges a man by the shine on his car. Especially since the Rambler was a gift from your grandpa, I understand why it's so important to you. Grandma Helen would have loved it."

Noah was relieved to know his car wasn't a problem for me. If we wanted heat on a cold night, we used my truck. Since we were sharing our lives, it was an amazing gift that Noah already owned a house. Not having to worry about maintaining a studio and an apartment gave me more time for my art. Owning a home without a mortgage gave him the freedom to be a musician and bring his creative gift into the world.

Noah had never worked in clay before, so I shared some techniques of hand-building bowls and the raku style of firing. I loved watching the fine attention to detail I saw in his music expressed in another form. His hands, which were strong and sensitive from his shiatsu practice, worked well in clay. For my birthday, he crafted a tea ceremony bowl, glazed in earth tones and blues. I thanked him with a dream-inspired sculpture – a mermaid in a lotus.

That night, our dreams converged in an image of walking over stones in a Japanese temple garden. The coincidence stirred my gypsy soul, and we both decided it was time to find a good deal on airline tickets to Tokyo. I found my Japanese phrase book and we practiced at night on the futon with a fire burning. Twice a week, one of Noah's neighbors helped us with the pronunciation, and she asked us to bring a small gift to her family in Nara. We of course agreed – it was the best way to thank her for giving us some access to the language. She told us about a temple in Nara where deer walked on the temple grounds. Her voice was very beautiful, like the spirit of the trees.

Noah and I were eager to visit the Zen potters of Kyoto, and we made a list of temples and shrines to see. Our first week in Kyoto would be a pilgrimage to Ryoanji, Yoshida Jinja, the Heian Shrine, and Ginkakuji. I had beautiful memories of walking in temple gardens and wanted to share these special places with Noah. We planned day trips to Nara and Sagano, with long walks on the Kamo River. We would arrive with the cherry blossoms, and take the train to Kyoto to see the Odori geisha dances by the Kamo River. We planned to hike up Mt. Fuji, with a pilgrimage to Sengen-Jinja at Fuji Yoshida. She was the Japanese goddess who walked into the fire and survived.

During our long years of solitude, Noah and I had been undiscovered treasures, like the Pennsylvania Dutch Star Amish quilt I had been saving in a cedar chest from my Grandma Helen. I brought my quilt to our house in Petaluma and unfolded it on our bed. As we planted seeds in the garden, Noah and I opened the box of long years when love was hidden like tule fog over a meadow. I was a calla lily remembering how to bloom. Noah was the whisper of an ancient promise, the writing inside the walls of a stone that had finally cracked open. Egyptian hieroglyphics with the code finally clear. Noah didn't understand why it took us so long to find each other, but maybe I needed those years alone to develop more completely as an artist before I was given that gift.

Sometimes, when my feet were tired from hiking or dancing, Noah gave me a shiatsu foot massage, which added a deep sense of peace to my dreaming. Our bodies, like sculpture, floated into the open space where our dreams created a private language. His hands, light inside a waterfall. Before I moved back to San Francisco, Robin had assured me, "When the right man comes, he will want to spend a lot of time with you." I knew it was true but didn't know if it was something I'd see in this lifetime. I had no idea that love would bring such a deep feeling of happiness and peace.

Chapter 75:

Hot Pink Cajun to the Core

When the season changed, Noah invited me to meet him at Zebulon's for a Cajun dance. I dressed flirty – short black skirt with two rows of ruffles in hot pink. Hot pink sweater. Emerald crystal earrings linked to a freshwater pearl. When I walked through the door, Noah was on the stage with his band. He hadn't told me his band was playing that night – it was one of those moment-by-moment surprises that continued to unfold since the night I met him. He caught my eye briefly as he played his violin, and from that moment I was filled with him.

Noah's music made me dance. I was a dervish spinning through time, a Sufi dream, a belly dancer at the edge of a tsunami. Whenever my dance partner dipped me to the floor, Noah's violin was in the cadence of the waterfall. Inside of every note, I felt him making love to me. And when my partner turned me upside down, Noah's music went hot pink to my face. His music turned me on from inside the core of my atoms, lit me up in a way that everything in the world became large, meaningful and symbolic. I felt his violin inside my womb. It didn't matter who I was dancing with – every dance was for him.

Noah's playing was passionate to the core. His way of making music was like a Rumi poem – sensual, artistic and mysterious. It was almost overwhelming, but at the same time, it put me in touch with the core of my being.

Close to midnight, Noah walked off the stage to waltz with me. As we orbited to *Valse Bebe*, he pulled me into a bear hug spin and whispered, "This is my dream you're in." But I know some of the best moments of life feel like a dream because they resonate so deeply with your soul.

The heart is intrinsically mysterious. I don't know why my heart opens to some people and not to others, but I trust it. There was something about Noah, about his music, and the way he was drawn to me. I don't know the whole story or need to know at this time. I know what I feel.

And our waltz... A melody walking down a mountain barefoot in a language I am only beginning to understand. The emotions coming from underneath the muscles. Memories from long ago, a recognition, a stream of light. Later that night when we found some private time and a private place, he found his way so deep inside me I didn't know I could be touched that way.

In the sky above the coastal mountains, we saw a full moon rising. A halo of memory. Above, the aurora borealis. Below, the heat of the earth. A wind swirling over the red barn next to a one room schoolhouse, a terrifying beauty that will blow the walls apart. An almost forgotten memory of the way back home. As Noah held me soft and warm under the moonlight, I felt the shattered sparks I had abandoned fly back home to the chalice of my heart.

Chapter 76:

Shooting Stars Across the Sky

ate that night, Noah and I got into my pickup truck and started heading north. Our travel omen, a shooting star streaking across the sky. In two weeks, we'd be flying to Kyoto. Everything seemed possible.

We wanted to sleep under the moonlight but felt that a campground would be too boring, so we climbed a fence to who knows where and put our sleeping bags out under the open sky. The sky was sprayed with the Milky Way, as we gave ourselves to each other under the constellation of Orion. I don't remember my dreams that night, except for a few images of redwood forests and rivers, but in the morning, it was clear that we had camped on someone's farm, as we were surrounded by a herd of Brahmin cows.

There was only one thing to do at that moment. Noah took his violin out of the case as I assembled my flute. We played *Wizard's Walk*, then *Jump at the Sun*, and *Far Away* to the cows.

Before we loaded the truck, we took a skinny dip in the pond and made love under water. Then, following the edge of the Pacific Ocean, we continued our journey.

About the Author

Diane Frank is an award-winning poet and author of six books of poems, including *Swan Light, Entering the Word Temple,* and *The Winter Life of Shooting Stars.* Her friends describe her as a harem of seven women in one very small body. She lives in San Francisco, where she dances, plays cello, and creates her life as an art form. Diane teaches at San Francisco State University and Dominican University. She leads workshops for young writers as a Poet in the School and directs the Blue Light Press On-line Poetry Workshop. She is also a documentary scriptwriter with expertise in Eastern and sacred art. *Blackberries in the Dream House,* her first novel, won the Chelson Award for Fiction and was nominated for the Pulitzer Prize.

To schedule readings, book signings and workshops, and to invite her to speak to your book club, contact:

Diane Frank
c/o 1st World Publishing
P.O. Box 2211
Fairfield, Iowa 52556

E-mail: GeishaPoet@aol.com
Website: www.dianefrank.net

Books by Diane Frank

Blackberries in the Dream House

Swan Light

Entering the Word Temple

The Winter Life of Shooting Stars

The All Night Yemenite Café

Rhododendron Shedding Its Skin

Isis: Poems by Diane Frank

Music and Recipes

Contra Dance Bands:

For music to accompany this novel, I recommend the CDs of my favorite contra dance bands: Airdance, Crowfoot, Flapjack, Groovemongers, Hillbillies from Mars, Latter Day Lizards, Lift Ticket, Nightingale, Notorious, StringFire, Stump Tail Dog, Wild Asparagus, The Moving Violations, and Uncle Gizmo.

Contra Dance Websites:

www.cdss.org
www.bacds.org
www.nbcds.org
www.HaywardContraDance.org
www.ltda.org
www.contradance.org
www.dancegypsy.org

More Music from this Novel:

These pages are also filled with music by Bare Necessities, Manring Kassin Darter Trio, and Sharon Bousquet.

Recipes:

For recipes in this book, check out *Eating for Two* by Robin Lim.